TALES OF KINGS AND GLORY

AN UNLIKELY
HERO

TRISTEN SNYDER

Cover art by Sina Pakzad Kasra.
Sinakasra.artstation.com

*****

An Unlikely Hero is a work of fiction. Names, characters, places, and events are products of the author's imagination or used fictitiously. Any resemblance to actual persons, living or dead, or events or locales, is entirely coincidental.

Parts of this work may be considered disturbing or offensive to the reader. Violence, sexual content, foul language, use of alcohol & drugs, and potentially sexist content is present. This work was written for mature readers and is not intended for children.

Reader discretion advised.

Getting here has been a long road.
Thank you to everybody who's supported and stuck
around for it.

This one's for you all.

◈ PROLOGUE

Two years ago...

His heart is beating fast, his every breath frantic. Hearing a loud rustling from the thick tropical brush, he turns nervously to find himself looking into the face of a pouncing jaguar. Midair the jaguar bites into the man's throat and thrashes his body to the ground, leaping to a predatory stance over its prey before it roars in victory. The rest of the members of the victim's party stumble backwards in fear—except for one: Templar Fortis.

A Commander in the Templar Order of *the White Sun and the White Tree*, Templar Fortis is clad in a suit of mastercrafted steel armour trimmed with gold. Covering the plates is a white tabard with a twelve pointed Sun resting in the branches of an oak, all embroidered in gold. Standing tall he draws his sword in one smooth motion. He takes a step forward into the rooty mud and the beast recoils in fear. Lunging forward, he swings his righteous blade at the beast. It bats the sword away with its spotted paw, howling in pain as it is sliced.

Another Templar thrusts the end of his halberd into the jaguar's hind leg. It snaps its head towards this Templar as its hind leg collapses. Another man stands in the back with bow in hand and arrow nocked. Unlike the armoured majority of the group this man is merely dressed in a beige tunic and dark leather trousers. Though the shot through the crowd between him and the jaguar is narrow, he lets his arrow fly.

*****

A man wearing a beige tunic and dark leather trousers emerges from the oaken tree line. Fashioned over his shoulder is his trusty hunting bow, and hanging at his side is a leather satchel. His light blue eyes dart around at the village; it has been a few months since he last saw civilisation. The tall grass parts around him as he manoeuvres between the stumps of trees cut down long ago. He brushes the sweat from his forehead before taking off his big fur hat, revealing his light blonde hair to the bright sun. *'Spring is here, no need for this anymore,'* he thinks, leaving it on a post out front of the rundown lumber yard.

The man cuts between the butcher and the bakery to get into town. Inside the town, it is bustling. A flock of washerwomen gossip as they scrub buckets of clothes clean, the clash of blacksmiths' hammers ring through the street, and a wagoner tips his hat at Milo as he rolls by. The town of Penkerdeen is an important locale in this part of Ateria, as it's where all the traders come down from the mountain to meet, trade furs, and exchange commodities. Penkerdeen is also built upon the only road that runs down the length of south-west Adros, a mountainous region so far left considerably untouched. Today the man is not here to trade his furs and other goods as he usually would.

He creaks open a heavy wooden door of an old apothecary shop. Stepping inside his eyes have to adjust to the shadowy interior. "Milo Khan!" The voice of an old woman cackles. "I haven't seen you, oh, since before the winter came."

"Good to see you Mabel," Milo answers, blinking and opening his soft blue eyes to try and see in the ill-lit room. "So I've been having these nightmares…" Milo's voice trails off as he recalls them.

For some time now he has been having terrible dreams every night. In one he stood at the base of a lonesome hill topped with a pale tree, drops of thick blood dripping from its thorny branches. In another he walked a black hall, seated in a Throne at the end of the hall was a mangled corpse clasping a rusting crown, seedlings of a dark spikey plant sprouting from his body. One dream above them all haunted him over and over again. It began on a normal day in the golden fields of New Adros. Then the world turned to red and the workers into rotting corpses eerily hovering over the fields. A pale steed would creep towards him, its rider a shadow. And there are others he cannot remember outside of faint slivers that reside at the edges of his memory.

"Everyone has been having them dear," Mabel tells him.

Milo raises a brow. "What do you mean everyone's been having them? You saying all the townsfolk been having nightmares as well?"

"Nay, the whole Kingdom. That's why they're here." She lifts her old skinny finger and aims it behind Milo.

Turning he looks through the door and across the street. Now before the inn opposite of the apothecary, a large group of Templars is readying their horses and loading supplies onto their wagons. Milo leaves the apothecary and heads towards the Templars, Mabel shouting after him: "It was nice seeing you again!"

He crosses the street and approaches the first Templar he sees, a tired man in plain steel armour and a tabard with a black twelve pointed sun. The man is gently brushing one of the horses as it eats the grass outside the inn. "Greetings stranger," the Templar says still brushing the horse.

"May I ask why you are here?" Milo asks.

"Because I have orders to be."

"I was told it had something to do with these nightmares I've been having? That everyone's been having apparently."

The Templar finally turns his head towards Milo and looks over him. "Talk to Templar Commander Fortis."

"Who's that?"

"Big Templar with gold. You gotta be pretty dull to miss 'im," the man says grooming the horse again.

Milo steps away and looks around the area in front of the inn. He could see no man in gold, only the same plain armoured men and a couple with silver tabards. Then he sees him. Sitting on a low limb of a tree is the Templar in gold. As he approaches the tree he can see why the man chose this spot. Not only does it give him a good view over all his men, but it gave him easy access to the apple he is chewing on. Walking up to the tree Milo looks up at the Templar and says, "Hail."

The Templar jumps from the low limb and lands pristinely. He is a tall, muscular man with a shaved head and a thick, yet well trimmed black beard. "I am Templar Fortis," he says extending his hand to shake.

Milo accepts the handshake firmly. "I am Milo Khan. What exactly are you doing out here?"

"Our great Vicar of the White Tree had a vision from the White Sun himself, my friend. The White Sun spoke through our Vicar and told us that we were to venture into the Bleaks to find the source of this evil and extinguish it."

"The Bleaks?" Milo asks in disbelief.

Fortis takes a bite out of his apple before telling him, "Aye, tis a wicked place. Its rocky terrain is the worst of anywhere; too many steep hills and sudden drops. They come out of nowhere too, hidden behind the unholy thick trees and vines. The most dangerous part, however, is the creatures; Jaguars stalk in the shadows, boars root at the ground, and colourful spiders weave their webs between branches."

"I know what the Bleaks is. I just can't believe that's where you're going."

"The White Sun commanded us, thus we go."

"You know what happened to Alexios the Second, right?" Milo confirms.

"After his coronation he attempted to prove himself as worthy as his father by surviving in the Bleaks. Before the end of the day only one of his scribes returned to say he had perished. I am aware." Fortis takes a bite out of his apple and chews it for a few seconds. "You look like a man who can take care of himself in the wild."

"I've lived out in these wild lands my entire life. Only really come into town to trade," Milo tells him.

"We're taking volunteers," Fortis says with an eager grin.

*****

The arrow Milo shot flies narrowly past one of the Templars, then gently brushes past a Dwarf's hair before entering the jaguar's skull.

"Oi! Watch your fookin shot!" The Dwarf yells at Milo.

Milo mocks back, "I'm sorry, I'm saving your life!"

The group shifts around nervously and scans the area for any more threats that may be lurking. Milo hears somebody say, "That man was in a frenzy since we first set foot in this jungle. Seems to me we're better off without him." Another shouts out, "That's the sixth man since we set out this morning!"

As if there wasn't any danger about, Templar Fortis says, "We need to keep on. In the name of Ateria, we cannot fail our crusade!" He throws a clenched fist up into the air and strides forward before anybody can contend. The group follows reluctantly. Overwhelming the terrain are bristling plants and vines, and outspread leafed trees create a thick canopy that blocks out all but the occasional snatches of light. As the day goes on the heat grows hotter and hotter, the water visibly steaming from the plants. The air becomes thick with humidity and their bodies slick with sweat. The animal paths they follow grow narrower and often end abruptly. The plant life grows thicker by the foot, seeming to swallow the group.

Their boots sink deep into the mud as the path becomes flooded with foaming water. The moist leaves brush against the skin exposed by Milo's rolled sleeves, some of the thornier ones scratching him. In the group's front is a Templar swinging a large machete to slash a path through the brush. Small insects bite at their skin as they fail to flick the swarms away. Travelling deeper within the hoots and screams of the jungle become more alien. As they exit the long stretch of flooded land, they enter a small glade in the thick jungle flora. For a moment the men get a reprieve from the oppressive branches and leaves enveloping the path.

Having let his guard down, one man walks straight into a large yet thin spider web. He flies backwards and frantically flails about screaming. Another one of the volunteers, whom Milo can tell is from Asbjarnarvik, becomes furious. The Asbjarnarviki grabs the man and throws him into a mossy tree. The man pushes off the tree and draws his sword screaming, "Fucker!" Templar Fortis moves in like the wind and parries the blade before most even realise what is happening. He shoves his knee into the man's crotch, causing the blade to slip from the man's hand, and pins him back up against the tree by his throat. The Asbjarnarviki begins to lunge towards the man, but another two Templars quickly leap and grab him by the arms.

"Now, are you going to fight?" Fortis questions the man, his voice booming through his greathelm. The man merely stares for a long time with his face twisted in anger before tears run down his cheeks from the pain. The man finally gives in and shakes his head. Templar Fortis lets the man go. "If I see any more fighting between any of you, I'll have you tied to the trees and left behind."

They get back onto the trail, tightly following the trail in a long column. The trail quickly begins to suffocate the group again as the humidity continues to rise and the gaps between the trees becomes smaller. Milo must begin slouching beneath the thick canopy despite the best efforts of the machete at the front. Everything aches horribly, and his entire body is soaked with sweat. Exhaustion is setting in, despite Milo having thought it had already. *'One foot after the other,'* Milo thinks over and over again. *'One foot after the other.'* He takes a drink from his waterskin, it barely a relief since it is so hot. *'One foot after the other.'* Time becomes a blur.

"Everybody setup camp. We're almost out of daylight and this is probably the most open ground we're going to find," Fortis shouts as they come to a stop. Milo sighs with relief. Everybody files into the fairly large clearing and begin unloading their packs. "We are to build a fire in the centre of camp. I know it's already hot as is, but this is not the place to sleep in the dark. Scribe Caereth will be assigning the watch order for tonight."

Milo rolls out his small bedroll close to where they will build the fire and sets his satchel and waterskin atop it. Fortis and a few other of the Templars approach him. "Hail Milo. We are assembling a crew to forage for some good firewood. Would like you to be on it?"

Milo nods his head. "Of course."

"We'll split into two teams of three," one of the men says. The men divide themselves and then head off into the woods. The men walk around a good part of the perimeter picking up any half decent pieces of wood, never letting the camp out of sight. When they return the other team has not yet returned. As Milo works on building the fire the other team returns, carrying molding and worthless wood. The fire starts to burn a little and huge clouds of smoke blow out, repelling the nipping gnats away from their most skin. After getting the fire really going, the men cook oats and boil water around the fire.

Templar Fortis pulls up a log and oils his sword. The sword is very simplistic and undecorated in design, as most of the Templar's weapons are. While this appearance may seem modest, this is only for this sake of mass production. In truth the *Church of the White Sun and the White Tree* is a powerful organisation with a lot of money, and the Templar Smiths are regarded as some of the best in Ateria, but only a few Templars are lucky to have individualised equipment.

"I suppose we were in luck to come across you in that village," Fortis says to Milo. "You were more collected today than half my Templars."

"Not as calm as you. I'd say you didn't even break a sweat, but it's too hot *not* to sweat. How are you so composed in this place?"

"I am a servant of the White Sun. I know he shall protect me."

"I wouldn't put too much faith in the White Sun's protection if I were you. Do you remember that man who died earlier?"

"The man was not a true servant of the White Sun. It might've been for the best, he was a coward and slowing us down."

Milo raises an eyebrow. "I thought you Templars were supposed to protect the weak?"

Templar Fortis sets his sword to the side and gives a dark look as he says, "The weak have no place here." There is a tense silence until Fortis changes the subject. "Perhaps you should get some sleep Milo?"

Milo looks over at the men, who are squirming and rolling around as they unsuccessfully attempt to sleep. "Do you really think we'll be getting any sleep tonight?"

"Even if you can't sleep, you need to rest. You will need your energy tomorrow."

"Fine, but know I'll probably be right back here in five minutes." He walks over to the bedroll he set down and checks around for anything that will kill him. Then he lays down and closes his eyes. The next thing Milo knows, he is jumping up from the ground and alerting the others.

"We have to head... Uh- That way." Milo points off into the Jungle. Through the shadowy canopy it seems daylight has just broken.

"What the fuck are you going on about?" One man says groggily, scratching his head.

"I had a dream. It said to go… Well, that way." Milo points again without knowing why he is doing this. There was no dream he could remember. His head is spinning in confusion of why he is saying this. His mouth is moving without him wanting it to. He doesn't even know where he is telling them to go.

"What makes you believe your dream has any actuality?" Templar Fortis asks with scepticism.

Milo stumbles on his words, "I- It's just- I don't know."

"Then why do you bother us with it?"

"I don't know…" Milo repeats.

A Templar of lower rank injects himself, "My apologies Sir, but we have no idea where we are, or where we head. How can following his dream be any different from the arbitrary choices you've made?"

"We cannot afford to waste time, Templar!" Fortis tells him.

"But…" the man says low.

"But..?"

"Could it be any more frivolous than arbitrarily wandering? It may be a vision from the White Sun."

Fortis looks at Milo through his greathelm, "Why would the White Sun give a vision to this commoner?"

"It is not my place to judge the actions of the holy White Sun."

"Aye I say we follow his dream!" One shouts, then more voices chime in "Aye!"

Fortis concedes, "We will follow his dream then."

While packing up camp the men scarf down some dried bread and oats from the night before. Clouds of mosquitoes buzz overhead a couple times before retreating to sleep out the day. "Fuck!" Someone shouts. "Garmund is dead!" Milo and Fortis run over to the site of the commotion. Laying on his side is one of the Templars, foam at his mouth and his eyes bloodshot. Milo inspects the body before picking up one of the arms and looking closely at it.

"Spider bite," he states.

"How can you tell?" Fortis asks.

Milo merely points to a small red bruise on the man's arm.

"Are we going to burn his body as the White Sun commands?" One of the Templars asks.

"No, we must continue. The White Sun surely understand our sacrifice." Templar Fortis says. He walks off and Milo soon follows his lead, leaving the Templar standing alone over his friend's dead body. Milo finishes getting his things together and the group hits the trail again. This time Milo is in the front, behind only the machete and Fortis. Milo guides Fortis through the various animal trails within the jungle, which are wider this day. As the morning gets hotter the large and spiky leaves of the surrounding plants steam.

At first nobody thinks much when a fog begins to creep in around them. They only begin to get disturbed as it grows thicker and the sounds of the jungle fade away into an eerie quietness. The men whisper prayers to the White Sun and become stiff with nerves. A ghastly shrill comes from further back in the group. Milo spins around quickly, his heart racing. At first he only sees the men standing in terror; then he notices the dark figures in the mist.

The men pack tightly together and clench onto their weapons ready for a fight. The world becomes still and silent. Milo can feel the shadows staring back at him. It feels like an eternity that the shadows stalk them; the world frozen in place. Then the shadows melt into the mist and disappear.

"What. The fuck?!" A northman whispers, breaking the silence.

"Demons," A Templar whimpers.

"Demons?" Another asks sceptically.

"Aye, only a demon could play this trickery on us!" Another shouts.

"They say a demon is a skillful wielder of illusions," yet another chimes in.

Templar Fortis moves to the front of the group, seemingly undaunted. "We cannot look to superstition in this! Demons are of the utmost malice. Thus they would have struck against more than our wits!" Despite his tenacious demeanour, Milo looks into his dark eyes and can see that in truth he is afraid.

"B-but... how can you suppose a demon's will? Can it not be foremost to torment us?" One Templar questions.

"Tis one of the church's parables! Dost thou dare renege the oath made to our church?" Fortis barks.

"I- No- It's just..." his voice trails off.

"Just..?" Fortis interrogates.

"It is just... how- how could anyone possibly know of demonic intent, even a man so holy and wise as the Vicar of the White Tree?"

"So thou dost deny the teachings of the White Sun! You heretic!"

Annoyed, Milo interrupts, "Oi, lads! You're both ugly, let's get a move on!"

"Are you too a heretic?" Fortis snaps.

"He's right! This is not the time to be fighting one another!" The Asbjarnarviki shouts. Walking away from the inflamed group and towards the mist he yells back, "I am heading after the shadow people." None dare follow him as he disappears into the myst.

The men wait apprehensively for what feels like an hour, but is in truth much less. The only man to sheath his weapon is Templar Fortis. Concurring that the northman isn't returning, Fortis gets the group moving down the path again. The path is surprisingly open and the myst still surrounds them. *'One step after another,'* Milo thinks to himself. His muscles are really aching, every fibre of his body screaming to just stop and lay down. But there can be no stopping. *'One step after another.'* Milo hears Templar Fortis ask something, but in a tired haze merely mutters, "Wuhn step aftuh anothuh."

"What?" Templar Fortis asks.

"The middle fork," Milo says in a tired haze, not sure where he got this answer from. They continue down the path for a tiring few minutes that feel like hours. Then the group stops, spotting an overgrown stone shack.

"Should we investigate it?" asks one volunteer.

"There doesn't seem to be anything else around," Templar Fortis responds, not quite answering the question.

"I'll go in," Milo says.

Templar Fortis holds out his hand towards one of his men and says, "Your sword." The Templar hesitates a moment before giving it to Fortis, whom in turns hands it to Milo. Milo gives it a strange look, not understanding why Fortis gave it to him. "Take it. Your bow wouldn't do you much good in such a small place."

Taking the fine yet plain short sword, he pushes on a rotting wood door. At first it does not budge, so he pushes harder. Suddenly he falls through the door. He finds himself not inside the shack, but back in the jungle. He bends over and puts his hands on his knees, his world spinning and his stomach feeling nauseous. As he recovers, he turns around to tell Fortis it is just more jungle, only to find nothing but jungle behind him. He turns around again perplexed by the occurrence and realises there is a mysterious cobbled road in front of him. A million thoughts race through his mind. *'Where am I?'*; *'What just happened?'*; *'Who spiked my drink?'*

Following the path, he halts for a moment when he sees a man hunched over in a dark cloak that drapes over his face. He shuffles towards the man and calls out: "Hail! Where are we?" The man suddenly vanishes from existence. The sight makes Milo's stomach churn and his head ache. *'How could things get any weirder?'*

Milo travels down the road slowly regaining his strength, soon finding himself at a fork. One path continues straight with nothing in sight, while the other veers off with the hellish tree from the dream in the distance. He takes a step towards the tree but a whisper echoes throughout, seeming to come from nowhere yet everywhere at the same time. "This is not your path to take." Despite his compulsion to head towards the tree, he finds his body moving back on the path straight ahead.

"Right, time to follow the disembodied voice to my doom."

Shortly thereafter the jungle suddenly ends, and he is somehow walking in the Adrosi capital of Varlebeck. Except it isn't the Adros he knows. The massive crop fields are ablaze and the buildings engulfed in flames. Monstrous howls unlike any creature of this world echo throughout the valley. He watches in dread as he passes by horrendously mutilated bodies of men, women, and children. Feeling something meekly grab at his pant leg, he looks down to a cadaverous man. Covering the poor man are wounds inflicted by claw and blade. Not muscle nor fat are present to separate bone from maggot infested skin. Through the ungodly amounts of dirt and mud that cover his skin, Milo could see many large buboes covering his body. Milo is in shock that this man is still alive.

"You are a beautiful sight, aren't you?" Milo manages to snap out over the nerves of the horrendous sight. He kneels to help the dying man, but all he can do is stare at the lurid sight. The man slowly raises his trembling hand up and places it in Milo's. With a faint voice Milo can barely hear he grinds out the words, "The dark one..." with a hoarse voice that hurts Milo's ears. Breaking out into a coughing fit, blood and spit are sprayed from the man's mouth. The man lets out a long, horrendous gasp for breath before his head slumps over, blood flowing from his gaping mouth. His open eyes remain filled with pain even in his passing. Milo lets out a soft gasp as he darts back from the man. Milo continues down the path, his world spinning as bad as a drunk's.

The same echoing whisper from earlier rings out, once again seeming to come from nowhere and everywhere at the same time. "You must stop him." The searing pain in his head is like none other and causes him to face to contort in pain and hold his head in his hands. When the pain dissipates, he finds that he had unknowingly fallen to the ground. "Can we stop with the disem…" He stops mid-word as he realises he is no longer where he was and takes a look around. Now he is in a large hallway supported by massive stone pillars. The room is shadowy, lit only by the rays of sunlight coming through the skylights. "Oh where the hell am I now?" Milo slowly takes each step down the hallway. He can hear a soft woman's voice echoing throughout, slowly speaking one word at a time, "*Honour. Valour. Loyalty. Wisdom. Compassion.*" Passing through the doorway at the end of the hall, he comes to see a naked woman facing away from him across the room. She is tall, has long blonde hair that curls near the ends, and a gorgeous form. A series of elegant swirling tattoos morph around her body.

"Do not forget these virtues," she tells Milo before vanishing into twirls and dances of smoke. Moments after this woman disappears, another dance of smoke appears and turns into a man. This man is average other than his striking ginger hair, glowing blue eyes, and luxurious suit.

"Thank the gods you aren't naked too," Milo says.

Speaking in a strange accent, the man says, "I am sure you are perplexed as of this moment, aye?"

Milo stares at the man questioningly. "Can everyone evaporate and reform at will here?"

The man stares at Milo for a few moments, then speaks again, "Well… Uhm- Nevermind that… Thou will understand what has just ensued in due time."

"Some incorporeal guide you are!"

Templar Fortis' voice booms throughout. "Milo?"

Spinning around, Milo finds that the group is standing in the temple's doorway. Everyone looks somehow even more baffled and tired than before. Fortis' face is grim and flushed of colour. Milo glances back towards the mysterious man, only to find that he has disappeared. "Well that was... peculiar..." He states to himself, his voice trailing off.

"What was?" Fortis asks faintly. He continues without giving Milo time to reply, "And in the name of the White Sun, what the fuck happened to you?"

"I'm not entirely sure myself. It was very *peculiar*," Milo responds whilst scanning the room, noticing it only had the one way in or out. He also takes note that the northman had miraculously returned.

"I don't think Ateria will be having any more nightmares," Templar Fortis says with hints of tremors in his voice.

"What makes you think that?" Milo asks.

This time Fortis' voice betrays him. "Can we just leave this god-forsaken jungle already?

I.

THE INSTIGATION . . .

◈ CHAPTER ONE

"Milo," a man's voice calls out. Milo Khan wakes up to a dazzling Sun shining in his face. He squints blankly into the sky before a dark figure fills his view. He blinks a few times to get his bearings. The air is hot, the sky is bleached by the sun, and he can feel the wagon he is in moving. In his nap he had dreamt of being in the cool night of the Adrosi woodlands, laying in a hammock looking at the stars; now he finds himself back in the heat that he has become so sick of. Sitting up he looks to the man he has been travelling with for the past few days. "We've nearly arrived!" The man cries excitedly. Milo looks out in front of the wagon and upon the barren sand dunes of the Pyrammian desert, which are glowing and shimmering under the hot sun. There are but a few trees scattered around the desert, mostly palms. This is quite the contrast to the wooden lands Milo is accustomed to. Looking closely to the horizon Milo can barely make out the large walls of Dalarus in the distance.

The trade capital of Ateria, Dalarus, is one of the richest cities in the entire world. Built entirely upon business, the city sits upon a strategic position on the trade route between the continents of Ateria, Accules, and Illyrium. Commerce constantly takes place in the bustling city streets, the taxes of which are what made the fortune of the great House Pyrammus. Ships from all around the world travel to Dalarus, so many that the Captains of the smaller ships constantly fight over the spots on the quays that there are never enough of.

And yet the already clamorous streets of Dalarus will be even worse today because of the city's yearly festival. Many would think it impossible for the streets to be more crowded than they normally are, but this day every year would prove them wrong. Throughout the city is an extraordinary amount of merchants from around the world peddling their goods; in fact, there are so many merchants during this time that it is common for ships become floating shops. Like any festival there is a number of games and other festivities.

Milo doesn't even know what they are celebrating. Hardly anybody does. In all honesty he doesn't know why he is heading there. Festivals have never been his thing; it was just a spontaneous urge in the back of his mind.

"We're late to the festival you know…" The other passenger whines. "It started this morning."

Milo shrugs, "Fine by me."

"But we missed the tourney!" It is a well-known tradition that the festival always begins with the year's grandest tourney in the Revan Pyrammus Arena.

"Being crammed into a noisy crowd isn't something I care too much about missing."

"Well you could've just stayed in the city…" The man says snarkily.

"There ain't anything interesting happening in the city during the tourney. It's a rule that there is to be no trade, nor any of the festivities until the Lords return."

Frowning the man says, "I wonder if Dequande the Bull won again…" When Milo doesn't respond, his fellow traveller looks off at the approaching city in the distance. After a long silence that Milo was quite happy with, he inquires, "Have you ever been to Dalarus?"

"One time before. Seem to remember something about a monkey and a thief. It's a little foggy. Not much out 'ere for me"

"I had thought there was plenty of work in Dalarus? Especially for a man of wealth such as yourself?" the man asks, a bit confused.

"Believe me, were I a man of wealth this conversation would be going quite differently."

"I see you have not only a bow but also a sword. Are you a Knight? A sellsword?"

"Nay, I'm just a man who's been around a while. Though I'd rather not talk of my life story." The man still doesn't seem to understand what Milo said, but he stays silent for the remainder of the trip.

The wagon nears the main gate of Dalarus and pulls off to the side of the road. "Oi! Why stop here, the gate is up ahead!" Milo shouts to the wagoner.

The old man slowly turns in the general direction of Milo and grumpily replies, "No wagons such as diss allowed in tah city. Lord Pyrammus' rules."

Milo hops out of the wagon before muttering to himself, "No need to be so angry. Not like I killed your pet goat." He heads straight towards the city gates, ignoring the various merchants of the outer market shouting impersonally for people to buy their wares. Following the flow of the crowd, he makes his way through the Blue Gates.

Inside the city is an entirely different sight. Well-trimmed palm trees grow everywhere, creating a comforting canopy that blocks out the harsh sun. Beautiful sandstone buildings are neatly pressed against one another, every one of them seems to either be a shop or have a stall up against it. Small yet lush gardens are placed in the gaps between buildings, all with plush couches for people to relax on. Milo sees children playing in some, women fanning themselves and chatting in others, and a young couple making love in another. Even the sound is different, with loud chatter and music filling the air.

Continuing straight Milo comes upon the Dalarus Mosque, a massive, elegant building with three tall towers on each side. And in front of it is a massive garden well-maintained by the Monks of the *Seven Winds*. In the centre of this garden is a large round pond with flocks of ducks swimming around. Here the Monks of the Seven Winds are selling barrels upon barrels of their fine wines.

The *Seven Winds* is one of the oldest religions in the world, somewhere in time having been worshipped predominantly. Yet in recent years its followers have dwindled. *The Church of the White Sun* was birthed longed ago in the northern realms of the continent Accules, and in the millennia since its followers have been forcefully destroying any other religion. Ateria was colonised primarily by the northron *White Sun* Kingdoms, while Pyrammus was colonised by the southron *Seven Winds* Kingdoms. After the colonisation of Ateria, a rift occurred in the Church of the White Sun. Many settlers of Ateria were those who wished to reform the church, and the Orthodox Church of the White Sun could not project their power across the ocean and onto Ateria; thus the churches split. Unlike their Orthodox counterpart, the *Church of the White Sun and the White Tree* was tolerant of heathens, allowing for the Seven Winds to remain in Ateria. Yet the belief of the Seven Winds is dying off, with more Pyrammians converting to the White Sun every year.

Milo turns right, away from the Mosque and into the main marketplace. Within the thick crowd, he blindly follows the current until he happens to end up at the stall of a blacksmith. Leaning up against a nearby tree to stay out of all the bustle and commotion, he listens in on the ongoing conversation between the blacksmith and two dirty peasants.

"If either of you want to purchase a sword, you are going to need the coin for it. I cannot make them any cheaper." The smith is acting patient but Milo can tell that they are frustrating him.

"But wee want a sword!" One of the peasants whines.

Pointing at a row of well forged daggers, the blacksmith tells them, "As I have already said, I have plenty of these. You might be able to afford them."

"Are yah sure dere is no swords fur cheap?" The other asks.

"Fine… If you really want it," the blacksmith says, his voice thick with spite. The two pesky common folk grin as if they had just seen the queen of Bordreaux's tits. The blacksmith drops onto the table the absolute worst thing Milo has ever seen in his life. The "blade" is somehow unsymmetrical, terribly proportioned, made of cast iron, and thin leather scraps hold the blade onto what one might call the hilt. The blacksmith looks as if he was dying from the plague just by looking at the thing. The buyer grins as he ostentatiously declares that he will buy it. "Ten Richters," the blacksmith states lowly. The man carelessly throws a single 10$\mathscr{R}$ coin at the table before the two take off with the abomination.

The blacksmith looks over to Milo, his expression lightening. "For reasons beyond me, every one of these peasants wants to buy a sword. They don't seem to realise that swords aren't cheap—or that they don't even know how to use one!"

Moving closer to the smith, Milo doesn't even try to contain a smile as he says, "Can't fix stupid sadly. Where did you get that … I'm not even sure what to call that, anyway?"

The smith lowers his head in shame as he tells Milo, "That is something I'd rather not disclose." Raising his head in pride, he asks, "However, would any of my other wares happen to interest you?"

"There is nothing I need right now. You are from Asbjarnarvik aren't you?"

The blacksmith nods. "It was the accent that gave it away, aye?"

"That… and you're sweating like a pig." At that the smith lets out a short yet hearty laugh. "Do you have a name or should I just call you smith?"

"I am Fenrir son of Harolf, renowned smith of the north. Who might you be?"

"I am called Milo Khan. I belong to no House—they would probably just dump me out as a black sheep if I did."

"Where does a man of no house obtain such a blade?" The smith says, throwing a glance at Milo's sword.

"As you said Master Smith, there are things one would rather not say," Milo says with a sly smile.

Milo Khan slips back into the crowd again. Blindly moving through the river of drunkards, he ends up standing before an expensively dressed man puffing on an opium pipe and flanked by armed guards. Milo uneasily asks what he is peddling, out of courtesy more than anything else. The man tells him in a broken Royce accent, "Some'a this, some'a dat. It'a make ya feel better." Summoning bells ring out, which tells the crowds that the Shaqif—the Pyrammian equivalent of a Duke—is going to be giving his speech. Uninterested in furthering the conversation, Milo abruptly makes his way to the palace gates.

Milo reaches the palace in time to get a decent view of the gallows, where the Lords are situated. *'What a lovely place to give a speech.'* Standing at the far end of the gallows is Shaqif Amir Pyrammus, an olive-skinned man with long brown hair, dark eyes, and square head, dressed in an exquisite Pyrammian style suit. Beside him is a taller man with lighter skin, short brown hair, and long of face; this would be Amir's younger brother, Lord Nasir Pyrammus. Milo notices a dark stain on the man's silks where he had recently spilled something on himself. Next to Nasir is a short, round man dressed more flamboyantly than either of the Lords, whose identity Milo cannot discern.

Another man trots up onto the gallows, this one dressed in an overtly ornate suit of gold-plated armour. His decorative helmet being visorless, he presses the silver mouthpiece of a masterfully fashioned, Pyrammian valved trumpet to his lips. The man takes a deep breath and plays a beautiful chorale in honour of House Pyrammus. The crowd silences at once and listens intently to the hymn. The man finishes with a bow and takes a long step backwards. Lord Nasir stumbles forward taking his place infront of the golden man. The crowd immediately begins chatting amongst themselves impudently, making remarks about the Lord being drunk for the speech the fifth year in a row.

"Thilenth. Lord Pyrammuth ith thpeaking," the man in the gold armour shouts over the chatter.

The crowd silences down again and Nasir begins his speech. "Men and women of *hic* Dalarus. Those who have come from all over the *hic* world. We gather for *hic* for this- Uh… great event taking place in our city. We have gathered…" The drunk Lord stands still for several moments before abruptly falling off the edge of the gallows. A number of Pyrammian Guardsman quickly swoop in and drag him off with shockingly practised precision.

Every Pyrammian Guardsman is dressed in a heavily engraved suit of *Zirah Baktar*—an armour made of steel plates woven into chainmail—a lobster-tail helmet with a sheet of mail in front of their faces, and an embossed *Dhal* shield. They always carry *Talwars*, and will wield spears when it is suited. The steel is entirely the high quality Dalarus Steel, recognisable by its distinct pattern of mottling and banding. This array of expensive equipment is coupled with years of intense training, making one Pyrammian Guardsman more expensive than a hundred regular soldiers.

A random man remarks, "Last year he was able to finish the speech!" Before retreating back into his palace, Shaqif Amir steps forward and tells the crowd, "I apologise on behalf of my brother. Enjoy your time in Dalarus!"

Milo wanders around the market, looking at all the wares and even buying some Kanafeh. After getting a good look around, he heads back out to the marketplace that resides outside of the walls. This outer marketplace is notoriously the place to buy second grade merchandise or make shady deals, but Milo decided to take a look around anyway. He quickly comes to the conclusion that people are right about it. After passing up a food vendor selling some not so appetizing meat, he stops by a stall displaying an array of foreign and intriguing objects. The peddler, a dirty man with big eyes and a short unkempt beard, gives Milo brief descriptions of each of his many wares, such as a lucky rabbit's foot and a few talismen. The peddler notices that Milo is unimpressed by his goods. Humming and scratching his patchy beard, the man thinks. Suddenly shouting "Aha!" the man dives under his table. He springs back up with an elegant tiki mask painted in strange hues of green and blue that Milo had never seen before.

"You see, this mask is very special. Hand carved by *the* master of the trade. Some would even believe that it has a sort of… power!"

"How much is it?"

"Shall we say… Fifty Richters?"

He gladly hands the man a single 50$\mathcal{R}$ coin. Milo wouldn't ordinarily think it worth that much, but there is something oddly captivating about it. The man gestures with both his hands at the mask, bows slightly, and tells Milo, "The mask is yours, my friend!" Milo hangs the tiki mask by a string on his belt and continues to look around the other shops. When he comes back around to the stall a short while later, the peddler has disappeared without a single trace of him ever having been there.

"Shady   dealers,   deplorable   wares,   and   now disappearing peddlers… Why did I bother waking up this morning?"

He heads back inside the walls and wanders around for several hours. He saw a lot of interesting items, but there was nothing he needed. He then tried to play some of the festival games. There was one where you threw some wooden balls into some holes at five feet away, though he found it boring. He tried a game of craps and won the first round, only to lose most of his gains in the next couple rounds. He also took part in an archery contest, but the game master forced him to use some cheap light draw-weight bow and it was too easy—that and he ended up being banned from it for being too good. He ended up exploring some far parts of the city, then listening to one of many bands that were playing, and finally watching some performers do tricks and eat fire for a time. After his many failures he begins to get frustrated; everybody else seems to be having a much better time than he is. Then he realises that they are also very drunk.

The Sun is close to setting. Summoning bells ring out. Someone tells him it means the Lords are serving food. Every year the Lords hire every chef and kitchen in the city to make food to be handed out during the festival. It would shock some to hear that they hand out thousands of plates of food for free, but the income the festival brings House Pyrammus greatly exceeds the cost of the food. Milo walks towards the palace, where hundreds of tables are lined up and covered with various foods.

Long after night falls, Milo is stuck waiting in one of the numerous lines to get food. When he finally reaches the start of the food tables, one serving boy gives him a wooden plate, two wooden mugs, and a wooden fork. When the line next moves forward, a serving girl plops down a huge spoonful of rice and a piece of Naan onto his plate. Milo is next given his choice of two meats, picking from Chicken Tikka Masala, Yellow Duck Curry, Goat Curry, Lamb Shashlik, and Lamb Palak; he picks the Tikka Masala and Duck Curry. The next serving girl asks if he would like wine, and instead fills one cup with fruit Sharbat after he declines. When he reaches the end, a chef pulls the lid off of a large metal pot, dips a ladle into it, and plops one then two balls of Gulab Jamun into one of his cups. He had been wondering why he was given two cups. A donation box sits at the end of the table, which he drops a 10ℛ coin into, despite having no obligation to do so. He then takes off to find a quiet place to eat his meal.

Milo happens upon an empty little garden and takes a seat there, lit dimly by an oil lantern. He gets halfway through his meal until a drunken man wanders into it. Milo is somewhat irked that he no longer has the place to himself, but then the man calls out, "Milo Khan, is that thee?"

"Would I happen to know you?" Milo asks, flustered.

"Dost thou not recognise me?" The man asks, using his fingers to pick at his plate of Shashlik.

"I do not."

"I'm Nathaniel Cheever. Remember, we went into the Bleaks to save Ateria from those dastardly nightmares?"

Milo remembers the event well enough, though even thinking of the thing still left him confused. At times he questioned if he accidentally ate some of those mushrooms that make you hallucinate. "Oh, that. If I'm to be honest, I don't remember you."

The man then takes a seat right next to Milo, despite there being several other couches just a few feet away. He takes a large gulp of wine and asks, "So how hast thou been? Happen to do anythin' interestin' since?"

"Just lived as I did before that mess. Coming here was a big change. I'm not too accustomed to settlement life. Don't really know why I even came."

"Thou may not understand it now, but thou will. Even when we don't know why we did something, it is all part of something bigger."

"Did all you Templars go through the same mystic *'your life is not truly your own'* class or something?" Milo says doubtfully, trying to eat his food.

"Oi!" The man cries out, laughing and spilling some of his food. Becoming serious again he says, "Tis but the truth. One day thou will find it to be so."

The two sat silent for a few moments eating their food before Cheever spoke up again. "Where would thou happen to be staying, my friend?"

"I don't know yet. I don't have much coin."

Cheever then procures a small sack and holds it out for Milo. Milo already knows what the contents are, but takes it and looks inside anyway. Confirming his suspicion, Milo tries to hand the coin-filled sack back to the man.

"I can't take this. You're drunk."

"Thou can take it and thou will. I know exactly what I'm doing and I still have plenty more."

Milo begins to object, "I-"

"Thou *will* take it," Cheever interrupts assertively.

Milo sighs and ties the bag to his belt. Cheever smiles at Milo, stands up, and pats him on the shoulder. "I will leave you to your food now. Until we meet again, my friend!" Milo eats the rest of his meal in peace.

◈ CHAPTER TWO

'It's hot. Again,' Milo thinks when he wakes up. The room he is staying in has a large canopied bed stuffed with wool, a desk carved in an uncomplimentary style, a big trunk for his stuff, and a painting by some insignificant artist. There is no hearth; nobody ever needs one in Pyrammus. Milo climbs out of bed, throws open the linen drapes, and looks out the narrow window. He can see the street has already become crowded, and the neighbourhood preacher crying from his box. Milo would normally wake right at dawn, but he has been waking several hours late since he came to the city. After quickly getting dressed, Milo leaves his room and goes downstairs.

The foyer of the *Silken Princess* is a small one. Some might call it sad, but Milo finds it cosy. It's also cool, with thick sandstone walls and small slits for windows. Milo spots Avannie behind the counter, facing away from him and washing a plate. Avannie is a timid girl with straight pale-brown hair, green eyes, and freckles. While almost every girl and woman in Dalarus wears low-cut, sleeveless dresses, Milo has only seen her in concealing Adrosi dresses. For his first several days at the tavern, he hadn't heard a word out of her. Now she talks to him from time to time, though he usually has to start the conversation. He enjoys having somebody to talk with, but her obvious crush on him always makes it awkward. A few nights ago she even tried to kiss him.

Milo casually walks up to the counter and says, "Hail, Avannie."

She jumps. Clutching onto the plate, she spins around and says quietly, "Oh, hullo Milo. You startled me."

"Would you happen to know where Griselle is?"

"Grammama is out back, feeding the goats."

"Thank you," Milo says, going around the counter and out the back door. Behind the *Silken Princess* is a rectangular courtyard made by the adjoining buildings. Pouring dried corn from a massive sack into the troughs is Griselle, a large old lady with only half her teeth and grey hair. Milo has been helping her around the inn lately, namely out of having nothing better to do.

"Hail Griselle. What was that one thing you asked me to get you at the market?"

Without looking at him, she growls back in that husky voice she has, "Stupid boy. How many times must I tell thee. Fenugreek! *Fenugreek*! Dost thou forget black pepper too?"

"No ma'am. It's just that I haven't heard of Fenugreek before."

Putting down the sack of corn, finished, she shouts at him, "Go get my Spices, or I go get my spoon!"

Milo quickly goes back into the foyer. It saddens him to see it so empty. A few weeks ago, after the festival, he found himself sleeping in a chair. A few men have come and gone since for a drink or thinking it was a brothel, but there has been only one other guest: a northman with a great mane of brown hair. Like Milo he had been staying in the tavern since the festival. A couple days ago Milo tried to chat with him.

"Hail. I am Milo. Who may you be?"

The man looked at him almost annoyed, "Aeris Wynterfang."

"I've seen you sitting here every day for the past week."

"So have you."

Milo shrugs. "I haven't had anything better to do. Why are you here?"

"My boss sold off his company during the festival. He got a position in one of them trade guilds in Corelyn," Aeris says, his voice bitter and full of annoyance.

Milo hasn't tried to talk to him since. Passing his hawkish glare, Milo leaves the *Silken Princess*. Across the road is the preacher, standing high above on his box dressed in the white gown and cape of a priest of the *White Sun*. He tries to pass the preacher unnoticed, but the man spots him anyway.

"You there! Come join us in prayer tonight, lest you be struck down with the rest of the heathens in this city! The White Sun must rise in the city of heathens!"

Milo ignores him like always and keep heading to the spice market. He comes up to the wide canal that encircles the palace, a great sandstone building standing five stories tall. Following the canal he reaches the *hara'asir*, a box of tall walls with two large wooden gates that guards the bridge to the palace island. Milo can see the Pyrammian Guardsmen hiding within the battlements in the walls, ready to strike down any threat with their composite bows.

Peering into the open courtyard, Milo notices the Pyrammus brothers speaking with men in dark green uniforms and berets. The Silverwood Rangers, he knows immediately. They are an elite force trained by House Silverwood of Astonbrough—the Grand-Ducal family of New Adros—for light combat and mountaineering. Milo can't help but wonder what they are doing in Pyrammus. Milo enters the courtyard without being stopped, but he knows he is being carefully watched. Standing casually off to the side, he spies on the ensuing conversation.

"-from there we will march on foot. We would soon begin an attack on the location. With the aid of your men hopefully," the Ranger finishes proposing to the Lords.

"I am sorry but we cannot spare that many men," Nasir tells the man.

"I see. However *any* support would help us defeat this terrible foe. He is quite capable."

"Thou did not even make mention of who this foe is?" Amir would inquire.

"In all truth, we are unsure of his identity. We only know that he is a threat to the Grand-Duchy of New Adros, perhaps even all Ateria if allowed to continue."

"House Silverwood has been a longstanding ally of House Pyrammus. I shall accompany thee, along with four of my Guardsmen," Nasir decides.

"Art thou sure that would be wise, brother?"

"I shall be fine."

"I assure you Lord Amir, your brother shan't be harmed. Alongside my fellow Rangers will be any sellswords that join us."

"I'll join you," Milo blurts out.

"Were you eavesdropping on us?" Nasir questions.

"No, I just happened by and discretely listened into your conversation."

"It is fine Lord Nasir! He is a volunteer. Thus he is a friend!" The Ranger says. He then speaks to Milo in a very friendly manner, "I am Ranger Dan."

"Milo Khan."

"Alright Milo. Gather your things and meet us at the docks."

Not wanting to get hit with Griselle's spoon, he gets the spices before returning to the tavern. When he returns he starts towards Griselle, but then stops and goes over to Aeris.

"You need some work, don't you?"

Aeris scowls at him suspiciously, "Why?"

"You're from Asbjarnarvik and have that nice blade at your hip. The Silverwood Rangers are here looking for sellswords to go fight something up in Adros. Thought you might be interested."

"What kind of something are they fighting?"

"I don't know, didn't ask them. Another one of those outlaw groups, perhaps. They're always coming down from Tyros and raiding northern Adros."

"Where do I go?" Aeris asks.

"They said meet them at the docks right after I get my stuff," Milo tells him.

"Perhaps I will."

Milo goes to the counter and puts the sack of spices down on the counter. Griselle opens it up and pulls out one smaller pouch at a time, checking them with one hand, her big wooden spoon in the other.

"Stupid boy isn't so dumb. Thou brings me everything I ask for."

Milo smiles for a second, then it fades away. "I am going back to Adros today, Griselle."

"Who will bring me fresh fish every afternoon now?" She says with a frown.

"I'm sure you'll find somebody."

"Avannie will miss you, you know," Griselle says with a wide grin. Her missing teeth make Milo uneasy, but he can't help but smile.

"Goodbye, Griselle. Mayhaps I'll come visit sometime."

"You best. Avannie needs a good husband," she says completely serious.

Milo hesitates, feeling awkward. "She's half my age, ma'am."

"My husband was thrice my age when I was wed to him—and I was younger than she is now."

"I'll consider it," Milo bluffs, already making way to his room. He gathers up his things. Extra clothes, his bow and quiver, his sword, and the tiki mask. When away from it he wonders why he spent so much on it, only to remember when seeing it again. After collecting his things he heads to the dock. Realising that Ranger Dan didn't specify where at the docks to meet, he paces up and down the docks trying to find him. Because of the crowds on the docks, it proves a task more difficult than most would presume. Thinking he hears somebody call his name within the dockside clamour, Milo looks behind himself for just a moment and nearly crashes into workers hauling a crate. Reaching the end of the docks for the second time, he finally spots Ranger Dan having a conversation with a cloaked man at the far end of the quays. Milo walks up to the Ranger just as he finishes his conversation and the hooded man walks away. Ranger Dan then gives a wide smile to Milo and says, "Ah, you made it! The others are onboard already!"

"Who was that?"

"Just an associate of mine. He won't be sailing with us. Go on now, climb aboard!"

Milo Khan boards the ship, a small galleon under the flags of a merchant vessel. The crew is running around preparing the ship to leave harbour soon. Milo spots Nasir drinking from a bottle of rum near the bow of the ship, guarded by Pyrammian Guardsmen. The smith Fenrir Harolfsson is also aboard and talking to the helmsman. Aeris is standing with a group of sellswords, none of whom Milo recognises. An hour later the ship leaves the harbour.

*****

It is the middle of the night and the ship is caught inside a vicious storm. Thrashed around by the violent waves, nobody is getting any sleep. Sitting in the forecastle with the others, Milo is quietly sitting and eating some bread. A Ranger barges in and screams, "We need all men out here!" As soon as he finishes, he rushes back out to the rainy deck whence he came. With exception of one one unfortunately seasick man, everyone quickly gets up and runs to the deck.

Walking upon the deck, everything is in chaos. The harsh storm is making it difficult to see. Milo is able to make out men running back and forth trying to remain in control of the ship, or standing at the gunwales with harpoons in hand. Above the roar of the wind and rain, Milo can hear men shouting about an attacking Lyndworm, a vicious sea-serpent that likes to attack ships. Moving his way across the violently swaying deck, he finds Nasir Pyrammus—of all people—just standing there.

"Can we go a month without some new strange occurrence?" Milo shouts above the clamour to nobody in particular.

Nasir stumbles over to him drunk. "Now where's the fun in that?" He takes another gulp from the bottle of rum he is clutching. "I heard something about a lindy worm from what I could make out. Have you ever seen a worm do lindy-hop before? I know I haven't."

"Don't you think you should go below deck, Lord over-drunk?"

"No, no! Tis fine. In other news, who might you be?"

"They call me Milo Khan," he tells Nasir, looking overhead as the Lyndworm travels overhead with a crew-member in its jaws.

"Well cheers to you, Milo Khan!" He then takes another large gulp from the bottle of rum he is holding. "What brought you to our great city?"

"We aren't in Dalarus, m'Lord."

Nasir's eyes widen and he takes in the chaos around him. "Oh- Uhh, when did we get here? Nevermind. Still, what do you think of Dalarus?"

"In all honesty? I don't really know."

"Well, I hope you find good fortune in due time! Would you care for a drink?" Nasir asks, holding out the bottle for Milo.

As this conversation has been taking place, the rest of the crew has been attempting to fight off the large Lyndworm. Harpoons are flying through the gale air, most of them fall into the churning sea rather than make it into the Lyndworm. Repeatedly slamming itself against the hull and arching its long body over the deck, the serpent has sent several crew-members falling overboard. As Nasir is holding the bottle out for Milo, the Lyndworm crashes its way straight up through the side of the hull and arches back into the water. Nasir stands oblivious to the havoc behind him, holding out the bottle of rum for Milo until the planks he's standing upon collapse and drop him into the waters below.

"The ship's a'sinkin'!" Someone cries out.

The men quickly run across the deck and to the rowboats. The surge sea of water is quickly flooding the hull. In a fury the men quickly release the rowboats tied to the side of the ship and drop them into the water. The ship is sinking fast and veering to its side. Quickly moving down the side of the bow, the men jump in and crash into their boats, causing them dip violently. One panicked man jumps into his boat from the top of the ship, breaking his ankle and causing the boat to tip so far down it begins to take in water. For a moment the men of the boat thought they were doomed, but in an instance of luck the current retracts and saves them from sinking. The angle of the sinking ship gets more intense by the minute.

Milo Khan lets the others get into the boats before him and is still looking around for more, despite the nearest boat drifting dangerously far away from the ill-fated ship. "Jump!" One calls out to Milo. He takes a last look around for any others. Nobody more coming, he takes his leap from the side of the hull—only to plunge into the frigid waters.

◈ CHAPTER THREE

All Milo can feel is the cold; his eyes are forced shut by the icy saline waters. He suddenly feels himself hit something hard and hears someone ask if he is alright. The men had managed to grab onto him and yanked him out of the waters and into the boat. He was so cold he didn't even feel the men grabbing him. Slowly he opens his eyes and coughs up some water. The men throw a wool blanket over him as he lays there.

*****

A few hours later...

The Sun has begun to rise and warm the chilled men. There are but a few clouds left in the sky and the waters have calmed. Sitting at the front of the boat in silence is Captain Isen Gale, his face contorted in ire. The navy blue uniform with gold buttons and piping is thoroughly soaked. Bitterly and directed to nobody, the only two words he has spoken have been: "My ship." Rowing the boat is a mercenary named Richard Rosenthal, a serious man with dark brown hair that is long in the back and armed with a Falchion.

The other mercenary on the boat is the opposite of him. Gerev Westman constantly has a mischievous smile and a look in his eyes that makes the others distrustful of him. His black hair is barely longer than his stubble beard and comes to a widow's peak that is just sharper than his beak nose. Hanging from his belt is a simple arming sword that bears the engraving of the Aterian army. Under his shirt, Milo can see a worn and rusted hauberk.

Also on the boat is a single Pyrammian Guardsman still ahold of all his equipment. Aeris Wynterfang is also aboard, laying against the side of the boat with his eyes shut. The last man on the boat, a Silverwood Ranger, is droopy faced and has dark bags under his eyes. His missing beret allows the blatant and uneven scissor lines of his haircut to be seen. He has only said his name is Forrest, leaving everyone guessing whether that is his given name or surname.

The men drift along with no idea of where they are at, or if they are even close to land. Several hours go by until they spot land. As Richard Rosenthal rows towards the shoreline, Milo makes out a forest of triangle shaped trees—conifers. They are sailing towards the province of Tyros. Located below the frozen *Asbjarnarvik* and above the *Redlands*, the land is almost always grey and melancholy from the clouds that roll overhead more often than not. These clouds cause summer rains to pour down and flood the land, while in the winter covering it with a thick layer of snow. When not buried in snow, mushy heaps of fallen needles and cones turn the ground soft.

Closing in on the beach, the group miraculously spots another boat that has already landed downshore. The men pull the boat onto the shore and walk to the other group. As they close in on the other men Milo can make out Nasir Pyrammus, Fenrir Harolfsson, another Pyrammian Guard, Ranger Dan, and another Ranger whom introduced himself to Milo simply as Smith.

"About time you bastards decided to show up," Nasir jokes.

"Well you know, we couldn't pass up the chance to let you miss us, now could we?" Milo responds smirking.

"Are there any others with you? Have you seen the other boats?" Ranger Forrest asks.

"No. This is all of us," Ranger Dan says.

"My crew!" The Captain cries out.

"Do not fret too much, Captain Gale," Ranger Dan tells him. "There must be another boat out there. Somewhere."

"What of the mission?" Ranger Forrest asks.

"This mishap was quite a setback, but we must head on."

"Do you even know where we are at?" Milo asks.

"Of course I do. We are in the Tyrosian forest. From the look of it, our destination is north of here."

"How would you suppose the ten of us will do this? We started with nearly thirty!" Richard Rosenthal exclaims.

"Now look you, this mission is paramount. If we fail, more than Adros shall be threatened by this foe," Ranger Dan tells him.

"You don't even tell who this foe is!"

"What does it matter to you?" The Ranger says sharply.

"Maybe we would like to know who we are fighting?" Westman questions.

Ranger Dan throws his hands up. "If you wish to leave, you may. We must get leaving, our journ' will take the rest of today and a good part of the morrow. We do not have time to stand here and argue."

"May I ask if we happen to have any food?" Nasir asks.

"Aye, I managed to grab some. We will have to ration it, though," Ranger Smith says.

"Shall we start our trek, then?" Ranger Dan asks.

"Are we not going to wait to see if any others arrive?" Milo adds.

"No, we shan't be doing any waiting. Let us go?"

Everybody looks at him blankly. Mumbling incomprehensibly, he ineptly marches up the beach, and the two other Rangers quickly bumbles after him. The group shuffles around nervously for a moment, then Milo says, "Well looks like we're going on an adventure." He then pursues the Rangers, and the rest of the group quickly follows. As they make their way up shore. Glancing into his lifeboat as they pass it, Milo shouts, "Looks like we forgot something in here." Peering in, it embarasses them to see that they had forgotten about the sleeping Aeris Wynterfang. "Aeris," Milo calls, but he doesn't wake up. He raises his voice slightly, but to no avail. Not wanting to raise his voice—to avoid attracting any unwanted attention—he climbs into the boat and gives him a reluctant nudge. In a sudden movement Aeris' hand lashes out as quick as a viper and twists Milo's arm back as he grabs for the knife strapped on his leg. Milo's heart beats so hard it feels like it is going to burst from his chest. But just as quick as it began, Aeris lets go of Milo.

"Shouldn't wake me like that," he says casually. Milo spots the faint twitch of a smile for a split second.

"I'm sorry, should we have just left you here?" Milo cracks nervously.

Aeris shrugs before jumping out of the boat. Milo follows, his heart beginning to calm. The group follows the shoreline for a short time, then heads off into the forest.

"Why don't we just find a nearby town? We could stock up on supplies, get more men," Westman complains.

"Do you know where we are at?" Milo asks the mercenary.

"I don't know. Some place with trees?"

"We're in Tyros," Nasir interjects. "There aren't any settlements up here, not anymore at least. And we'd be better off not seeing anybody else."

"What do you mean?" Westman asks.

"Did your parents teach you nothing? Since the discovery of Ateria, Tyros has been left mostly ungoverned. Too rocky and cold to grow most crops. With no nobility to keep the land civilised, it became the land for anarchists and criminals. Occasionally this Lord or that Lord would become tired of the savages raiding them and strike against them, but none desired to invest in maintaining these lands."

"That's a surprise. I thought you lord-folk claimed everything and anything they could," Westman mocks.

Nasir ignores the insult and says, "Worthless hills and savages aren't something many lords care to fight for control of."

"I thought the House of Malbose ruled Tyros, though?" Richard Rosenthal inquires.

"House Malbose did not come about until centuries later, not until Alexios the Great united Ateria. When he reorganised the realm, he established the Duchy of Tyros and gave rule over it to his general, Cyprian Malbose. House Malbose kept Tyros somewhat under control, but it was never strong enough to domesticate it. And any order that there may have been was lost after the Malbose Revolt. I hear that..."

Nasir's voice trails off and the group comes to a halt. Slowly approaching them is a massive bear. Milo slowly takes the bow from his shoulder, going to knock an arrow. Fenrir Harolfson and Richard Rosenthal slowly draw their blades. Then the three Rangers draw their swords in haste. The bear stops its approach and roars ferociously before getting onto its hind legs, standing fifteen feet tall. The group and the bear stand at a tense impasse for a long minute, until the bear goes back on all four and wanders off into the forrest.

"That was a big fucking bear!" Westman exclaims.

"Lord Nasir, I believe you forgot to tell Westman here something," says Milo.

"What?" Westman asks.

"That there are many monsters here, I believe is what Milo is referring to," Nasir answers.

"Aye," Milo affirms. "That there was just one of them; the Tyrosian bear, the largest in the world. Along with Thrymers, Wyverns, Griffins—and not the kind of Griffins like down in Adros. Monarch Griffins; the kind that will tear a man apart."

"Don't forget about Goblins," Richard Rosenthal adds.

"Goblins? Them little green imps my mother used to say would eat me if I was bad?" Westman scoffs.

Nasir then explains, "Imps? Nay. The Imps were hideous, aye, but they were bound to serve us, and were some of the most benevolent beings known to this world. The Goblins are dark beings. For millennium they have warred with the Dwarves and ravaged Human lands. They are a parasite that plunders the toils of higher beings, for they cannot make their own steel or sow their own seed. The settlers of Ateria thought they would be free from the scars of the Fracture, yet they found the same monstrous beings inhabiting these lands, and down from the mountains came the Goblins. They expand through their vast cave networks, infest abandoned buildings, and hide in trees awaiting to rob the misfortunate Human who happens to pass by."

"A splendid speech my Lord. And here I took you for just another drunkard," Milo jests.

*****

The group sits under the moonlight around a campfire, a boar roasting on a makeshift spit. Everybody is wolfing down their share of the boar Milo killed, except for Ranger Dan. Instead, he picked only a few parts of the meat before leaving more than half of it uneaten. "Tomorrow we continue on, we should reach our target location a few hours before the Sun sets," he informs the group.

"Where exactly *are* we heading?" Nasir inquires.

"Our adversary is held up in the Division."

The entire group all stops their frenzied eating at once and looks at him in concern. The Division is the behemoth mountain range dividing the frozen wastes of Asbjarnarvik from the rest of Ateria. The range spans across the entire continent, reaching all the way to the oceans on each end. Blocking the freezing winds of Asbjarnarvik from the rest of the realm are its massive peaks.

"Fret not. He isn't too deep in or high up."

"They better not be. You ought to know that we aren't goats," Milo remarks. Ranger Dan bitterly stares at him unamused for a moment.

"My ship..." Captain Gale mutters to himself with no clear reason.

"Oh? The fuck of it?" Gerev Westman snaps at the man, annoyed that he keeps saying that over and over again.

"It was all I fuckin' had!" Captain Gale lashes out, but then his face turns to sorrow and he buries his face in his palms. After a moment, he looks back up, his face plastered in misery and asks Ranger Dan, "Do you think the Grand-Duke will reimburse my losses?"

"I don't think so," he says ashamed.

Captain Gale moans and buries his face in his palms again. A few minutes later, he takes his face from his palms, but his head still hangs low.

"You see, that ship was my life. When I was a boy, I worked selling oysters at the docks of Lord's Port. Neither me nor my mother had a fuckin' coin to spare for anything. Dirt poor, living in the fucking slums! I got out by working on a ship, my dream since I was just a wee fucking child!"

"I don't understand where you are heading?" Richard Rosenthal quietly asks.

"I'll get there. I jumped from one ship to the fuckin' next. But eventually, I made it from just a swabbie to somehow being my Captain's first mate! His first fucking mate! You see, after he struck big-" The man goes silent for a minute before continuing, "After he struck it big, he made me Captain over that damned ship."

The group sat in silence for a minute until Gerev Westman began to speak. "Shut up, you well off prick. I grew up as a simple farming bloke. Sat in my tiny village for years, didn't even chance to take any of the harvest to Lord's Port. It was about what? My thirteenth year, I think it was, when some pricks wandered into my village. I don't quite know what occurred that night, but they ended up burning down half the village. It killed old Ida in her sleep. She was about to 'ave been sixty-four or sixty-five—I don't remember all that well. I don't recall any others having gotten hurt from the fires."

"So you took on the sword and vowed to avenge them? Like in the tall tales?" Richard Rosenthal snarkily interrupts.

"Let me finish! At first I went to rebuilding the village and right back to working the farm. Problem arises a few months later, when I find the girl I had been a'love with for the past few years had become with child!"

"So you got her pregnant and ran away from home, then?" Richard interrupts, again.

"Damn it stop interrupting me! Thing is, I had never laid with her. Hell, I hadn't even seen a tit yet! After some hard pressing I found out one of the assholes had forced himself on her that night! Guess they burned down the village after her da whacked 'em behind the head. Didn't save her the trouble though. After that I thought I could track them down and kill 'em by joining the King's Legion. Boy, what a mistake. I took some equipment and tried to track them down on my own."

"So you deserted?" Nasir asks disapprovingly.

"No! I hadn't finished training yet. Most I'm guilty of is thievery."

"Hmmm," Nasir hums, then allows him to finish.

"Soon after I realised that they weren't just gonna let me to track 'em down, So I fled and tried to track them down on my own. Damn I was naive to think I could find them. I never did. Likely never will. To make some money to feed myself, I took to being a sellsword. You see, I was one of them few lucky ones who got trained with a sword rather than a spear."

"Thy story sounds a little like mine. Well not really, now that I think about it," Ranger Dan states.

"I think we would all be interested in hearing how you became a Silverwood Ranger," Nasir says.

"Yeah, do tell us how you went about becoming a Silverwood Ranger," Richard Rosenthal says.

"Aight. I guess I should start with that my father was a drunk. A mean drunk. He seldom touched me, but my mother wasn't as fortunate. He beat her nearly every night. Forced himself on her too, only not when... Well, you know."

Several members of the group look to him questioningly, not knowing what he was referencing. So the man informs them despite breaking couth, "When she bled." Everybody understands, some of whom it embarasses.

"It's surprising that the old bastard never fathered any more children. I think I may have been five at the time and my sister less than a year when this happened. It was late at night when I was awoken by the slamming of the door. He had spent his night drinking, damned if I knew where. My room didn't have a door, so I saw and heard *everything*. My mother quietly began to reheat supper for him. At first he just drank even more, staring menacingly at her. But then he grabbed her and turned her around. I can still remember her face, so scared. And his words: 'There's something else I want...'" His voice trails off, and a tear slides down his cheek.

"You don't have to continue," Nasir tells him him sympathetically.

"No, tis fine. I laid there in bed, watching as he forced himself on my mother. But then, my sister began to cry. Made the old bastard stop for a moment to curse at her. My mother pleaded for him to let her calm my sweet sister. He reluctantly agreed at first. She was shaking and crying as she tried to calm my sweet sweet sister. The old bastard said that *she* was making my baby sister cry! *Mother*! Not *his* yelling and raping her!"

He once again pauses for a moment with a look of pure hatred in his eyes. "He grabbed my sister by the leg and tried to rip her from my mother's arms. They struggled for a few moments that felt like years to me then hit mother in the face. Her yelp of pain..." He stops again and another tear runs down his cheek. "Then he threw my sweet sweet baby sister into the wall and... killed her. He became furious and strangled mother while telling her to look what she did and that it was *all her fault*. She was very beautiful, but her face was now all puffy and covered in blood." He sobs for a moment before continuing on. "I remember little after this, only that the house was on fire. I remember the scorching heat. Next thing I can remember a man was carrying me out of the burning house and telling me everything would be all right from now on. He was the man who trained me to be who I am now." The man then starts to cry a lot, and Milo can tell the men are feeling guilty for asking.

"He made you a Silverwood Ranger?" Richard Rosenthal asks.

"No, he-" After a sudden stop he nervously stutters, "Well... Yes."

Milo doesn't say a word. There is nothing for him to say. He gets up from his seat on a rock, throws down a blanket, and tries to sleep, his mind swimming from the sad story. Many members of the group follow his lead, those who don't sit in tense silence. It is going to be a big day tomorrow, and nobody other than the Rangers know what is happening. If it weren't for the depressing story, Milo would have demanded answers *tonight*.

Milo wakes up at the crack of dawn. Arguing over the ashes of the fire are the two mercenaries.

"Nay, you can't eat it now. It has been sitting out all night," Richard Rosenthal tries telling Gerev Westman.

"Oh come on, sure you can." Westman picks off a piece of meat, only for Rosenthal to slap it out of his hand. "It was over the fire all night. It's just like that smoked beef we have with us."

"No, it's not the same."

"He's right," Milo interrupts. "I would have had to prepared it properly for it to be safe to eat. If you eat any of that now, you'll likely get sick."

Westman wanders off mumbling to himself.

"Should we wake the others?" Milo asks Rosenthal.

He shakes his head, "Nay. This mysterious enemy can wait a little longer."

Milo takes a head-count of the sleeping bodies and finds Nasir is missing. "Where's the Lord?"

"Uh, I think he went to go take a piss. Now that I think about it, he's been gone for some time."

"Crap. Which way did he go?"

Richard Rosenthal leads the way into the woods, where they search the nearby perimeter to no avail.

"Dammit, where could he have gone?" Milo says.

"Something may have ate him," Rosenthal thinks out loud.

The two look at each other afraid of what that would mean. Then they hear a faint voice coming from nearby. Making their way through the brush they find a small clearing, where a greying ancient Forest Troll is standing before Nasir. The green giant is an astounding several heads taller than the men, and about as large as the boulders situated in a circle around him. A lone hawk's call could be heard echoing throughout the forest as it flies through the pines. In its talons is a small tortoise, which is promptly dropped and heard loudly cracking on the Troll's skull. The Troll doesn't seem phased by it. It leans over and picks up the tortoise's shell, tapping it with his fingers.

"Hawkses drops rockses likes theses on Dirg's head verses much. Dirg noses likeses bub... shells pretties." The Troll would speak as he peered upon the man he had caught with his pants down quite literally before him. His snout's muscles contorting instinctively as he caught the scent of the nearby men and peered over with his small dark brown beady eyes, speaking with a deep rasp in his voice, "Humanses comes sees Dirg's rockses works?"

"I apologise Dirg, but I believe I must be getting back to my group," Nasir tells the ageing giant.

"Dirgs says always welcomses to see rockses." The ageing giant would state as he overlooked Nasir, picking some large beetle out of his nose before flicking it off into a nearby fire as he blinked his eyes down at Nasir, "Does manses haser smallses peckers? Others manses smells strongers thanses yous."

Watching from the brush, Richard Rosenthal finds himself unable to contain his laughter. Hearing the hysterical laughter, the Troll and Nasir turn and look towards their two onlookers. The Troll just looks upon his onlookers dumbly, pursing his lips as he lowers his right hand to scratch his rear, letting out a large waft of gas and filling the air with what smelled like a mixture of wild onions and roasted stew.

"Dirg markses territory, now go beforeses mans become oneses with Dirg."

Nasir backs away from the Troll, clamping his nose tightly. A man whose face is so contorted that he hardly resembles Richard Rosenthal gasps as he says, "Come with me, my Lord." The two flee from the stench and towards the camp. But Milo, vainly pinching his nose to keep the smell out, remains to ask the Troll, "Wait. How old are you? I've never seen a Troll so aged."

"Dirgs err... not sureses... er, but woodsies pointsied ships Dirg rememberses invades lands long time agos... if says how oldses Dirg is." The Troll says as the men hear the sounds of something exploding near them, and what appeared to be the remains of stew is splattered across the rock circle. He'd turn and blink off at the source of the explosion, "Dirgses thinks Lamias soupses doneses."

Milo nods as he says, "Enjoy your breakfast." He then runs back to camp, trying to escape the noxious air as quickly as possible. He, Nasir, and Richard return to the camp together, finding that the others have all woke up.

"Where were you three?" Ranger Forrest questions.

"Nasir decided he wanted to chat with a Troll," Richard says.

"I was taking a piss when the thing came up behind me!"

Fenrir Harolfson walks up to the men, "A Troll eh? Lucky we ain't in my homeland. The Trolls up there are terrible. About half a decade ago my people fought a great war against them." Aeris' face twitches slightly and his eyes fill with rage at this comment.

"Gather your things. We must be on our way!" Ranger Forrest says, irked.

The men collect the few things they have and set back onto their march north. Continuing north they are met with a small river, but luckily an old tree has rolled into the river and can use it to cross it without getting wet. First Ranger Dan goes, taking each step slowly. Then Milo goes, faster than the Ranger but still taking it slow as the log shakes. After him follows Aeris, who very quickly gets across it, all without a sound. One at a time the rest cross slowly and successfully. The very last one is Ranger Forrest. Despite inching slower than Ranger Dan, he still shakes and wobbles horribly. Right before finishing his painfully slow crossing, Ranger Forrest loses his balance and falls into the water. He flails about in the foot deep water as if drowning until Milo and Ranger Dan pull him from the stream.

After crossing the river, it is a fairly easy travel north. Further up into the rocky hills they journey, yet they follow a dry riverbed with ease. After some time the riverbed turns east, and the men turn off it and towards the north-west into densely forested foothills. Most of the remaining rations are eaten on the move, and there is little in the way of conversation for several hours. That is until Westman speaks up.

"Do you ever talk?" He asks a Pyrammian Guardsman.

"Yes."

"When? This is the first time I've heard you speak. *Ever*."

"I speak when it is relevant."

"Is having a conversation relevant?"

"When it is relevant."

"Boy, what did they do to you in Pyrammian Guard training?"

"Oi! We train them to have disci-" Nasir begins before being cut off by Ranger Dan.

"Could you both keep it down? This part of the forest is crawling with Goblins. We don't want to-"

A large rock flies through the air and fall into Ranger Dan's legs, crushing them. Milo spins to the direction that the rock had come from, and sees a large force of Goblins with a small catapult. He quickly nocks an arrow and takes aim at one of the Goblins that is reloading the catapult. Loosing the arrow, he shoots right in its neck. The Goblins, who vastly outnumber the group, charge whilst release irritating screams. In the hands of each one of them is a crude knife or axe. The group stands in a tight line ready for battle. Milo once again nocks, draws, and looses, this time sending the arrow into a charging Goblin's chest. He repeats this once more before realising that it is futile. Within seconds a Goblin is atop Richard Rosenthal and brutally sinks its blade into his stomach several times. In swift, decisive movements Aeris Wynterfang cuts down the Goblins in droves. The Pyrammian Guardsmen keep a wide area under the guard of his spear to protect Nasir, who in turn takes off into the forest alone. Nobody seeming to have noticed but him, Milo sighs and says to himself, "There goes Lord Drunk. Again." Milo decides to goes after him.

The two men run through the rugged forest until they believe they have made it a safe distance away, only to find out they are horrible wrong when several Goblins jump down out of the trees ahead. Milo shoots an arrow into one, but then feels something crash down onto his back. He knows it is a Goblin.

◈ CHAPTER FOUR

Nasir reacts almost immediately, sinking his Yataghan into the Goblin's back and chopping through bone. The creature falls off Milo's back with a hideous yelp. He spins around and looks down at the flailing creature, then up to Nasir, who gives him a nod. Milo nocks another arrow, points it towards Nasir, and shoots the arrow.

Nasir's face turns to shock, only to quickly realise what had happened. This time Milo had saved Nasir; a Goblin had run up behind him and was about to plunge its knife into him. Goblins coming from the nearly all directions, the two run further into the forest. After several minutes, Nasir stops and hunches over, gasping for air.

"I think we've lost them," Nasir says.

Milo scrutinises the surrounding woods, an arrow knocked in case anything is out there. "And the rest of our group."

"Should we try to find them?"

"There is no way to know which way they went. If any of them even got out alive."

Nasir nods his head. "We aren't far from the Division. If we travel north and don't find the others, we can follow it to Korvun's pass."

"Korvun's pass? Why would we want to go there?"

A chuckling Nasir reminds Milo, "Did you forget that my brother is the Shaqif of Pyrammus, and my sister the Queen of Ateria? The Jarl of the Pass will certainly help us get back to Dalarus."

"Right," Milo says, taking note that Nasir said *us* in spite of speaking to a commoner. "This way, my Lord."

Milo leads the way with bow in hand and arrow knocked. As they venture through the forest, they keep a nervous eye out and up the trees for Goblins. For a long time they see nothing but trees and hear nothing but birds. Then they hear the close screams of a man.

They rushed through the forest as quietly as they could. Halting at a distance, the men watch from the cover of the treeline as a great Tyrosian bear rips Ranger Smith apart. Violently it tears his body nearly in half, flinging his entrails across the forest. After it finally decides it has thoroughly mauled the Ranger, the great bear wanders off into the forest with a cub in tow. When the bear is long out of sight, Milo and Nasir nervously approach the carcass. Suddenly the grotesque figure's head twitches in their direction.

"Help me," it wheezes out.

Whereas Nasir takes a step back, Milo kneels down by the man after a moment of hesitation. "There's nothing I can do for you, but there is something you can do for us... Can you tell us where the others are?"

"A cottage. To the... east."

"Thank you," Milo says melancholily. He stands up and walks towards Nasir, but then the man whimpers to himself, "He will be angry..."

Milo stops in his tracks and looks over his shoulder. "Who will be angry?"

"F-father," he gets out before his head falls limp, finally dead.

Milo feels a strange sense of calmness and malevolence. He gently places his hand on Nasir's shoulder, his head pressed up against a tree.

Shaking his head, the Lord says, "Jurzai protect us. This is a wicked place."

The two turn east in search of the cottage. After even more wandering through the woods, they find a derelict water mill sitting upon a small cliff, its wheel turned by the small waterfall created by the adjacent stream. Hanging from a nearby tree is a dead man. Whether brigands were the ones to hang him or if it was at his own hand, Milo could not determine.

The men pull themselves up the rocks and boulders of the cliff, and approach the building. Inside they hear men shouting heatedly. Milo swings open the door. The shouting stops immediately as the entire room draws their blades.

"Bloody hell, we thought you were more Goblins," Westman spits.

"Then fix your eyes. And your volume," Milo says as he takes a head-count. There is himself, Nasir, Westman, Ranger Forrest, Fenrir Harolfsson, and Aeris Wynterfang.

"Dar'ak didn't make it..?" Nasir ask, though his tone says he already knows the answer.

"Derrick? Was there a Derrick amongst us?" Forrest asks confused.

"It's pronounced Dar'ak. He was my Guardsman."

"I'm sorry, he held the Goblins off while we escaped," Forrest says sincerely.

"I watched as the Goblins swarmed him. Bastards stabbed him a lot. Or that might've been the other one. I don't know, they all look alike," Westman states indifferently.

"What were y'all arguing about when we came in?" Milo interjects.

"The Ranger here wants us to continue. I believe the rest of us think that's a bad fucking idea," Westman sneers.

"This is a fucking catastrophe!" Fenrir Harolfsson snaps. "How does he think we can go on? We started with twenty-six. Now we have just six."

"I thought someone said we started with thirty? I guess thirty to six doesn't sound as good as twenty-six to six," Milo says.

"I know we are worn, but we must continue on! For the sake of Ateria!" Forrest says trying to sound inspirational but failing pitifully.

"And why is that? You won't tell us why we are even here!" Westman prods.

"We are nearly there. Just a league or two and we can begin the attack!"

"Earlier you worried if we had enough men! Have you really grown so arrogant to think we could do it *now* after all that has happened?" Fenrir says.

"We must! It does not matter what I think! We must head for the cave!"

"Men! Enough have died to get us here. This man, a Ranger of the House Silverwood, says that this is of our utmost concern. Do you all really wish to put your own lives above that of all Ateria?" The men listen intently to Nasir, taking his words into heavy consideration. "If you don't wish to come, just leave now and start the trek back to Adros or wherever it is you hail from."

"I shall stay," Westman proclaims, his head lowered slightly in shame.

"I shall stay, too," Fenrir says.

"Ain't like I have anything better to do," Aeris answers.

The men look towards Milo questioningly. Milo says, "Don't look at me, I've been with you this whole time."

"It's settled then," Ranger Forrest says.

*****

Even from far away they could see the colossal mountains reaching far above the trees. Seeming to Milo as if it is the man's second nature, Ranger Forrest leads the men to a trail that winds up the mountain. The men stand around anxiously, their heads snapped back as they stare up towards the tremendous peaks. If there were any doubts in their minds, they now all know that the chances of returning from those spires are slim.

"Are you all ready?" Ranger Forrest asks the group.

One at a time each member of the group says, "Aye."

"Then..." Ranger Forest begins, but his voice trails off. He lets out a sigh as he too peers up into the peaks, "Let it begin."

Swords in hand, the group begins the trek up the path. In the lead is Ranger Forrest, followed by Westman, then behind him Milo, then Nasir, then Aeris, and finally Fenrir at the rear. The path is clearly man made, but Milo can only wonder who built it and why. They slowly march up the path, winding further and higher into the vastness of the Division. The wind to get stronger and colder. Curving around the ridges nobody can tell where the path ends, nor can they see where it began. Milo looks down and sees they are on the edge of a great cliff. A menacing screech echoes throughout the bluffs, powerful and menacing. Most members of the group look as though they have no idea what creature made that noise, but Milo knows exactly what it was—the scream of a King Griffin.

They look around frantically for the source of the sound. From behind a spire it suddenly appears and dives straight towards Ranger Forrest, who is looking the other way. Milo tries to warn the Ranger, "Run, Forrest-" But the Griffin has already swooped down and grabbed the man with its great talons. "Oh, he gone."

The group has fallen to five men. In the span of two days they lost more than twenty men. And now they are moving to fight an enemy whom none other than dead men know anything about.

Despite this, the group pushes on, watching the skies for the Griffin's return. The path goes over a steep slope, a hike that felt like hours with the great beast lurking about. Once over the top of the ridge they find themselves in a small valley. In the centre stands the Griffin, devouring the flesh of the former Ranger.

Either hearing or smelling the approaching men, or both, the griffin stands defensively over its catch and screeches at the men. It slowly and cautiously moves towards them, though not afraid of them. The men stand in a line, swords drawn and ready to fight the terrific beast; except Milo, who has taken off to the side. Contrary to the others, he sheaths his sword. He then pulls the bow off his shoulder and nocks an arrow. The griffin moves at a steady pace towards the men, it growing quicker with each stride. Milo puts the arrow between the beast's eyes, the steel head penetrating the hollow bone with ease. The winged monster crashes to the ground with a loud thud and a cloud of dust.

The men move around and encircle the beast cautiously, weapons still drawn in case it it still alive. After assuring themselves that it was dead, they look around for what it is they are supposed to be after.

"Where in fuck's name are we supposed to go from 'ere? There's nothing but cliffs in sight." Westman curses.

"That cave, perhaps?" Nasir responds, pointing at a cave in the nearby cliff face.

"What cave?" Westman says as he squints to try and see the small entrance.

"Don't look much like a fortress to me," Aeris says.

"There is nothing else around," Nasir says disgruntled.

"Is the so terrible force hiding in some dank cave?" Westman asks rhetorically.

"How much could it hurt to check it out? If he isn't there, oh well. If he is, it couldn't be any worse than if he was in a fortress," Fenrir says to the group. "We at least owe it to those who died trying to get here to at least look, don't we?"

The group looks to one another in hesitation before going over to the cave. They enter the mouth of the cave. The air is thick with moisture and has a repugnant must. Deep within the tunnel they can see a faint light. Milo takes a few minutes to realise that they are walking down a staircase carefully carved into the stone and not merely eroded rock.

The men reach the end of the staircase and turn a corner, meeting two peculiar rock structures that resemble the form of large overweight Humans. It is as if they are guarding the room that lies behind them. At first Milo thinks these rock figures were a pile of stones someone had mortared together, possibly as a warning. This changes when one of the statues smacks Fenrir Harolfsson several feet back, his lamellar clinking loudly as it collides with the stone floor.

Aeris, whom was standing right next to Fenrir, instinctively draws his sword from its scabbard, cutting one of the stone figures as he does so to no effect other than a spectacular array of sparks and ruining the blade's edge. He pauses for a moment to get a bearing of his situation. "The fuck?" He ducks as the stone figure swings for his head. Fenrir Harolfsson slowly rises again. With a half limp and axe high, he charges, shield readied to take another blow. It does not help him. As soon as he enters the figure's arms reach it smacks him again, this time throwing him into the cavern wall with a loud crack.

Nasir picks up a large rock with both hands and chucks it at one of the stone figures with all his might. It crashes into it with a loud and powerful thud, but the figure merely absorbes the stone into its form.

Milo stands back calm and observes the area. He notices that nearby is a high ledge he could climb up onto. It doesn't run past the statues, but it is just high enough that he should be able to jump over them. Climbing up the ledge, Westman shouts to him, "The fuck do you think you're doin'?" Milo just ignores the astringent mercenary and pulls himself onto the ledge. He makes a leap and dives over the statues. He feels his foot hit one statue, but he clears it and lands with a roll. Jumping up, he quickly looks around. The room is fairly round with a domed ceiling, from which hangs many braziers. Milo wonders how whoever lives here keeps them all burning. In the centre of the room is a steep stone tower, with a flat top. He hears another strike of metal against rock ring throughout the cavern.

Before the tower stands a stout pedestal carved right from the stone of the cavern. Running up to it, he finds a stone tablet lays upon it. Through a swath of strange symbols carved into the stone he realises tell the stone is merely a case for one mass of dark crystal. For the first time since the Bleaks, he hears whispers echo through his mind, as if coming from everywhere yet nowhere at the same time.

"The Tiki mask," the voice tells Milo.

After getting a grip on the world the voice had just sent spinning, Milo asks, "Could you be any less specific, oh disembodied voice?"

He believes he hears a sigh, then it continues, "Use it."

"How do you suppose I use it, eh?"

"Well you- Just figure it out!" the voice snaps in frustration.

"What is it with my incorporeal guides? Come on people, learn to do your job will ya!"

After several moments he realises the voice isn't responding to him anymore. He scrambles to untie the tiki mask from his belt, knowing the others aren't going to last forever. First he puts the mask up to his face, yet nothing happens. Flustered, he turns it upside down. Milo lets out a long, heavy sigh and moans, "Couldn't this have come instructions or something?" He then holds it out in front of him, near the tablet and mumbles, "C'mon, do yer thing!" The Mask vibrates momentarily. Angered that the mask did nothing but shiver, he groans in frustration. Only then does he hear the sound of falling rocks. Spinning around, he sees that the stone figures are now just a pile of slate. The cavern grows completely silent and Milo feels a sharpness in his heart believing it was too late. Then they appear over the piles.

"I don't know what you did, but you fuckin' did it," Westman exclaims.

"What *did* you do?" Nasir asks.

"I- You see …" He pauses for a moment and thinks. "It's awful complicated."

"What were those?" Aeris asks.

"I think they were something called… The fucks the word?" Westman asks himself, unable to remember.

"Golems," Nasir tells the group.

"Golems?" Westman asks.

"Aye. They are… things made by magic. They are often used as guards or other forms of servants. It takes great magic to create one, and seldom even are tales of those who made one without a fragile crystal core within their chest. Someone like this could certainly create one with a higher task, such as blacksmithing."

"I was thinking Gargoyles. You sure they aren't Gargoyles?" Westman asks.

"Nay those are those bat things you find on cathedrals."

"I think the important matter at hand is who made them," Milo interrupts.

"I made them," a voice booms throughout the cavern.

They all spin around to an old man standing atop the tower. His short grey hair is balding and a long beard reaches down to his stomach. He is dressed in a long red robe made of silk with a black belt wrapped around his stomach, and a pair of ugly round glasses sit on his nose.

"I am Albus DéFreur. I had thought you would all die by this point, as the others before you had," the man tells the group.

Milo is not amused. As Albus talks, Milo takes an arrow from his quiver and nocks it.

"It seems I have found-"

Not caring to let Albus finish, Milo shoots his arrow into the man's heart, knocking the old man backwards and off from the tower with a particularly disgusting splattering sound.

"What did you do that for?" Nasir asks Milo.

"What? Did you want to listen to the madman?"

"Well not really. But perhaps we could have learned the truth of this all before we killed him."

"Come here," Aeris calls from around the tower. Making their way around the tower they are met with Aeris' hawkish scowl.

"You sure you killed him?" Westman asks Milo. The body is nowhere to be found.

"It pierced straight into his heart. And from the sound of it alone I doubt he'd be walking away."

"If that's so then tell me... Where the fuck is he?" Westman asks.

Milo looks around the cavern for the man. If he did somehow manage to crawl away, he couldn't have made it far. To his dismay he can't find the man's body anywhere, but he does notice a small doorway carved into the wall. He makes his way to it and finds there is a small room behind it. On one side of the room is a bed made from straw and some wool cloths, and a large trunk on the other. Directly ahead is an alcove, with a display of several objects: a steel warhammer, it's handle engraved with symbols unlike any Milo had seen before; an old Asbjarnarvik style helmet; and a disturbing, hand stitched doll of some man.

Milo hears steps enter the room behind him. "Whoa! That old bastard was into some creepy shit!" It's Westman. Milo turns around to to find him with a foolish grin. Westman then looks over to the trunk, saying, "I wonder what's in this thing." He then kneels down and flips open then latches. He places his hands to open it, but pauses to look at Milo. "Let's see if a Goblin or something jumps out." He quickly slams open the lid, but only finds it full of clothes: a funny pointed hat, more colourful robes, a cloak, and a lace lingerie. Westman's grin fades to a look of disappointment as he digs through it. Disenchanted, he stands up and leaves the room, shouting back, "I'm going. This place is a crackhole." Milo grabs the warhammer from the shelf and takes it with him.

Leaving the dreaded place, Milo climbs over the rock pile from the Golems and finds Nasir and Aeris struggling to move the injured and now Fenrir. After helping get him as comfortable as possible Milo quickly examines him.

"It seems you've dislocated your shoulder, break one leg, roll the other's ankle, and either break or bruise several ribs," Milo tells him.

"How long do you think I'll take to heal?"

"Couldn't tell you, I'm not- Wait, be quiet."

"What?" Westman blurts out.

"Shut up, I think I heard something."

Barely audible to his ears, numerous footsteps are descending towards them.

"I think I see a light," Aeries whispers.

"Aye," Milo confirms.

The four healthy men quietly position themselves around the room and draw their weapons, and Fenrir pulls his dagger for a last stand. The footsteps get closer and the light grows brighter. The light comes feet away from them and stops, it dimly flickering onto several figures on the shadowy staircase. While Aeris coils up to strike the mysterious arrivers like a viper, the others tense up for a desperate defence.

◈ CHAPTER FIVE

"Is everybody alright down there," a voice calls out.

The men hesitate but do not let their guard down. A man holds the lantern out and squints trying to see the group. Milo's eyes adjusting to the new light, he can make out a squad of Silverwood Rangers accompanied by Gale. After looking over the five men then his own uniform, the Ranger says, "Lord Silverwood would like to send you his dearest apologies, Lord Nasir."

The men remain in silence until Nasir speaks up, "How are we to trust you? How did you find us?"

"I assure you we are the actual Silverwood Rangers."

Nasir repeats himself slowly, "How did you find us?"

"We have been searching Tyros for you ever since we found survivors of the shipwreck. We came across Captain Gale here who told us of the Goblin attack. While he couldn't tell us the direction you went, he led us to the site of the attack. There we found a man who had been stabbed in the gut. He was able to tell us the direction you ran."

"Was it Dar'ak?"

"No. It was the mercenary named Richard Rosenthal. He died a few hours ago sadly."

"Continue telling how you found us here. There is still a great amount of land between the attack and here," Nasir asks, still suspicious.

"We followed the trail of corpses and footprints. First to a cabin, then here."

"Hold up, I still don't understand why your fellow Rangers led us here?" Milo asks.

"The men you met were not Silverwood Rangers. A few months ago we found one of our patrols murdered and robbed of their uniforms. We thought they were merely trying to hide the identity of the bodies, but now we see their uniforms were stolen so those men could pose as Rangers. Why they led you on this spurious mission, I could not begin to tell you."

"I think we might know more than you do, though no less enigmatic," Nasir says.

"In any case, the Grand-Duke has ordered us to escort you all to his Ducal Authority," the Ranger tells the men.

*****

The men roll into Lord's Port in a seated wagon. A large wagon with wooden benches, it is nothing splendid. Inside sit Milo, Aeris, Nasir, Westman, and Gale; and laying in a makeshift bed of straw between the benches is the recovering Fenrir. Trotting alongside the wagon are two Silverwood Rangers escorting the wagon.

Like most of the big towns in the Grand-Duchy of New Adros, the city of Lord's Port sits on the massive bay within the middle of Ateria, known as the Noble Bay. However this city is infamous for its high traffic, due to farming villages shipping their taxed crop across the bay to Lord's Port, where it is then sent either sent to the capital of Varlebeck by wagon or shipped up to the frozen lands of Asbjarnarvik to feed their population.

The men hauling their harvests and other goods throughout the cobbled roads of the city stare at the wagon. Not only are the Silverwood Rangers renowned heroes amongst the Adrosi, but the Silverwood Rangers escorting the brother of Shaqif Nasir and Queen Arianna is a site to behold. Lord Nasir cheerfully waves to the common folk. As they pass one dirty beggar and who they can assume to be his daughter, Lord Nasir flips a 50$\mathscr{R}$ coin towards him. "Thank you," the man whispers hoarsely. Smiling brightly, the man and his daughter smiling admire the crystal coin, which is carved out of the common dull-green Erezold crystal.

"So this is Lord's Port," Milo says.

"You have not been here before, Milo?" Nasir asks.

"Nope. I'm from Southern Adros, and I don't get to the cities a lot."

The wagon rolls past a flock of whores who wave and call at the men. Their bright red dresses stop just below their fannies and have their chests cut out to reveal their bosoms. One whore blows a kiss at the wagon, and another barely has to lift her skirt to show the men her merchandise.

"Ah fuck it," Westman mutters to himself before jumping out of the moving wagon.

"Where are you going?" Milo shouts after him.

Looking over his shoulder he shouts back, "To fuck some whores!"

"What about-"

Nasir interrupts him, "Just let him go."

The wagon continues through the streets, the busy working streets still staring in awe as the cart passes by. The tall tudor buildings recede as they approach the citadel of Lord's Port. Ascending high above the city on a hill is a great square tower, watching over even the farthest expanses of the city. A great hexagonal wall surrounds the tower, each point of the hexagon tipped with a round bastion.

"So this is the Keep of the Red Lion," Milo says.

"Doesn't look red to me," Aeris says.

Fenrir says with a chuckle, "Not very much like a Lion either." Then he groans in pain.

"It's not supposed to look like a red lion," Nasir begins. "This part of Ateria was colonised by Bordreaux. Their flag was the face of a lion embroidered in red onto a white field. The locals began calling it the Keep of the Red Lion for the large flag flown over the gatehouse, and soon the name of Citadelle de la Voiçont faded into history. It's this same reason why this narrow strip of land between the Noble Bay and the Sea of the Turquoise Dawn is called the Redlands."

"You really like history, don't you Lord Nasir?" Milo asks.

"Aye, ever since I was a small child. I find it so fascinating how greatly the things of the past have shaped our world. Many people live their entire lives never knowing why the world is the way it is."

A small portcullis clatters and shakes as the men inside the gatehouse manually crank it open. Flying over the gatehouse is the banner of House Blount, a field of orange bordered with light blue and a deep blue trident in the centre. The horses pull the wagon up the gentle slope of the hill and pass through the wooden portcullis with barely enough headroom. The huge wooden doors of the keep swing open and a man flanked by a couple Guards comes out. With his fingers he combs back his lush brown hair, then pats down his coarse ginger beard. The wagoner tugs on his reins and the horses pull the wagon off to the side, then he gives another long pull and the horses stop. As Milo, Nasir, and Gale exit slowly through the back of the wagon Aeris vaults elegantly over the side.

The man brushes the miniscule dust that might have been there off of his cream and orange striped tunic before saying, "Greetings Lord Pyrammus. It is good to see you have arrived safely."

"Thank you, Lord Blount. With me are Milo Khan, Aeris Wynterfang, and Captain Gale."

Fenrir shouts from his bedding within the cart, "And Fenrir son of Harolf!"

Speaking towards the cart but unable to see Fenrir, Lord Blount says, "My riders told me of your condition, Harolfson. My court physician will tend to your needs until you are fit to return to Asbjarnarvik."

"And as a token of our appreciation, House Pyrammus will grant a tax reduction to sell your wares in our city. I believe you will find it quite generous," Nasir says.

Milo snorted in his attempt to suppress his laughter. Everybody looks at him as he awkwardly tries to hide a smirk.

Bryan Blount speaks slowly, still watching Milo suspiciously, "Grand-Duke Silverwood is waiting for you inside."

Nasir nods and disappears through the two grand wooden doors. The others stand nervously until Lord Blount gestures for them to also enter. Facing away from them on the dais is a man with his hands clasped firmly behind his back. He inspects the Throne of the Keep of the Red Lion carefully. It is a simple chair with eloquent carvings of the forest on it, and mounted atop it a pair of antlers bigger than any Milo had ever seen before.

"Enter Lord Nasir of House Pyrammus and company. They stand before Hrothgar of House Silverwood, Grand-Duke of New Adros," the Herald of Grand-Duke Silverwood announces.

"I would think from the name, the Elk Throne, it would be so much grander," he says as he turns around. His hair is a shiny grey, but this is inconsistent with the youthfulness of his face. "Who are these men with you?"

"These are the men who too were lured by the dark mage. I doubt I would be here today without them," Nasir tells him.

"This is all of them?" He asks.

"All who made it out alive, I'm afraid," Lord Nasir says lowering his head in remorse.

"I must apologise to you all for this horrible incident. I never would have imagined that somebody would steal the identity of one of my Rangers, lest use their identities to lure so many into such a terrible escapade. I can only hope that you can pardon my fault in all this."

"You are at no fault my Lord," Nasir tells him.

"Thank you Lord Nasir, though I wish I could have avoided it from having ever happened. As a token of my atonement, I will have my personal ship take you all back to Dalarus. It has been stocked with plenty of foods and wines—including a rare vintage from the vineyard of Emperor Carlisle von Clausewitz-Silberholz during his exile in Mordavia. I'm sure you'll find the history as great as the taste."

"Pardon me Grand-Duke Silverwood," Gale begins. "My ship was destroyed because of this... escapade as you called it. If you truly wish to make it up to us, would you recompense me with a ship of equal value?"

Hrothgar Silverwood's face turns dark. He steps close to Captain Gale and gently touches one of the gold buttons on the man's naval coat. "You may wear gold on your uniform and work on the seas in the stead of fields, but do not think that you are in any more of a right to make demands of a noble." He returns his hands to behind his back again before turning around and taking five paces away from the men.

"My ship," Gale whispers to himself in defeat.

Milo rolls his eyes, "Oh not this crap again."

The Herald cries loudly, "Exit Lord Nasir Pyrammus, the risque sailor, and company!"

The men take the que and leave the Throne room. Back outside they find Fenrir has been disappeared, most likely taken into the castle to tend to his wounds. One of the Silverwood Rangers comes up to the men and says, "I am to escort those who are returning to Dalarus to the *Pelikan von Adros*."

Nasir looks to the men, "Who's coming?"

"Better than starving on the streets of Lord's Port," Gale says melancholy.

Aeris shrugs, "Why not."

Nasir looks to Milo and waits for a response. After a long while of silence he finally asks, "Are you coming back to Dalarus Milo?"

◈ CHAPTER SIX

Reading from a book is a man with a red slicked-back undercut and a pointy ducktail beard. His right eye is icy blue, while his left is bright green. A wolf pelt is wrapped around his shoulders, and beneath it he wears simple off-white shirt and pants. Strung around his neck is a golden harp pendant. Sprawled across the massive, eloquently carved desk he is sitting at are various scrolls and tomes. Leaning against the desk is a beautiful Sabre with a golden swept Guard and a shark leather grip, sheathed in a scabbard just as eloquent as the sword itself. Built into the walls surrounding the desk are tall bookshelves, each carefully carved in a style complementary to that of the desk, and seamlessly transition into the vaulted ceiling. Many of the books are texts, a few of them are tales, and some have to do with the arcane. He learned to read and write from his old mentor, and he hasn't stopped reading since. Even if it's re-reading the same text for the tenth time.

A gust of icy wind blows down the chimney of the fireplace in the middle of the room. For a moment Valdus feels a slight chill on the bare back of his head, then the fire blazes hotter than before. The castle of Valketten is built in the high north of Ateria called Asbjarnarvik where year long it is a vast frozen wasteland. It is nearing summer, yet a blizzard rages outside. Valdus can hear the ensuing brouhaha from the canteen. Normally this is the time to be eating with his men, the Vallin Knights, but he has been so intrigued with what he was reading—despite having read it a few years ago—that he decided he would eat later.

Suddenly voices fill his head, many whispers speaking as if in a crowd. *'I see a pale horse,' 'he is free,' 'the dark one,' 'the lamb has broken the first seal.'* He becomes nervous and flustered. His first thought is he lost his mind, as that is not unlikely for a man such as himself. But fighting to think through the discord that overwhelms his head, he recalls that he hasn't used the Eldritch in months. The voices stop. All becomes silent except for the crackling of the fire. He stares blankly for a moment, finding himself afraid for the first time since he was a child.

Three booming knocks pound on the door. His head snaps towards it. Slowly he reaches for the nearby Sabre. Rapidly somebody pounds on the door and does not stop. He stands from his chair in a quick and quiet movement. He knows it is likely just one of his Vallin Knights, but why would one pound on his door like this? And, with the madness that just occurred, he doesn't want to take any chances. The pounding stops as fingers touch the knob. He swings the door open and finds it isn't a Vallin Knight on the other side.

Instead he is face to face with a cloaked man in shackles. Staring into the dark eyes of the strange man, Valdus finds himself unable to move or speak. Suddenly he is falling and his vision delves into blackness. He feels himself hit the ground on his back. Looking around as he gets up he finds that he is in a shadowy corridor of prison cells, each one containing dark and menacing figures. He walks down the dimly lit corridor. Through the darkness he sees a shadowy figure unlocking a cell. Valdus can make it out to be Albus. The cell door swings open and the shackled man emerges. Dragging a ball and chain behind him, the man walks down the seemingly endless hallway. Valdus tries to pursue them but the distance between them merely grows further with every step. Valdus suddenly finds himself standing in the middle of Valketten's canteen.

"Albus you old fool!" He screams.

◈ CHAPTER SEVEN

Milo wakes up in the darkness of the night to something crawling into his bed. He jolts up and reaches for his sword. Through the narrow windows and thin canopy, just enough moonlight gets through that Milo can barely make out the figure sitting on his bed.

"Avannie?" Milo cries. Albus has been creeping into his dreams lately, further heightening the alarm he felt.

"Oh I- Yes. I'm sorry, I- I didn't mean to wake you," she says.

"Why are you in my bed?"

"We can get married tomorrow. White Sun or Seven Winds, I don't care."

"Avannie-"

"Grandmama said she'll give us the tavern," she cuts him off. "Or- or we can run off. If you'd like."

"Avannie-"

"I can start my wifely duties tonight even. I've never done it before bu-but I'm not afraid," she stammers. She clumsily begins to pull her nightgown over her head.

"Avannie!" Milo snaps, grabbing her nightgown and pulling it back down. "What the hell?!"

Even through the dim light Milo sees her eyes beginning to tear up. She gracelessly takes flight from Milos's bed and runs out of the room. A heavy sigh escapes Milo's mouth. He slowly dresses himself, having only been in his knickers. Leaving the Silken Princess he takes a stroll through the city. He found he had been sleeping too much since returning to Dalarus, leaving him in a dull lethargy.

As he paces down the street he worries about returning to the wild. The city seems to be getting inside of him, ruining everything he is. Every day he finds himself saying he will spend just another night, a promise that grows harder to fulfil by the day. Somehow the city is more energetic and intoxicating, yet brings a feeling of unfulfilment and depression that only Milo seems to acknowledge.

And in recent days something has been happening in the city. The crowded streets have thinned and the Guard patrols have increased dramatically. Milo found that many were staying indoors rather than venturing out because of whispers that many have gone missing. Tonight Milo has seen nobody walking the streets but Guards in the distance, which is unusual for Dalarus. He ponders different and somewhat absurd scenarios before getting stopped by a group of four Guards.

"You there! Why are you out here?" A Guardsman says.

"Just going for a stroll. I always see people out here at night."

"The Shaqif has ordered all citizens off the streets. Go back to whence you came."

Milo raises an eyebrow. "Can you tell me why?"

"The Shaqif will make an announcement soon. Now please, go back inside."

Milo heads back to the Silken Princess. As he makes his way up to his room, he faintly hears the crying of Avannie. Before entering his room he sighs at the poor girl.

He wakes up late the next morning. Sore from getting too much sleep, he stumbles his way over to the narrow window. The Sun has almost reached its zenith. Despite the streets below being almost entirely devoid of life, the preacher is once again standing on his box. Annoyed and tired of this city, Milo gathers up the few things he owns. As he is leaving the tavern he stops when sees Avannie across the room awkwardly smiling as she serves wine to a kindly old man. She looks up and sees Milo. Her face darkens with blood and her smile contorts to a frown as she droops her head low. Confusion and frustration overcome Milo as he leaves the tavern. Aeris' hawkish eyes darting between the two in curiosity.

As Milo exits the building the priest begins shouting at him. "You there! The White Sun is punishing the heathens of this city! Come pray with us my child, lest the White Sun disappear you as well!" Milo furrows his brow and clenches his jaw, but keeps walking.

Milo finds the city eerily empty. Few are on the streets, most of whom are nervously rushing around the city. Ominous murmuring replaces the typical cheerful clamour. As Milo looks around, even the most colourful things seem monochrome. He approaches the city gate prepared to leave once and for all. As he passes by a small group of people speaking in low tones, he overhears that Shaqif Amir is planning on speaking shortly. Once again his curiosity gets the best of him.

Thus he heads over to the gallows—for some odd reason the Lords always deliver their speeches there. After about twenty minutes of waiting, an official of house Pyrammus is escorted out of the palace by three Guards. Milo looks around to see how many people showed up; to his surprise it was only a few dozen. One of these few is Aeris Wynterfang, who gives him a strange look. The official and two Pyrammian Guardsmen climb atop the gallows. One of the Guardsmen signals the crowd to quiet down, to which they do.

"I am Xavier Anatolli. Shaqif Amir Pyrammus has appointed me to inform ye of the current situation here in Dalarus," the man's voice booms to the crowd, his voice filled with confidence. "I am sure ye have all been wondering why we have told ye to stay indoors. This is because of the disappearance of numerous people of Dalarus." The crowd murmurs but it is little disruption. The man continues over the crowd, "Seventy-six of our good people have disappeared." The crowd booms, talking frantically amongst themselves and incomprehensibly screaming questions at the speaker. The Guards get the crowd to quiet down again and Anatolli continues, "Until the scourge responsible for this upheaval is discovered and dealt with, we-"

A strange screech from above interrupts Anatolli. The sound was similar to that of a bird, but hideous and otherworldly. Everybody looks towards the sky for whatever made this sound. The nervous chatter is dominated by another screech, closer this time. Milo can't see anything, the tall buildings and palm trees block out vast portions of the sky. Another hideous screech pierces their ears. Before anybody sees it coming, a terrifying beast like nothing of this world lands on Anatolli, digging great raptor-like Talons deep into his shoulders. The creature pierces his skull with another set of talons and rips off the top of his skull. All within mere moments it bites into the man's brain with its toothed beak, eating a large chunk before the taking off with its massive wings. The two Guardsmen dive off the gallows in terror. Anatolli's body crashes down with a disgusting thud. The creature lands back on the body and ravenously tears into the man, swallowing chunks of flesh with disgusting gulps.

Milo quickly fires an arrow into the creature's side but it merely screeches in pain and takes off, guts dangling from its beak. It disappears behind the numerous obstructions again. Many run for their homes, leaving only a handful to fight the creature. These men are looking up into the skies trying to spot the creature before it attacks again. From behind a nearby roof the creature drives straight down at Aeris.

As if he could sense the creature he looks up at the beast with a fierce scowl. Right before the creature plummets into him, he moves out of the way like how a hawk moves through the forrest. When it hits the ground he springs like a viper and tackles it. He pulls his dagger from his belt and stabs the creature in the neck. The creature claws at his chest, ripping his tunic to reveal a layer of chainmail hidden beneath. Aeris stabs it in the neck again. The beast lashes out at his face. He jolts in pain for a moment, then in one powerful stroke of fury takes its head off.

"Do you always wear that?" Milo asks. Aeris looks down at the exposed chainmail before nodding, shaking drops of blood from the sheet over the left side of his face. From the bridge of his nose and across his cheekbone, his skin sliced as if from a razor.

Pyrammian Guardsman circle around the dead creature and stare at it puzzled. Everyone is asking what is it. And for once Milo doesn't know. The strange being is the size of a small child, with two legs, two arms, and two wide spanning wings from its back. Most of the body is covered in coarse red-brown hairs, except for the feathered wings. The worst part was the intense odour of rotting eggs that surrounded the creature.

One Guardsmen shouts, "Come with us!" The Guards quickly get into formation and march back to the palace. Milo and Aeris follow closely behind the Guards, along with another man that Milo doesn't recognise. The gates of the *hara'asr* open for them and they pass through without resistance. On the other side of the *hara'asr* is a long bridge to the palace island. Across the bridge is eerily peaceful, a lush and well-maintained garden with roses and tulips and small ponds. The Guardsmen lead the men up the thirty-five steps of the palace and into the Throne room, a large hallway with two grand tables on each side and surrounded with balconies. Seated in his Throne on a raised platform at the end of the hall is Shaqif Amir Pyrammus. The three make their way halfway across the Throne room before stopping. The third man bows flamboyantly to the Shaqif and waits to be spoken to, but Milo and Aeris only give simple and brief bows.

"Who are you?" Amir asks.

"We are here to help," Milo answers.

Amir thinks for a moment before telling them, "Come closer."

The three approach to three-quarters of the way across the room, and the third man bows again. "My brother Nasir would usually be in charge of a situation such as this, however he is out of Pyrammus on business. What is happening out there?"

"Some sort of bird thing attacked your man," Milo informs Amir.

"A bird?" Amir asks.

"Well, it wasn't like anything I had ever seen before."

"Aye, it didn't seem to even be from our world," the third man adds.

"Where in the name of the seven winds did it come from?" Amir asks rhetorically.

"The sky. How should I know?" Milo says.

"Do-" Amir begins to say, but a Guard rushes into the hall and interrupts him. "More of the creatures have been spotted coming from the abandoned mining pit!" Amir takes another glance over the three. "You may join my men in the fight if you so desire. And you shall not go without reward." The three turn to walk out of the hall. Aeris suddenly freezes and a moment later the others freeze as well. Standing before the great doors of the palace is a mysterious figure shrouded in a dark cloak. The doors slam themselves shut. Milo feels something brush against his side. Looking down he sees that someone has stolen his arrows. "Hey, those are mine!" he shouts as he turns around, only to find nobody behind him.

The men reach for their weapons, and in response the figure raises both his hands. The numerous Pyrammian banners and tapestries on the walls spontaneously ignite. The men look around the burning hall in horror. The other two draw their swords as Milo looks up to see a chandeliers falling. He jumps back and barely manages to get out of its way, though falling in the process and landing painfully on his tailbone. Milo jumps up only to stare in horror at the crushed pulp that was once Aeris. The many doors of the Throne room burst open and massive hordes of bats pour in like water through a bursting dam. Within seconds they fill the room. Swarms of bats land on every body part of the men, tearing through their clothes and sinking their fangs into their flesh. Milo jumps to the ground to minimise the area the bats can attack. Abrupt silence fills the room. Looking up, the palace is just as it was before. No longer do bats fill the room, nor are the tapestries burning. Aeris stands in the middle of the room while patting himself as if trying to determine if he was a ghost. Before his Throne Nasir gazes around the room puzzled and confused. Pyrammian Guardsmen attempt to keep their composure as they nervously patrol the room.

"People live here?" Milo spits.

Milo hears a terrifying screech outside the Throne room. Milo and Aeris run through the palace doors as the other man picks up the sword he had dropped. They stop atop the steps of the palace. In the middle of the garden three Guardsmen stab their spears up into the air at another flying creature. He grabs at his quiver, only to remember that the dark figure stole his arrows.

Milo draws his sword, but Aeris is already ahead of him. The creature dodges another spear and dives at the Guardsman. The creature lands on the man, securing its talons into the leather of his armour. Before anybody could do anything it rips off the man's helmet and breaks his neck. As the body collapses to the ground, the creature takes flight again. Before it could get away however, Aeris strikes the creature. The blade goes through its hollow bones and halfway down the wing, and the creature falls to the ground with a meek screech. Aeris quickly sinks the tip of his blade into the base of its skull.

Aeris runs across the bridge and through the open gates of the *Hara'asir*. Milo and the other man follow after a moment of hesitation. As they chase Aeris through the city, all is eerily quiet with the only sounds being the monstrous sounds echoing from the distance. As they near the outside of the city, the screams of men and monsters grows louder. As they approach the great Mosque of Dalarus they realise the sounds are coming from within. The men run through the grand garden that surrounds the Mosque, its vibrant flowers and gentle ponds now bloodied by the slaughter of monks.

Peering inside the Mosque, the men witness the creature defile the shrine of Hudan, inciting further rage in Aeris—a follower of the Asbjarnarvik variant of the Seven Winds. He charges down the hall at the creature. Taking flight over a large fallen candelabra, he impales the beast with his sword. Aeris pins it to the ground with his sword as flails and screams, especially enraged by the blood dripping from the wound on his face.

As Milo and the other approach, Aeris twists the blade slightly, causing the creature to scream in agony. The three observe the pitiful creature for a moment, then the other man decapitates the creature with two hard swings of his backsword.

"Perhaps you could do a little more work?" The other man says to Milo.

Milo mumbles to himself, "Why do I even bother helping these morons?" Then, out loud tells the man, "Yeah sure. Who are you anyway?"

"My name is Arnold."

A strange man carrying a large bag stumbles into the Mosque. His hair is long and a mess, and his beard isn't much different. The man holds himself very awkwardly, and walks stiffly and slouched. He stops awkwardly close to the men and slowly rubs the massive bags under his eyes with his wrist. The men watch the man in perplexity as he stares off blankly. Suddenly he twitches as if just remembering he is there.

"I am Rhymus Lombard, the alchemist of House Pyrammus," he tells Milo specifically, offering his hand. Milo hesitantly gives the man handshake, which lasts uncomfortably long. "Are any of you hurt?"

"Uh? That guy is?" Milo says, pointing at Aeris.

The strange little man twitches his head at Aeris as if just noticing he was there. For a second Aeris looks confused. He touches his cheek and looks at the blood on his fingers. "I'm fine," Aeris testily tells Rhymus. "I had already forgotten about it."

Rymus puts down the bag he is carrying and squints at the wound as he adjusts his glasses. "Ach muj. Tsk tsk." Removing a vial filled with a clear liquid from his bag, he pops off the cork and dabs a small amount onto a towel. He proceeds to not very gently clean the wound. Aeris' face twitches slightly, but other than that his face holds its usual scowl.

"Luckily only the epidermis was penetrated. Some bleeding, yes, but no real damage. You are lucky, those talons could have easily caused more damage."

Rhymus puts the bottle back into the bag then pulls out a needle and some thread. He proceeds to stitch up the wound, his fingers surprisingly nimble. A pair of Guardsmen come into the Mosque. Seeing the men they ask, "Are you the men the Shaqif sent to assist us?" The men nod in accidental synchrony. "We are grouping at the gate. The monsters are coming from the old mining pit." The two then turn around and march back out of the Mosque. Rhymus quickly finishes up the stitching and tells Aeris, "Find me in my laboratory in four or five days and I will remove the stitches." Aeris gently brushes his fingers over the stitches and nods.

Leaving the Mosque they find forty or so Guardsmen concentrating by the city gates. The soldiers push open the great gate and march out in formation, Milo and the others follow. Outside the city walls the sound of the gentle breeze again existed, along with the methodical sound of marching. Yet Milo found the strange serenity just as chilling as the ghastly silence.

The soldiers make their way through the outer market. Following close behind the formation Milo looks over his shoulder to see Rhymus leisurely following them as well. Suddenly a monstrous howls echoes from the vast sand dunes. Exponentially more and more creatures begin howling and barking—and they are fast approaching. Milo feels like he's heard them somewhere before, but he doubts that could actually be. The soldiers continue marching without missing a step.

Behind the great rolling dunes a great pack of creatures emerges. It first looks to be a great stampede of large boars, but the creatures are too lean and sharp featured. The great formations of the Guardsman dissolves into a chaotic rush to form a shield wall. The creatures close in quicker than any creature Milo has ever seen. Hideous snarling and barking pierces the air as they show off their rows of shark-like teeth. The Guardsmen scramble to hold the creatures at bay, but the strikes that they do not dodge merely glance off their hard pinkish scales.

Milo, Aeris, and Arnold stand behind the disorganised wall, safe for the time being. Leisuring lagging behind is the strange alchemist. A Guardsman in one of the lesser ranks stabbing his spear from over the first rank glances behind his shoulder. Seeing the men merely standing around shouts, "Get to the pit! I don't know how long we can hold the beasts!"

Milo and Aeris take off along with three Guardsmen who were doing little for the ensuing skirmish. Arnold looks around before spitting, "Bloody hell," and quickly taking after the men. They quickly become drenched in sweat, the summer Sun bearing down from above and reflecting from the wavy sands. Reaching the top of a sand dune the Guardsmen stop. Out of breath and missing the que of the Guardsmen, Arnold continues over the dune and down the side. Realising his mistake he tries to stop, only to slip and slide down its face. He tries to use his heel to stop, but this only throws the fine sand into the air and his face. Finally stopping he sits up. Mere feet away from where he stopped is a hole plummeting deep below the surface. Moving backwards like a crab he quickly distances himself away from the hole, before turning onto his stomach and skittering back up the dune.

"I take it this is the place?" Milo asks the Guardsmen.

"Aye."

"And how do you know this is where the beasts are coming from?" Aeris asks sceptically.

The Guardsmen points at the towers protruding from the great walls of Dalarus in the distances. Milo looks at the wall briefly, then behind him. The figures are small in the distance but he can tell many have died; what the outcome would be, he couldn't determine. Bumbling up the hill at a leisure walk comes the alchemist.

They carefully make their way down the sandune and to the pit. Hanging off one edge of the pit is an old elevator platform. Thick rotting ropes run through a complex system of rusting iron mechanisms and into the abyss where the cage has sat for decades. Two of the Guardsmen begin cranking at the derelict system.

"You can't seriously be thinking of taking this thing?" Milo asks in disbelief.

"We would never make it down the ladder with all our gear," one of the Guardsmen replies.

"And if one of these decrepit ropes snap?"

"Then we get there faster," Aeris responds.

"Somebody will have to stay up here to release the mechanism," the Guardsman says.

"And that somebody will be me?"

"Sounds like you want to be," Arnold says with a shrug.

The men finish cranking the cage up, an aged box of rusted iron and warped wood. Seeing the cage makes Milo sure that he doesn't want to ride it down. "Everybody get in," the Guardsmen orders. Everybody except for Milo packs into the rundown box. As the Guardsmen secure the door shut, Milo sees Rhymus pull a bowl out of his bag and begin to pick at whatever is in it with his fingers. Pulling a series of three levers, Milo sends the men down into the depths.

He then makes his way over to the other side of the elevator platform where he finds the ladder. The wood creaks and screams as he gets on it. "Great, the ladders just as likely to kill me, if not more likely." Slowly he descends down the ladder, carefully putting his weight down on the next board to make sure it will hold.

Ten feet.

Twenty feet.

Thirty feet.

The sky was getting farther away with his every step, yet the depth below him remained indiscernible. He pushes his foot down on the next board. The board he is holding onto screams as it jolts backwards. Milo's hand slips off in the jolt and his arm flies backwards. The bow slips off his shoulder and slides down his arm. In the last possible moment the nails catch the stone again, but not before the bow takes flight into the abyss. Milo quickly gets his hands off the broken board and onto a secure one. He continues his decent, this time more hurried.

When he reaches the bottom he is surrounded in blinding darkness. From within the darkness he sees sparks fly. He makes his way over towards the sparks, guided by their occasional and brief presence. As he gets close he begins to make out the silhouettes of the men. One of them is striking flint and steel, trying to light a torch.

"Does the torch have any fuel on it?" Milo asks.

"Aye. We managed to find a sealed barrel of alcohol.

"Give me that," he says as he grabs at the barely visible silhouette for the flint and steel. Taking it from the man, he sends a great array of bright sparks flying, lighting the torch with a single strike.

Holding the torch above them, Milo looks around at the men. Most of them cover their eyes before getting a bearing of their surroundings. Rhymus gapes at the flame, picking single grains of rice from his bowl. *What a strange man,* Milo thinks to himself, but he knows that soon enough they may need him. "Everybody make it down all right?"

"Aye. Though something did hit me on the head as I was exiting the cage," Arnold says.

Milo doesn't tell him what it was. He lights a second torch for the group before going to find his bow. When he finds it he sees that one of its limbs is badly cracked. He tosses the worthless hunk of wood and rawhide back onto the ground. He then returns to the group.

"Where to now?" He asks.

"Only one way to go," Aeris says.

They descend deeper into the mine, following a narrow shaft. They follow the shaft for about forty feet before it widens. Placed into the opposite side of the room is a stone gatehouse, a black portcullis set within and blocking a brightly lit room on the other side. The perplexed group cautiously approaches the gatehouse.

"I'm guessing that shouldn't be here?" Milo asks rhetorically.

"No," a Guardsman replies.

Milo goes to shoot the Guardsmen a look for answering, but sees a face emerging from the shadows. A tongue flicks out between external lion like teeth. Silently emerging from a near shaft, Milo can make it out to be some giant lizard. It stands low to the ground yet nearly up to their waists. Covering its body in stunningly articulate patterns are numerous great plates.

"What are you looking at?" A Guardsman asks Milo as he turns around. The creature bites into the Guardsman's leg with great force and pulls him down to the ground. It lunges forward with great speed, pinning the man down with its foot, crushing his ribcage and sinking its claws in deep. The Guardsman flails and grabs at the lizard, but it is futile. The creature bites at his neck, ripping away flesh and chunks of chainmail alike.

Another Guardsman dashes to the great lizards side and attempts to stab it. His spear merely glances off the thick plates. Before he knows what happened, a great ball of spikes crashes into his side and pierces his armour and ribcage. He falls limply to the ground with a wet scream.

Meanwhile Aeris and Arnold wisely retreat to the far side of the room, and Rhymus looks on eating his rice.

The creature darts forward with great speed at the last Guardsman. He manages to stab the creature between its plates, but it is too late. With a single swipe the creature rips apart the man's groin. Then a warhammer goes through its helmet-like skull plate like an eggshell. The attack was much more effective than Milo had expected. The creature collapses to the ground with a loud thud.

Rhymus gently sets his bowl of rice down and runs over to the men. After determining that the other two were dead he examines the wounds of the man whose groin had been destroyed. He mutters to himself in a foreign language that is harsh to Milo's ears. Over the cries of the man begins a loud rhythmic sound of metal. Turning their attention away from the man they see the portcullis raising. It slams to a halt. The men wait for somebody or something to emerge, but nothing happens.

"You stay here and take care of him," Milo whispers to Rhymus. After he nods his head in agreement, Milo quietly moves towards the portcullis and peers in. Aeris and Arnold cautiously approach as well and peer from behind him. The sight is sickening. Men and women of all ages are chained up to the walls and hang from the ceiling. Their clothes and flesh alike are shredded and torn away; fed upon by the otherworldly creatures Milo concludes. In the centre of the room is some strange cast iron contraption. It isn't a cage, nor does it seem to have any purpose—it's just a huge, contorted mess of iron forming a poor circle. And in the centre of the contrapture is a pool of molten rock. The men slowly enter the hall, taking in the carnage around them.

"What evil has occurred here?" Arnold says.

"Fucking…" Aeris spits.

A small clawed hand rises out of the magma pool, and then another one. Pulling itself out of the molten rock, a head appears, followed by wings. One of the winged creatures slowly drags itself out of the pool. Screeching weakly it tries to flap its wings. Just as it begins to gain its strength, Arnold strikes it with his backsword. The creature falls backwards, part of its body entering the molten rock. The creature then is pulled back into the magma by a mysterious force.

From behind the contraption they see something move. A man had been on the other side of the metal jumble, yet somehow nobody had noticed him there before. He makes his way across the room and sits down in a chair. The men cautiously make their way around the metal contraption and over to the man.

"I am Albus DéFreur," he says, gesturing to Arnold. "Now Milo, please don't try to-"

Milo has already closed in and, before Albus can finish, he slams the warhammer down into his skull. His flesh bloats, turning rotten shades of green and black. It begins cracking and turning into dust, withering away until nothing but bone was left. Soon the bones too begin to crumble until there was nothing. "Was that..?" Aeris asks.

"Yep," Milo responds.

"You know him?" Arnold asks.

"Aye, he's an old… adversary of ours," Milo says.

"Think he's actually dead this time?" Aeris asks Milo.

"Something tells me that would be a no."

"Hold up, are you saying that this isn't the first time you've killed him?" Arnold asks, baffled.

"Nope."

The men begin to look around the cave, trying to ignore the urge to vomit at the stench of the bodies. Milo pushes open a door placed into one of the walls. On one side of the room there is a contraption of tubes and glasses, surrounded by strange powders and items. Loose papers and books are sprawled across the room. Milo crouches down and looks at some of them. Picking up a book he reads the title: *The Three Empires of Old*. He picks up another tomb, this one titled *The Tower of Evening*. He tosses them both across the room. Gathering up a few of the parchments, he tries to read them, but every one is written in a language like none he has ever seen. Some of them have partial drawings of creatures, some have blank spaces where Milo can assume drawings would be. Throwing the papers back to the ground he goes over to a crudely made desk. Across the table are more parchments, all written in the same indiscernible language. Just as he is about to leave one catches his eye. He stops and picks it up. Between scattered blocks of foreign text is an unfinished drawing depicting a cloaked man, chained and bound. In a flash the memories of what happened in the Bleaks come back to him: the cloaked man he approached only to vanish. Then he realises he saw the same cloaked man again earlier, when the palace went mad.

"Milo, you should come see this!" Arnold shouts from the doorway. Milo sets the papers back on the table and follows Arnold to another room. Entering, it appeared to be a bedroom identical to that in Albus' cave. He approaches the shelf that is carved into the rock with a shiver. Sitting on the shelf are a fine yew shortbow with a rawhide string—an exact replica of Milo's—a hand stitched doll of his likeness, and a half finished drawing of him that was eerily too lifelike. Milo picks up the drawing and sees there is writing on the other side. Turning the parchment around, he reads:

Dearest Milo Khan,

> *It appears thou hast once again attempted to bring my death. But that is fine, I shan't hold it against thee. I couldn't do that to you. Not now that you have finally come to me, my champion. The sisters whisper to me. "Blood, blood, death," the hag says. "One great and like none else," the nymph says. There was nothing I could do, they made me do it. I know you shall succeed, my Milo.*

> *~ Yours truly forever and ever and ever,*
> *Albus*

Arnold looks over Milo's shoulder and reads the note. "Looks like you have an admirer," He remarks.

Milo ignores him and shoves the note into his pocket. He mutters to himself, "Doesn't that bastard have anything better to do than stitch dolls and write me love letters?"

"Let's get the hell out of here," Aeris growls.

"Agreed," Milo says.

As the other two leave, Milo grabs the bow and draws it. *'A worthless replica. Great.'* He tosses it on the ground as he leaves and misses it shimmering magically. Exiting the portcullis, they find Rhymus sitting in the middle of the room, eating one grain of rice at a time.

"What happened?" Arnold asks the alchemist.

Rhymus jolts as if he just became aware of the men's presence. "He bled out, there was nothing I could do."

"Come on then, we're leaving."

The four make their way back up the narrow shaft. They slowly and cautiously climb up the old ladder, it creaking and screaming worse than before. *'It's surely going to break this time,'* Milo thinks, but before he knows it he is climbing onto the surface. Overcome with a feeling of nausea and disorientation, Milo takes a look around. The world had become grey and monotone, a thick cloud layer now hiding the sky as far as one can see. Behind crumbling city walls billows of smoke are rising up across the city. Horrific screams of both man and monster can be heard in the distance. Milos head begins to pound terribly. He finds himself laying in the sand.

"Are you alright?" One of them asks, though which one he could not determine.

Getting up he takes a look around. The sky remains to be inexplicable overcast, but Dalarus is the same as always. "Yeah. Probably just heat stroke." After helping Milo up, they begin the trek back to the city. But before Milo follows, he sees something in the corner of his eye. Looking out into the vast desert he sees a dark figure standing in the distance. He could feel it watching.

"What the hell is wrong with this world?"

◆ CHAPTER EIGHT

It is a sunny day in Asbjarnarvik, not a single cloud in the sky. Valdus' footsteps crunch as he walks over the thick slab of permafrost, the snow steaming in the hot day. He is dressed in a dark red overcoat with matching trousers, and long black boots that go over his calves. At his side is his trusty Sabre. Walking next to him is one of his Vallin Knights, Vladimir. Draped over his shoulders is a fur cloak, hiding beneath it a lamellar vest over a hauberk, and finally a heavy gambeson. Teeth are embossed on his helmet to form a hellish grin, and two small horns protrude from the forehead. The eye slits are cut to look angry, but the eyes within are devoid of emotion. Six more Vallin Knights follow them dressed similarly to Vladimir, though their helmets have blank expressions, round eyeholes, and no horns.

They approach the Dalrgatt, a wall running across the valley they are in. Atop the twenty foot tall wall is a large roofed structure to keep the men within out of the elements. Smoke billows from the gatehouse, but none of the other chimneys are active. The entourage approaches the gatehouse, the top structure protruding as it is machicolated so that the men can shoot anybody below the gate. This machicolation is unique to the gatehouse, as they rebuilt it after the Troll Wars. A large portcullis blocks their path.

"Halt!" A voice shouts from up in the top structure. "State your business."

Valdus looks up at the gatehouse with a bored look; his men continue to look forward. "I am here to hire a ship."

"You may enter, but the Vallin Knights must remain outside!" The voice demands.

Vladimir speaks just loud enough for Valdus to hear, "We can return at night and scale the wall."

"No," Valdus responds as he takes off his overcoat, beneath it a matching red vest over a white wool shirt. Handing the coat to Vladimir, he orders his men, "Return to Valketten, I was expecting this."

Vladimir marches back into the snowy plains whence they came, the other ghostly figures quickly falling into line. When they are a fair distance away, the portcullis shakes. Slowly it raises and when it is high enough, Valdus passes through, it slowly rolling back down behind him. He walks through a large open valley, nothing in it but the frost and a few trees. It was almost strange to see the snow not red with blood. Across the valley he walks up to the Storrbalkr, a fifty foot tall wall of pure stone and now a crumbling relic.

Emerging on the other side of the wide mouthed-tunnel through the derelict wall he finds himself in the city of Bjartrtun. The builds of the city are giant, their steep roofs as large as the buildings themselves. Men shovel and chop away at the snow and ice from prior storms, piling wagons with snow to be dumped elsewhere. The road itself is a thick layer of gravel, years' worth buried beneath his feet from constantly being walked on and pressed into the permafrost. In Bjartrtun the city square is desolate, the only reason its citizens go outside is to get from one place to the other, or to work. Valdus passes by the massive statue of a legendary figure in the centre of the squire, not giving it any mind.

Turning left he heads south. In a few minutes he finds himself at the edge of seven-hundred foot cliffs. Bjartrtun is built high up in the mountainous peninsula of North-West Asbjarnarvik, the southside of which is made up almost entirely of cliffs. He looks across the bay and out into the open ocean. After taking a moment to appreciate the beauty of it all he heads down one of many giant staircases descending down the cliff face. Built at the bottom on the gravelly shores within the bay is more city, though here exclusively are warehouses and other naval oriented buildings. Long piers stick out into the dark arctic waters, many working ships docked to them.

The docks are fairly busy with sailors loading and unloading cargo. In Asbjarnarvik nobody is loitering around, there is always work to be done. Valdus approaches a couple fishermen hauling in barrels full of crabs they had trapped.

"Excuse me," he says politely.

The men look at the red man suspiciously. "Aye?" One asks.

"Would there any ships heading to Dalarus soon?"

"Hm. Nay." The first one says.

"Actually…" The other man rubs his bearded chin. "Find Ugligr. His sail has a green serpent on it."

"Thank you. Best luck on your next voyage," Valdus says.

He wanders the docks trying to find a green serpent. Hiding behind the forward sail of a small galley, he finally spots the green serpent. Making his way up a creaky gangway he boards the ship and wanders to find the Captain. First he searches the Captain's quarters but nobody is there. He spends some time examining the cut-rate possessions of the man, then reads through his logs. Valdus eventually leaves when the Captain never comes to his quarters.

Hearing grunts and moans from the forecastle, he heads up the stairs. At the top he finds a fat man with a naked woman bent over the wheel for him. Her clothes were literally ripped off her body and thrown all across the quarterdeck. The man pounding away at her is still dressed, poking her from his fly. His nose is bulbous and eyes tiny. Lips pulled back like a horse as he breaths heavily, Valdus can see his rotting crooked teeth. Stringy peppered hair drapes down to his navel and his greasy beard looks like it hasn't been washed in weeks.

Without taking his eyes off the woman he snarls, "If yer gonna watch, ya better fuckin be payin."

"Are you Uggligr?" Valdus asks.

The man puts his manhood back in his breaches. Slapping the woman hard on the ass, he says, "We'll continue later... Er, what was your name?"

The woman walks away without answering him, disregarding her shredded clothing. Valdus does not look at her, completely disinterested.

"She your wife?"

"One of my slaves. Bought 'er on my last expedition to the northern shores of Kovera. Wild place, the far west."

Something within Valdus' mind makes him feel a sharp anger. "It is not honourable to lie with a slave."

"The fuck about honour? What do ya think I am, a fuckin' Knight?"

"I hear that you are sailing to Dalarus," Valdus says, refocusing in his mind to the task at hand.

"Nay, I'm not. And if I were you wouldn't be coming along. I know who you are. Just because you and the Jarl are lovers or whatever the fuck now ain't mean shite. And saving the city from those Trolls back then ain't gonna make us forget what yah've done."

Valdus walks back down the stairs. "Patricide!" The fat man spits after him.

II.

THE DETOUR. . .

◈ CHAPTER NINE

Milo stands in a flat and endless plane. It isn't warm nor cold. Not even the slightest breeze exists in this world. The silence is cruel. He can faintly hear the thuds of his own heart beating. He looks around trying to find something—anything. A huge shadow engulfs him, a great creature with wide wings and a beak that comes to a point akin to a rapier. Milo looks up only to find an empty blue sky. Feeling something stab at his ankle, he looks at his feet to be met with a rooster squawking at him.

Heavy footsteps echo throughout the vast empty from behind him. Milo spins around. The word blackens and torrential rain crashes down. The wind howls through thrashing trees. A giant man twice the size of him swings a great club towards him. Milo throws himself backwards to avoid the club, falling on his back in a pool of mud. Lightning flashes and the figure is gone, but hordes of twisted beings charge from the woods. Lightning flashes again and standing before him is the chained and cloaked figure. "There are some tasks you must do for me," the figure says. Milo gets up from the mud and approaches the figure, trying to get a look at his face. He can almost make it out when he wakes up.

Milo sits up in his bed and looks around the cave that is his room. *'This place is cursed. Why did I decide to stay here?'* After the chaotic events that transpired he got ownership of the cave—once they removed the bodies that is. After helping put those killed to rest, he burned liberal amounts of incense. He even bought himself a whole new bed, not wanting to sleep in Albus'. *'Looks like that didn't work,'* he thinks.

He dresses himself and heads to the main room. Grabbing a bowl and a spoon, he goes over to the cauldron he placed above the still molten rock, having found it to be a good source of heat for cooking. Taking some leftover stew from the previous night, he sits on the floor and eats. It is nearing his time to leave Dalarus; he can feel it. But something that he cannot describe is keeping him here. Perhaps city life is addictive—and just as harmful to the soul as any other addiction. He would leave soon. But for now he decides he needs a day off; he had spent too many days working on the cave.

Milo's thoughts are interrupted by Aeris filling his bowl with the thick stew. He also sits down on the floor, a fair distance away from Milo, and begins wolfing the bowl down.

"You must really like two-day-old stew," Milo jests. Aeris squints and glances at Milo in the corner of his eye. Unreceptive of the joke, Milo asks him, "So what are you planning on doing? We can't stay in this cave forever."

"Don't know yet."

Accepting the hopelessness of making conversation with the man, Milo finishes his bowl and puts it off to the side. Milo makes his way up the mine shaft and up the ladder. Despite being reinforced since Milo's incident, he is sure that one of the creaky boards will end up killing him. As he pulls himself onto the platform, the glowing sand dunes blind him. Blocking the Sun from his eyes with the back of his hand, he looks about. Nothing around except for the great walls of Dalarus, the glowing dunes, and the Sun bearing down on him. He makes his way around the city wall, dripping with sweat. He pushes his way past the shouting venders, trying not to get trapped by one of them. "Jewellry! Fine Jewellry!" A shady and dirty old woman screeches about her cheap wares. Another vender with long unkempt hair and rotting teeth tosses smelly meat in a sooty pan, "Freshly made Kapooray! Get some before it's all out!" Just before getting through the market and into the city, a man with a terrible stench steps out in front of Milo.

"A potion for your health, m'Lord?" The man asks, his breath worse than his body odour.

Milo glanced at the nearby stall and saw dirty viles full of disgusting sludge. "No, I'm feeling fine," he tells the man while trying to step around him. The merchant steps back in front of him.

"Are you sure? My potions will keep your health good long after being drank!" He pleads.

"Yes," Milo says as he tries to step around again, only for the merchant to block him repeatedly. The merchant opens his mouth to speak again but Milo cuts him off, "Get out of my way before I am forced to hurt you." The merchant scrambles back behind his stall and Milo enters the city.

Passing through the gate, the world becomes refreshingly transformed as always. The air is cooler within the shaded city and has an air of respect contrasting that of the outer marketplace. He takes a minute to look at the great Mosque down the road, a great domed building surrounded by the lushest of gardens. But Milo would not be going there today.

At a slight oblique, he walks through a small gap between buildings. On the other side of the small gap is one of the small gardens sprawled around the city. The plants had grown unmaintained and wild, seemingly forgotten by the world—except for the signs of flowers having been recently plucked from the plants. Milo goes over to the old couch in the garden, worn and partly overtaken by plants, and sits back. He closes his eyes and thinks about a cool Adrosi night, hanging in a hammock. His mind wandered to his father, to his first hunt, and to his first time pulling his father's bow back.

A woman's voice pulls him out of his reveries. "I see you've found my secret spot."

Milo quickly glances her over. The woman is young, around twenty years Milo guesses. Her skin is the olive tone of a Pyrammian, lush wavy brown hair, and two soft eyes in a heart-shaped face. "Didn't realise this was yours. Are you evicting me?"

"Well I don't own it. I've never had anybody here before though. You mind some company?"

"Fine with me. The only person I've had around has been a grumpy mute."

Smiling and raising an eyebrow, she makes her way over to the couch. She sits down at an angle before putting her legs across the couch and Milo's lap.

*****

Milo quietly makes his way through knee high brush. He has tracked a great Red-Tailed Hawk for a great distance. Across a river delta and over a snowy mountain he followed it, then lost it in a storm a short time ago. It had landed here during the storm he somehow knew. A sudden patch of snow came into view as he made his way through the dense thicket. As he neared, he found a chickling ripping the flesh away from the great bird. Milo lazily wakes up rubbing his head.

'All this sleep is giving me bad dreams,' Milo decides. Looking around the garden he finds the woman, Asya, has already taken off. He very much enjoyed her company. But it doesn't matter anyway; he will be leaving Dalarus soon.

Squeezing between the buildings again he leaves the hidden retreat. The bustling sounds and sights of Dalarus return, however they were not the same as when he entered his sojourn. This time a crowd had formed around the gates and there was an excited murmur. Milo pushed his way through trying to see what they were swarming around for, the crowd reluctantly making way for him. Finally getting close enough to see, he finds a man dressed in plate and a Pyrammian tax collector going back and forth. Still he cannot make out what is being said over the crowd's chatter. Off to the side of the argument is a wagon accompanied by two more similarly clad men and a boy, the group seeming to be embarrassed by the ordeal. Milo finds himself unable to get any closer and frustratedly tries to make out what the men were arguing about, to no avail.

Then Arnold approaches the two. He says something to the armour clad man, who there out ignores the riled taxman's existence. The man's face turns bright red and contorts to the point of hilarity. "Thou dare disrespect me? I am a worker of Zacchaeus!" he screeches at the top of his lungs.

Laughter erupts through the crowd and Milo manages to break through and takes a step towards the men. His attention changes as a huge man pushes his way through two gossiping women. An incredibly muscular, shirtless man standing at seven feet tall, he is the biggest man Milo has ever seen. Milo watches the behemoth raises the taxman into the air by his collar. The man released an undignified screech and flails about.

Before Milo can do anything, numerous Guardsmen come pushing out of the crowd. A short and chubby man stomps out behind them screaming. *"Arrest everyone! Take them by force if need be!"* Milo stays still, watching the soldiers grab Arnold and the mysterious men. Some Guardsmen go to grab the hulking man but hesitate, unsure how to. The man puts his arms up and they walk him off. Then Milo feels himself being grabbed by the arms and drug backwards.

"Why do I even bother waking up on days like this?" Milo mutters to himself as the Guards drag him away.

*****

Milo leans against the wall of a dark and dank cell within the bowels of the Pyrammian Palace. There were two wooden benches shoddily secured to the wall of the cell. The giant man was taking up one and Arnold was laying across the other staring at the ceiling.

"Why don't you sit down? You've been standing there for how long now?" Arnold asks.

"I'd rather just get out of here," Milo says sorely. "Save the city from primordial forces, get a slap on the back and a 'good job.' Walk around at the wrong time, lockup."

"Don't blame me. I was trying to see what the problem was. Big fellow over there's the one who bloody picked up the little bastard."

"I was only trying to help," the man says, speaking for the first time.

"Yeah, and good job that-" Arnold begins to say only to stop when they hear the voice of Nasir Pyrammus outside the cell.

"No arguing Zacchaeus."

"My Lord, they assaulted one of my men! One of your men!"

"You locked up Dequande you fool." With a chuckle, he continues, "And from what I hear all he did was pick up the miserable sod."

"We cannot let-"

"Enough! Let them go. All of them." Nasir snaps.

A few moments later the cell door swings open. On the other side stands the chubby man, who couldn't be much over five feet tall. He momentarily stares angrily at the men with wide eyes before stomping off. Milo cautiously leaves the cell first. He looks to his left and sees Zacchaeus standing before another cell, his face red and jaw clenched. Grinding his teeth, he strains to speak, "You. Are." He groans. "Free to leave."

The stranger boldly steps up to Zacchaeus and says, "See little man?" This makes Zacchaeus become even more infuriated, beyond the point of what Milo thought was humanly possible. He attempts in vain to shove the much larger man back into the cell, who doesn't even flinch. Milo turns around to head back into his cell before things become much worse, but the voice of Nasir Pyrammus calls out. "Let the prisoners go Zacchaeus. Now!"

Zacchaeus reluctantly steps out of the way, visibly shaking in anger. The man walks out as if nothing had even happened, followed closely by his shaken men. Zacchaeus storms back into the bowels of the palace, passing Milo with his angry stare. Milo eagerly makes his way out of the dungeon. Passing the strange men collecting their gear, the man who had gone up against Zacchaeus stops Milo.

"I would like to apologise for getting you threw in here. Let us meet at the tavern, eh?"

"I don't-"

Milo is cut off by the man.

"I insist, my friend."

Milo realises it is an opportunity at learning who this man is—and an opportunity that is far from Zacchaeus. "All right, if you insist."

"Good! Meet me at the Arid Temptress, aye? Long and far I have heard of this mythical tavern."

Milo nods and continues on his way hoping to catch Nasir Pyrammus. Emerging from the dungeon he finds Nasir, but the circumstances are startling. The Lord has stripped naked in the magnificent garden outside the Palace. He walks to the retaining wall at the edge of the island and climbs atop it. The man takes an elegant swan pose and dives off into the waters.

"He's drunk again, isn't he?"

As he walks to the tavern Milo wonders if his curiosity is worth the risk. The Arid Temptress is the biggest tavern in the city; a rouse wouldn't be unlikely. And it wouldn't surprise him if Zacchaeus were to in and arrested them all again out of vengeance.

Then he sees Asya walking towards him with a friend. His thoughts turn from the stranger to her within an instant. He stops in place and watches her approach, but she does not seem to notice him between the crowd and the conversation she is having. Before getting close enough to notice him, her friend and she turn down an alleyway. He follows her but keeps his distance; he doesn't know what he would say to her. On the other side of the alley is a small market, in the middle of the square is a small pool with a bridge. Asya and her friend cross over the bridge watching a performer play the flute while Hopak dancing. Milo watches her from the other side of the pond.

"You care to look at my goods?" A deep yet gentle voice asks. Milo looks to his left and finds he is standing obnoxiously in front of a Dwarves stall. The Dwarf smiles softly, "Genuinely made in good ol' Bjekadir."

Milo looks over the array of leather and metal items. "You're not like the other peddlers. Not so obnoxious."

"Aye, my products speak for themselves. Nothing's quite like the stuff from the homeland."

"Get a lot of business? A lot of people still share their ancestors' hate for the grip the Dwarves held on the economy."

"People can talk shite all day, but when it comes down to it, they always choose Dwarven wares. Besides, they merely traded the Dwarves for House Pyrammus." As Milo picks up a beautiful sheath and looks it over the Dwarf says, "Fine lass you were eyin'. You know her?"

Setting the sheath down, he looks over at Asya, who is still watching the performer. "Met her earlier today. She's amazing." The performer finishes with a showy bow and the crowd claps, and Asya walks off with her friend.

"Why don't you go over to her instead of creepily staring?" The Dwarf says with an uncomfortable, forced chuckle.

Milo's feels the warmth of blood rushing to his cheeks. After a second of being embarrassed, he nods his head and chases after the two as they turn down another alley. He follows them into the alley and the air becomes strangely chilly. The two women take another turn and Milo tries to follow them. Seemingly out of nowhere a decrepit hunchback hobbles out in front of him. Holding his hands out in a cup the man asks, "Mastah, spare any coin can ya?" Milo searches his pocket and gives the man a 10ℛ coin. "Thank'sa mastah," the man says as he moves out of the way. After Milo walks past, the hunchback takes the coin and pushes it down his throat with his fingers.

When Milo turns the corner after her, she is gone. Disappointed he turns back and heads down the alley. He looks for the hunchback as he passes by again, but he too has vanished. He goes back to the Dwarf's stall.

"I take it didn't go so well?" The Dwarven merchant says.

"Lost her around a corner," he says with a nervous shrug.

The Dwarf sighs. "Perhaps tis for the best, my friend. Looks to me like some rich merchant's daughter." After a long silent pause the Dwarf asks, "Still interested in any of my wares?"

Milo picks up the sheath from earlier. "How much for this?"

The Dwarf thinks for a moment. "Let's say seventy?" Milo hands him two 50$\mathscr{R}$ coins. The Dwarf opens a drawer and begins sifting around. "Got some change somewhere around here."

"Keep it," Milo says.

The Dwarf stops sifting through the drawer and looks up at him. "Are you sure?"

"I'm sure," he says with a nod.

Milo goes on his way back to the Arid Temptress with the new sheath in hand. Approaching the door he can already hear the ruckus within; men are banging on tables and chanting for drinks. Milo stops and wonders if he should just turn around now. He enters.

As soon as he opens the door, he watches the giant man bang his table so hard it collapses. At the table next to him the stranger spots Milo and waves him over. Milo walks across the colonnade and through the pillars into the open courtyard that is the bar. Almost immediately, a skimpily clad wench is atop him with a flirtatious smile.

"What kinda drink would ya like, sir? We 'ave almost anythin' you can think of."

"Nothing."

The woman furrows her brows as she cocks her head and gives him the look that he knows means *'Why did you come here then?'* She proceeds to target another sailor to charm into buying a drink. Done with the distraction Milo looks over to the stranger, who is laughing hard at something. His eyes are light blue, his hair is golden brown, and he has a well-maintained beard.

"So who are you?" Milo asks.

The man fights to contain his laughter. "I am Sir Carwood Winters, dutiful representative of House Hale."

"House Hale? I've never heard of them." Milo says.

"Aye. Few know it," Winters states, his expression souring. "Now my friend, who are you?"

"They call me Milo Khan."

Winters opens his mouth to say something, but the giant man speaks first. "I am Dequande." Several scars run across the man's bare chest, and one stretching from his temple and down to his jaw. His black hair is very short and thin, having not been shaved for some time.

"The gladiator?" Milo asks. There is seldom one who has not heard of Dequande the Bull, but Milo had never seen him until now.

"That'd be me."

"Is it true you have never lost a fight?"

Dequande shakes his head. "Not since I was wee."

"There is nothing more exhilarating than a good sword fight!" Winters exclaims.

"I prefer using a mace or axe," Dequande responds, pulling his large battle axe out from his belt and showing it off with pride.

"My friend, a sword is much more graceful!"

"I prefer my bow," Milo pitches in.

"Ah, you're-" Winters begins to say, but out of nowhere a man holds a flask in Winters' face with a grin. "Would you care to try a drink?" This man's appearance is striking, with an exquisite pencil moustache sitting atop his lips and wide reddish-hazel eyes. He is wearing a black doublet over the whitest shirt, and matching black pants.

Winters stares at the man for a few moments trying to figure him out, then slowly takes the flask. He cautiously brings it up to his lips and takes a sip. Immediately as it touches his tongue, his mouth violently forces the fluid out. He holds the flask back out to the man, his face covered with disgust. "That shit is fuckin' wicked!"

Bitterly taking the flask back, the strange man mutters, "Rectified Spirits. What you just spit out was worth more than your weight in gold."

"*Who are you?*" Milo questions.

"Call me…" His voice trails off as he thinks. "Alexander," he eventually decides.

Winters yawns heavily. He then announces, "It has been fun, but I believe it is time to sleep. I have important business I must attend tomorrow." He quickly finishes a mug of Ale and stands up to make his way up to the room.

Alexander steps in front of him.

"Are you certain you want to leave so soon? The fun is just beginning!"

"Aye. I am."

The two stare at each other for a few tense seconds before Alexander steps out of the way. Winters marches up a staircase, and Milo watches him walk across the balcony overhead the bar and enter his room. Despite not being fond of the drunken hubbub, Milo doesn't leave yet.

"You really haven't lost a fight since you were a boy?" Milo asks Dequande.

"I lost most fights when I was wee."

"How d'you become undefeated?"

"I lost most fights."

"*That's it?*" Alexander asks with a raised eyebrow.

"Mhm. The more I lost, the more I learned what not to do. I soon started winning from my size, until the younger Torunn beat me. So I learned there's more to it than size."

"And how d'you become *the* champion of Pyrammus?" Milo asks.

Dequande looks down, his eyes watering a little. "My parents sold me, too much burden. For years my masters forced me to fight. I beat champion of Pyrammus, and they wanted me to take his place. After I told them I was a slave, they were revolted by it and freed me. I've been their champion since."

"What about you Milo?" Alexander asks. "You're an archer, if I am not mistaken?"

"Eh, I'd say more so a hunter than an archer. But yes, my father taught me when I was young."

"You live out by yourself in the woods, yes? How does one get arrows out there?"

Milo squints at Alexander, not being able to recall telling him that. "I make them."

"But how do you get the arrowheads?"

"If I need, I'll visit Penkerdeen and trade with the smith. You can reuse them though. Also I can make them out of stone if need be."

Dequande drops his axe on the table. "I have an axe!"

Milo furrows his brow. Alexander opens his mouth to speak, but something peaks his interest and he looks to the balcony above. A loud crashing sound from one room along the balcony then sends the bar into silence. A moment later there is a thud followed by a grotesque gurgling sound.

"Prolly just someone gettin' it on rough," one sailor remarks.

Then Winters screams combatively.

"Maybe not," Milo tells the sailor.

He jumps from his seat and dashes upstairs to investigate. Dequande promptly follows, and an unperturbed Alexander takes his time.

The first thing Milo notices when he gets up the staircase is a pool of blood coming out from Winters' room. Milo looks down at the empty sheath in his hand. *'What the hell am I going to do with this?'* When Milo looks into the room, he sees where the blood is coming from; one of Winters' men lay dead with his throat slit. Standing off against a masked attacker is Winters, dressed only in his knickers and a sword firmly planted in his hand.

Dequande gently pushes Milo aside and walks into the room with giant strides. The attacker goes to swing their dagger at Winters, only for Dequande to grab their arm. The massive man yanks the attacker so hard that his shoulder dislocates, and swings them with tremendous force into a wall. His skull cracks loudly as it impacts with the limestone.

Alexander claps. "Bravo!"

Winters approaches and picks up the dagger from the floor. "Flip him over Dequande," he says, the attackers face still planted in the wall. Dequande turns the attacker over and rips off the crude sack mask off his head. Through the blood dripping from the attacker's cracked forehead, the men have a hard time making out what lays behind the mask.

"Is that..?" Milo asks unable to say what he thinks he sees.

"...A woman?" Dequande gasps.

Winters appears unperplexed. "It is. In Tyros the women aren't the most lady like."

"Tyros?" Milo asks.

"Yes, Tyros. Where I am from."

"You didn't tell me *that*."

Winters ignores him. "Would any of you know how to... extract information from this assassin?"

"I could break some bones," Dequande answers after a period of silence.

"Broken bones will do you no good. If you wish to *actually* obtain information, I would suggest that *I* work with *it*," Alexander speaks up, seemingly vexed by Dequande's proposal. Milo is starting to wonder how demented everybody in the room is.

Winters thinks hard for a long time before finally deciding. "You do it, Alexander was it?"

"Then I must ask for all of you to leave and give me some time."

As they leave the room Alexander gently strokes the woman's cheek and tells her, "Wake up, darling." She wakes up and cries out in agony. Like a trapped cat, the woman claws at Alexander's face, but all he has to do is grip her wrist.

"Do you need me to hold her down?" Dequande asks.

"No. But do close the door. And could you make sure I am not disturbed?"

With Dequande clicking the door shut, the woman's cries and wails instantly turn into screams that chill Milo's bones. The men wait. Within a few minutes the tavern clears out except for the wenches who are obligated to be there. Ten minutes go by of persistent screaming, broken up only by brief moments of whispers none could make out. Milo looks off the balcony and into the tavern below. A pair of Guardsmen look around for the source of the woman's agony before spotting them. "Ah fuck," Winters spits. He descends the staircase and Milo follows. The Guardsmen grip their Tulwars anxiously but do not draw them.

"What the fuck is going on here?!" One Guardsman growls.

"I was attacked by a masked assassin. We are now performing an interrogation. Nothing to worry yourselves with, my good soldiers."

"Torture?! You cannot just torture somebody!" The other Guardsman shouts.

"Well you can go tell them to stop, though Dequande the Bull has been instructed to not let anybody interfere. Or you can go tell our Lord Pyrammus that a representative of House Hale wishes an audience."

The two Guardsmen look to each other in fear. "We will inform our commander right away," the first Guardsmen says, and the two scurry out of the tavern.

Time passes slowly, the horrifying screams of Alexander's victim turning every minute into years. Milo's stomach churns and his heart beats heavy with each persistent scream. Winters paces around anxiously, and Milo works on fixing the broken table with some tools he finds behind the counter. Just as Milo finishes fixing the table all goes silent. At first Milo thinks it is just another brief eye of the storm, but then the door opens. Milo and Winters rush upstairs. Alexander appears nonchalant, but Milo notices a faint twitch at the corner of his mouth that may be him hiding a grin.

"What did you learn?" Winters asks eagerly.

"I'll sum it up for you. It claimed to be a... freedom fighter for the people of Tyros. It said it caught wind of your mission and wanted to stop any chance at diplomatic agreement between your House and House Pyrammus. I saw that it looked at itself as a sort of... martyr against the tyranny of government."

"Was there anything more?"

"No, not that I can recall. And I have impeccable memory."

"Does she have any accomplices? Know of any further plots?"

Alexander shakes his head. "I can assure you it was not aware of anything more. Intentional I would presume."

"I should ask her some questions myself," Winters says as walks towards the room. Alexander extends his arm and puts it in front of Winters' chest.

"My friend! It died shortly after I finished up. You need not worry about the mess either—there is none!" He becomes more cheerful with every word. He asks with a grin, "Shall we have a drink to celebrate?"

The men stand in silence, astonished by the man's demeanour.

The grin still plastered over his face, Alexander looks back and forth between them. After several long moments his grin disappears. "No?"

"I believe I must be going," Winters says, his face plastered with repugnance. He quickly makes his way down the stairs. Alexander watches in shock and confusion as Winters storms out of the tavern. Then the rest of the men stand in a tense silence. Milo and Dequande feel anxious as Alexander silently smiles at them. After a long minute of this Milo slowly turns to leave. Dequande follows in his suit. To their dismay, Alexander follows them.

Exiting onto the dying down streets of the night, Milo notices a man with a big chin leaning against the tavern wall. They stare at each other for an awkward moment before the man shifts his gaze to Alexander. "Hello *Alexander.*"

Squinting his reddish eyes at the man, Alexander walks up close to him and leans in to whisper something. Alexander then steps back and turns to Milo and Dequande saying with a sly smile, "When we meet again." Then he takes off into the night.

"Prick," the man with the big chin mutters as he takes off in the other direction.

"I hope I never see them again," Dequande says when both men vanish into the night.

"Agreed."

◈ CHAPTER TEN

Milo is woken up by a scowling Aeris. "You sleep fucking late. Get up." Milo gets out of his bed and starts dressing. "Somebody was looking for you this morning."

"Who was it?" Milo asks as he laces his boots.

"How the fuck should I know? Some guy tramping around in a suit of armour asking around about you."

Winters. Milo knows it has to be him. "Great. I wonder what trouble he's going to get me into this time."

Aeris leaves his room saying, "Don't. Fucking. Know."

Milo quickly scarfs down another bowl of the same stew and repeats the tiresome trek out of the cave and towards the city. Perhaps this is why his body doesn't want to wake up, he wonders. He routinely passes through the market, ignoring all the venders. Just before the gates is the cart in the same place as yesterday, Winters' accomplices loading it up with supplies. As Milo walks over to it a dirty old man wearing naught but an open robe steps out in front of him. He pulls a few cigars out from inside his greasy robe and holds them out to Milo.

"Cigar, young man?" He rasps.

Milo looks down at the cigars but quickly looks away, wincing at the sight of the man's cigar shaped appendage. "Why are you people always stepping out in front of me?!"

The man looks at him blankly before asking, "A cigar, yes?"

As Milo slowly turns back to the man, he sees Winters' man come up behind the merchant. "Get out of here, old man."

The exposed man slowly turns to face Winters' man. "Cigar?"

"Are ya deaf? The fuck outta here," he says as he gives him a shove. As he slowly trots away, the old man gazes back before going on to harass somebody else.

"I'm Reynard. You're the one called Milo, yes?" The man asks.

"Rumor is Winters is looking for me. What does he want?"

"It'd probably be best if he told you himself," Reynard says.

"Well, where is he?"

"Eh... Back at the Temptress, I believe."

As Milo makes his way through across the city and towards the Arid Temptress, he daydreams about seeing Asya again, what he would do, how things would play out. While he knew that it was very unlikely he would see her, he was still somewhat disappointed when he arrived at the door of the famous tavern. With a sigh he enters the tavern.

Inside is quite beautiful. Designed by famous architect Yazid Pyrammus, ornate pillars and arches hold up the rooms above that peer down into the quartyard. The main area of the tavern, this quartyard has vines growing across wooden beams to form a sunroof. Paintings from throughout the ages hang on the walls inside the colonnade, pieces from the best artists to come out of Dalarus. But what had happened here last night was not beautiful. Nor is the expression on Winters' face.

"You look upset," Milo says taking a seat across from him.

Winters takes a hearty swig from his tankard. "Did I happen to tell you why I am here? I can't recall."

"Nope."

"As I am sure you know, Tyros is crawling with rogues and monsters. It has always been a nightmare, even when House Malbose was there to keep it in order." Winters pauses and stares off in deep thought. "And things have only gotten worse since the revolt. Much worse. A few months ago my Lords had enough and decided to take up the impossible task of cleansing it. Knowing all too well that we lack the manpower to do it alone they sent me to speak with the King."

"Let me guess: he denied your request?" Milo tries to finish.

"No, he agreed to send men."

"Then the problem is..?"

"The King agreed he should send one of his Legions, but not in cooperation with us. They know little of Tyros. The last time was against armies under an 'arch-duke'. And our people don't much trust the monarchy after all that's happened."

"So you came down here to ask House Pyrammus, is that it?"

"Aye, but they declined sending any men at all. The only thing I can think of now is to gather volunteers."

"Oh no, don't look to me. I helped mysterious strangers with their 'mission' before, and that turned out *fantastic*."

Winters is taken back. "The Lords said practically the same thing. Though they were less sarcastic." Winters takes another swig from his tankard. "My friend, we need every man we can get. We want to change the world for the better. I saw the way you handled last night, and I have heard stories about the attack on this city. Your heroism. What is a man like yourself doing wasting away in this city?"

"No. I'm not doing this again."

He remembers last time, the Rangers, Albus, everything since. All logic is screaming at him not to; but something inside him urges him to go like a whisper in the back of his head. This can't possibly be any good.

"Please Milo," Winters pleads. "We can do good."

"Fine. But if anything gets fishy, I'm out." It was time to leave the city. He felt it now.

*****

Milo and Aeris approach the wagon unmolested by the pesky peddlers for once. With him is everything he owns. Clothes and other small items are in his satchel, while his sword is fitting loosely in its new sheath on his belt, and the warhammer is mounted to his back. The wagon is now loaded and a couple mares are hooked up to it. Along with Winters and his two is Dequande, who is petting the horses like a big child.

"I've brought a friend," Milo tells Winters. Aeris looks at Milo in the corner of his eye as he says the word friend.

"Oh? I am Sir Carwood Winters. Who may you be?"

"Aeris Wynterfang."

"Wynterfang, eh? A good name," Winters says with a laugh. "You can throw your stuff onto the wagon. If you're both ready to go, we can start our long journey in once Reynard returns with the last of the supplies."

House Kyverhan took the Throne from House Julich, everyone expected the road's name to change again, but it never did. It would be this great road that would take them from southernmost Ateria to the northern land of Tyros. The first night into their long journey they stop and sit under the moonlight. They are all exhausted from a day of walking under the sun, but they stay up eating fruit and talking.

"So Milo," Winters says.

Milo is watching crocodiles sleep on the beaches of a distant oasis. "Huh?"

"Have you been to Tyros before?"

"A few times. I don't like it up there; a tad too dangerous even for me."

"Well we shall change that, shan't we?" Winters says with a sad smile

"Shall we toast to Tyros?" The boy shouts.

"Fucking Paulin, if you weren't my sister's kid you'd not be a fuckin' squire. Mine or otherwise."

Paulin tries to say something, but in his nervousness forms no comprehensible words.

"Would you tell us about your Lords?" Milo changes the topic.

"Of course. Where to start... Xandercus Hale is the head of the house. His wife Lady Margaret is very ill. Bedridden in fact. No healer has been able to help her."

"I am sorry to hear that."

"They have five children. The oldest is Bartholomew, heir to House Hale and all that. The second eldest is a girl named Elara. Sweet and kind and pretty too. Born after her were a pair of twins: Dylan and Sarah Hale. One took off and joined some druids, and the other took up the sword."

"I would love to duel this boy when we get there," Dequande says.

Winters corrects him, "Ahem. The *boy* is the druid. The *girl* is the warrior,"

"A female warrior? Are you trying to trick me?" Dequande asks in disbelief.

"I am not. Things are different up in Tyros."

"I must meet this girl!"

"Their last child is a little girl, no telling yet how she will turn out."

"Do you have a wife and children?" Milo asks wanting to learn more about the man who is taking him back to Tyros.

"Are you asking to court me?" Winters laughs. "Nay no wife, no children. Not sure if I ever will at this rate. You don't have a family do you Milo?"

"Nay," Milo says.

"Does the glorious Dequande have a family?"

Dequande stands up and starts walking towards the wagon. "Where is the alcohol?"

"Other side, near the front."

*****

The cart pulls into a small town square. Winters had the group veer off of the Alexios Highway and down a long winding road into the woods. He wouldn't say where they were going, and his two were just as clueless as Milo.

"Y'all stay here, I'll be back in just a few. Got a surprise," Winters says excitedly. The men affirm with slow, unsure nods and Winters takes off into the town.

"You know where we are Milo?" Reynard asks.

"Well, the sign said Dermott. Never been here before if that's what you're asking."

Milo looks around the town square. A butchery, Gaunter's Mirrors, a lewd looking place called "A Beer and Beth," then something catches his eye. Milo starts walking towards it.

"Oi, where ya going? Sir Carwood told us to stay 'ere." Reynard asks.

"I'll be back in a minute," Milo says over his shoulder.

Reynard looks to Aeris and Dequande as Milo hurries off. Aeris just shrugs and Dequande obliviously pets the horses.

Milo walks up to the storefront, where a man is chiseling away at a block of wood. Not ceasing work on the block for a second, the man says, "Hail stranger. Can I help you?"

"I see you're a carpenter. You wouldn't happen to be a Bowyer as well, would you?"

"I am." The man glances at the Milo still chiseling. He stops chiseling and says, "Francis Yewcarve. You a soldier or something?"

"Or something," Milo says.

Francis sets down the chisel and pulls off his thick gloves and apron. "One moment." The man then disappears into his shop and comes back out with a longbow. He hands it to Milo. As he looks it over Francis says, "Tis the bow I make for my Lord's men." Milo draws the bow with ease and gives it a long feel before easing off the string. It is better than most of the bows he finds in the service of Lords, but he feels it doesn't quite suit him. Francis seems to sense Milo's dissatisfaction.

"Would you consider yourself a master of the bow?" he asks.

"I don't want to sound too full of myself, but I've been using a bow for longer than I can remember."

Francis takes the warbow back from Milo and heads back inside his shop. He emerges again with another bow and hands it to Milo. It is the most beautiful bow Milo has ever seen, a compound bow made of perfect Yew wood and bull horn.

"Tis two hundred," Francis says.

"Richters?" Milo asks.

"Nay, pounds. None have been able to use it, not even the best archers of the King's Royal Legions." Francis reaches into a box, pulls out an arrow, and raises an eyebrow.

"Might as well give it a try."

Francis points high into the branches of a tree. "See that nest up there in the tree?" Taking the arrow Milo nods. With a heavy heart he knocks it. Slowly he empties his lungs, and a single heartbeat later he takes a deep breath as he draws the bow. He brings the string to his cheek. His heart beats once as he makes sure he is on target. Before it can beat again, he releases his breath and the string with it. The nest explodes with great force, the eggs within splattering far and wide. He gazes at the branches in a euphoria of amazement and triumph. The sound of clapping pulls him back to reality, though it is not Francis.

"Not even the best of the King's Archers have been able to control that beast," a man in a black doublet says, Winters beside him. "Francis, I believe this good man has earned the bow."

"I can't take it," Milo says.

"It is an honour for you to take it. None other can wield such a bow," Francis says.

"You may go now, Francis," the man in black says.

"Aye my Lord," he says, going back to the block of wood.

Winters then speaks, "Milo, this is Lord Eddon of Dermott. He has offered us a seat at his table this eve and bed for the night."

"Tis the least I can do for an old friend. And from what I hear of your long journey, it is well needed."

"Thank you my Lord. We are grateful for the hospitality you show us," Milo says.

"I should get back to the keep now, lest my wife not know that more needs to be cooked. I shall see you and your men shortly, yes?"

"Yes you shall Lord Eddon," Winters says before bowing. Lord Eddon turns around and starts walking off. Milo and Winters walk in the opposite direction towards the cart.

"So how do you know this Lord Eddon?" Milo asks.

"Do you know of the Battle of Tornister?"

"Yes." The Battle of Tornister was one of the most infamous battles of the Malbose Revolt. The Tornister River was flowing violently and none could safely ford it. After the forward army crossed the only bridge on the Tornister, the Malbose forces hooked around and captured the bridge, cutting off three hundred men for several weeks.

"My Lords remained loyal to the King. Downriver I led men across in boats, many of which capsized. We were supposed to attack at daybreak, but shortly after sunset they marched prisoners out of the camp to for execution. I decided we had to save them, plan be damned. We charged out of the woods and saved the prisoners, one of whom was Lord Eddon. Thinking the entirety of the King's armies had found a way to cross, the rebels began to panic. It descended into pure chaos after a fire broke out. We took the bridge that night, and Lord Eddon and I fought together to the end of the war."

The two approach the wagon and Reynard jokes, "Telling war stories, eh Sir?"

"Remember that surprise I said I had? Well we are to spend tonight as guests of the Lord," Winters says cheerfully.

*****

Two young servant girls enter the dining hall. It is a small room with a large table crammed into it. Four candelabras burn across the table, though only one of the middle ones look it has ever been used, and in the wall between the dining hall and Throne room is a two-sided fireplace. The straw haired servant carries a large sizzling platter of brown bulbs. The other, a frizzy brown haired girl, makes around the table pouring wine into each cup. As she pours Milo's cup, she gives him a flirtatious smile. Moments later Lady Abigail sets down a dish stacked with large slivers of meat before taking a seat next to her husband. She has a beautiful face and gorgeous red hair, but her body is thin as sticks and womanly features flat.

"For you my dear friend Sir Carwood I had one of my bison freshly slaughtered for our meal tonight," Lord Eddon says.

"Thank you my Lord. You are very generous," Winters says.

Lord Eddon forks some of the meat onto his plate, cueing everybody else to take food as well. Milo tears off some bread from the loaf, waiting as the others stumble over one another for the meat. After he gets some of the bison onto his plate, he sticks his fork into one of the strange brown bulbs. He raises an eyebrow at the feel of the fork squish in, and slowly puts it on his plate.

"The bison fascinates me so. They used to be quite populace over on Accules as well, but the Acculeans have driven them near extinction," Lord Eddon says.

Cutting into the strange food with apprehension, Milo speaks up, "I don't mean to interrupt your history lesson, but *what is this?*"

"Oh yes! That is what they call a Po-ta-to. Though I first discovered them in an Adrosi village on my way to Lord's Port, they are indigenous to the Royce. They are quite hardy and seem to grow anywhere. I believe they will soon become a future staple of the Aterian diet."

"If you say so," Milo says before eating the slice of potato.

"It's good, yes? Say Carwood, I don't believe you have introduced your companions?"

Winters holds up a finger as he finishes chewing on a slice of bison. "This here is Reynard. The little one there is my nephew, Paulin. He is Milo Khan."

"Khan? As in the nomadic troupe that once inhabited northern Celethrand?" Lord Eddon asks.

"Take an interest in Celethrandrian history, m'Lord?" Milo responds.

"Since I was a child the story of the Fomorians enthralled me so. Otherworldly beings, ancient pure Elves, and the lost heir of a dead House returning after being raised by the Khans. I often wonder how the monks came up with this stuff." Lord Eddon leans forward intently. "Do you know the tales of Karth Valarain, Milo?"

"Aye, my mother would tell me stories about him."

Lord Eddon sits back in his chair. "Enough about old legends. Tell me, who is this giant who sits at my table?"

"I am Dequande," he says with his mouth full.

"Ah I should have guessed! Dequande the Bull, famed champion of House Pyrammus."

"That is me," he says before washing down the potatoes with an entire cup of wine. Dequande slams the cup back down and Milo pours the wine from his cup into Dequande's.

Winters speaks up, "And the man at the very end is Aeris Wynterfang."

"Since we've been on the subject of the etymology of names, can somebody explain to me why some Asbjarnarviki are whoever's son, while others have some random surname?" Milo asks.

"I see how it may come off as a little confusing," Lord Eddon begins. "It is a deeply rooted tradition. When an Asbjarnarviki boy is born they are their father's son. The son of Bjorn would be Thur Bjornson, for example. Similarly a girl would be the daughter of the mother, such as Ingridsdottr. If they ever leave Asbjarnarvik, they have forsaken their roots and no longer hold their family name. Thus they take up a surname of their choosing."

"I met an Asbjarnarviki smith in Pyrammus who still called himself Harolfson?"

"This tradition is not very easy to explain. It is not so much if they physically leave. They can go trading, on expedition, to war, and even enlist in the King's service. It is more of if they leave the land behind."

"So you left your home? Why?" Paulin asks Aeris. Oblivious to what is coming, the boy gets slapped in the back of the head by Winters. "Ow! What was that for?"

"That was bloody rude to ask," Winters growls.

Milo looks to Aeris, who is shoveling food into his mouth, never for a second letting it be foodless. His eyes are focused down at his plate, but for a brief second they flick up at Milo with a fierce rage that Milo had never before seen in them.

The brown haired girl comes up to Milo with a bottle of wine. "I see your cup is empty, Sir?"

"No more for me, thank-"

Milo is cut off as Dequande finishes off his cup in a huge gulp and bellows, "More wine!" The girl fills his cup half way. "More!" He cries. She finishes the bottle filling his cup.

"Damn you, now we have to wait for another bottle," Winters says as the serving girl retreats back into the kitchen. He looks over to the Lord and Lady solemnly. "I haven't wanted to ask, but I find myself needing to…" He stops takes a deep breath. "Where is Belany?"

Lady Abigail's body shakes as she says, "Belany is no longer with us." Her voice is weak, barely audible across the table.

Lord Eddon takes her hand. "Some weeks past she grew ill. We don't know when it started, but by the time we noticed there was nothing we could do."

Winters looks down and shakes his head, "I'm sorry, I shouldn't have asked."

Lady Abigail speaks with a weak voice, "It was not wrong of you to ask. The two of you were always quite fond of each other." She looks down in her lap. "Do you remember that doll you gave her?"

"Of course… My sister made it for her."

"She loved that doll so. I thought it was creepy, but she loved it…" Silent tears roll down her cheeks.

Lord Eddon stands up, placing his hand gently on his wife's shoulder. "I think it is time we take our absence. I hope you have enjoyed supper." His wife stands up and they exit the room, Eddon firmly clasping her small hand.

The servant girls come in and begin to take away the trays of food. Winters stands up slowly, his head hanging low. In a soft voice he says, "I am going to retire to my room. You all may go into town if you wish." As he leaves the room the others stand.

"We're gonna go to that tavern, care to join us Milo?" Reynard asks.

Milo shakes his head, "Nay. I'm going to go sleep as well."

"I wanna go!" Paulin cries.

He exits the dining hall and enters the Lord's Throne room. Carved to look like tangles of tree branches and cushioned with a dark red velvet, the brief appearances of the Throne in the flickering light of the two-sided fireplace disturb Milo. He shakes off the feeling of the chair lurking in the shadows and crosses the room to a staircase.

He follows Winters' steps up the staircase and up two floors. Entering a shadowy corridor, light pours through an open door, guiding Milo to the room they had shown him to earlier. Right before he can reach the handle, Winters shuts the door and everything goes dark. Milo feels around in the dark until he can find the handle. Swinging it open, an iron barred window sits in the thick castle walls, illuminating the room with moonlight and a cool draft coming in. Milo swings to door shut behind him. He jumps into bed and quickly drifts off.

Milo is suddenly woken up by the bulky wooden door slamming into the stone wall. Jolting up, he sees Dequande bumble into the room and slam the door behind him. The giant flops onto his bed, and almost immediately he begins snoring loudly. Milo lays back down and drifts back into a dreamless sleep.

Milo's once empty dreams are invaded by the soft sound of a girl's singing:

> *"Life shines brightly,*
> *As a brilliant facade.*
> *But take not lightly,*
> *That it's all just a fraud.*
>
> *Breathe of wind in the lungs,*
> *Shine of grass forms a crown.*

Her eyes shine, reminiscent of suns.
Water gives life, yet too much will drown.

Oh I am lost,
Oh I am lost.
Yet in life should be found…
Yet in life…
Should be found."

Slowly he opens his eyes, the room dimly lit by the glow of the moon. But his eyes are heavy; his awakening does not hold. To the soft tune of the girl's voice he drifts back into slumber.

"There's a promise of glory,
Of a finishing story.
To warriors bold,
Of the conquests of old.

There's a promise of wealth,
To those who live life void of self.
To the priests and the nuns,
To the gods holy daughters and sons.

There's a promise of joy,
To the young girl and boy.
Of the coming of spring,
To take life under their wing.

Promises left unfulfiled,
In the silence, breath is stilled.
Life it lies to you and I,
Life itself is just barely getting by.

Oh I am lost,

Oh I am lost.
Perhaps Life's end is nigh.
Perhaps...
To begin life, it must end."

Milo pulls himself back awake. His heavy eyelids drift open. Quickly they shut again for a long moment as he fights to stay awake. Sitting up he stumbles out of bed towards Dequande. The voice continues:

"A shadow softly falls,
Upon upturned cheek it aligns.
Not one of heaven's glorious signs,
But rather earthy and low in design."

Standing over the giant, Milo tries to shake him awake. Without his eyes opening, Dequande slaps away Milo's hand and rolls over. Milo leaves the room and follows the voice as it faintly echoes through the silent halls.

"A shadow softly calls,
Yet no promises does it make.
Freely admits to that which it takes,
Lays plainly that which is at stake."

Chasing after the voice he goes down the staircase, his every footstep nearly suffocating its lyrics.

"A shadow softly enthralls,
Its nature is to gently hide.
When truly it only wishes to confide,
For we all have the shadow inside."

Finally he tracks the voice to within a room locked with a heavy iron latch. Throwing the latch up, he gently creeks open the door and peers in.

"The Shadow softly consumes all,
Gently caresses the soul.
Flows along my body and yet leaves it whole.
The shadow even now takes upon itself the toll."

A girl sits in the corner, perhaps fourteen or fifteen years of age. Silky auburn hair drapes down her back; and black iron chains from her wrists into the wall.

"Oh I am lost,
Oh I am lost.
But I wish not to be found,
For to that lovely Shadow I am bound."

Slowly standing she turns towards Milo. Her skin is pale and flaking, her eyes large black voids. Around her neck hangs another chain. Through dark red lips, every word she speaks shows batlike teeth intermittent with Human teeth.

"I am lost,"

She raises her arm to take a look at the iron bracelet clamped around her wrist.

"I am bound."

Sprouting from her fingertips are long, sharp claws.

"Why doth thou think I would wish to be found?"

Moving towards Milo slow at pace yet with sudden strides, her voice becomes ever more agitated with every word.

"Fear not, for thine own heart even now doth mine Shadow surround."

At this point she is screaming rabidly, foam forming in between her jagged teeth. On her last lyric the chains of her iron necklace catch her mid-stride. She extends her hands the few inches forward that her chains allow for and wiggle her gruesome fingers.

In the doorway half across the room, Milo slowly steps backwards. Slowly he closes the door. Footsteps stomp down the hall. He turns to see Lord Eddon and two Guards storming his way.

Lord Eddon screams at Milo, "You have upset Belany!"

"That's your daughter?" Milo asks befuddled. "What happened to her, my Lord?"

Lord Eddon stops a couple feet away from Milo. His face twitches in anger, then his face mellows as he sighs and rubs his head. "Vampirism."

Milo raises an eyebrow. "Vampirism? How'd she get such a rare disease?"

"We don't know." Lord Eddon shakes his head. "One day she began acting strange. More irritable, less sociable, sleeping away most of the day and wandering through the night. We thought it was just the age… Then she attacked one of the village men, and we barely realised something was wrong. It wasn't until she started to lose her teeth and her fingers began to burst open that we realised."

"And you haven't been able to cure her?" Milo asks.

"Our physician said once the physical effects set in, there is no cure. We consulted doctors and druids and scholars from across Ateria to no avail."

Milo points a finger at the door. "So you've just chained her up, leaving her to suffer?"

"A man came to us a fortnight ago. He told us about his cousin in the Vostokov who's been cured of Vampirism. We paid him most what we have to find the doctor who cured him."

Milo sighs for the Lord. "I think you know you've been scammed, my Lord."

"He will come back, he swore on the Sun!"

"You said yourself that Vampirism can't be cured. And you just paid some random man a fortune for a miracle cure supposedly on the other side of the world."

"Would you have me do nothing?" Lord Eddon groans.

Somberly Milo shakes his head. "No. I'd have you end her suffering, my Lord."

"She is my only child!"

"She is not your child anymore. It is the best you can do for her now."

"If you were to… could you do it peacefully?"

"Of course. I'll get my bow."

Lord Eddon stands silent for a long moment before giving Milo a nod. "We will be outside the keep."

Without another word, Milo turns back down the corridor. Walking away he hears the men behind him creaking open the door to the girl's chamber. He is dreadfully aware of every step he takes up the staircase. The halls feel extra empty and solemn as he goes towards his chambers. In utter silence he enters the room. Before picking up the bow, he pauses and takes a deep breath. He makes his way back down the staircase, his every footstep heavy and echoing loudly. Passing through the Throne room with the only light being the soft, warm light of the dying embers, the Throne is now clouded in darkness, yet he can feel it watching him, judging him.

The doors exiting the keep are left wide open. He emerges from the darkness of the hall and the glow of the moonlight bathes him. The two Guards stand with the girl's chains tight in hand, using their feet to pin the girl on her knees. She faces away from him, her shadow stretched long before her. Milo approaches, nocking an arrow. He touches the arrow to the base of her skull. Lord Eddon winces in despair.

The girl giggles. "What a funny moustache he has," she says, her voice soft yet twisted.

"That who has?" Milo asks her. He looks at each of the men, but every one of them is clean shaven.

She giggles again. "Your shadow, silly."

Milo glances at his shadow, which is now overlapping hers. He furrows his brow and hesitates. Then he pulls back the string, his world slowing. Releasing his breath and shutting his eyes, he lets go. There is a sickening cracking sound, followed by the chains rattling, then complete silence.

Milo slowly opens his eyes. The girl hangs limp at the chains, the men still holding her. Lord Eddon stands a few feet away, his eyes glossing over. Giving a sharp nod to Milo, he turns away to hide his tears. The entire world moving in slow motion as if to torment him, he returns to the keep in dreadful silence

*****

The men are back on the road—they have been for some time. Long since they have left the core New Adros, and they have already passed through the narrow and rivery Redlands. Now the sharp hills and tall conifers of Tyros surround them. Milo hasn't spoken a word about what happened in Dermott.

The pair of horses pulling the cart trot along, Reynard sitting at the reins and drowsily looking down the Alexios Highway. Paulin sat in the wagon next to the crates of supplies, staring wide eyed at the world around him. Everybody sorely marches alongside the wagon, Milo seeing that the heavy Dequande is suffering the worst. Winters stops and turns to his left. "Ho!" he calls out to the horses. They stop and Reynard stretches as he looks over to Winters.

"Why'd we stop?" Milo asks.

Carwood Winters ignores his question and walks over to a stone circle between some trees, a four foot tall monolith made of loose squared stones in the centre. He takes a seat facing the monolith on one of the larger stones. Milo stands a short distance behind him, curiously taking in the scene.

"Today we turn off the Alexios Highway," Winters says.

Stepping into the stone circle, Milo asks, "What is this place?"

"It's a circle of worship built by the druids. They say it's built on a site of good energy."

"You're a druid?" Milo asks.

"No I am not. But this circle tells me that we only have a couple more leagues to go until we turn west."

"Can we get going now?" Aeris says from outside the circle, his eyes scanning the surrounding woods.

Winters stands back up. "Aye, best go before something attacks us."

Reynard is slouched over fast asleep, and both Dequande and Paulin are feeding the horses a couple carrots. Winters returns the bits back to the horses' mouths and clicks twice. Reynard jolts awake as the horses start walking, and they are back on their way. The farther north they travel the more unmaintained the Alexios Highway becomes. In the more developed parts of Ateria the road is cobbled, yet past Lord's Port it turns to a purely dirt road all the way to its terminus at Korvun's Pass. The road has become quite overgrown and piled with pine needles. It can only really be followed by the light signs of foot traffic, and the occasional decades-old milepost that is still standing.

"Hey Reynard, do you have anybody back home?" Milo asks as the man groggily drives the wagon.

"Aye. There's my wife and together we had two small girls. When I left we had another on the way. Dylan Hale said they're gonna be a boy."

"Why do you do this then? That's a long time to leave behind your family."

Reynard shrugs. "Well I guess somebody has to."

"What did you leave behind in Dalarus, Dequande?" Milo asks.

"I do not have much."

"You never did say if you had a family?" Reynard asks.

Dequande's face droops in sadness. Closing his eyes and slowly shaking his head he says, "I... I don't want to talk about it."

"I'm sorry. I won't pry."

Reynard looks to Aeris to change the subject. "Do you have anything back home?"

Aeris glances at him for a moment before scowling back down the trail. "No. I don't have a home."

Reynard shifts awkwardly in his seat. He tugs slightly on the reigns and guides the horses through a curve around a steep hill. "And you Milo?"

"Me? I-" Milo starts to say, but it is all he gets out. They hear shouting from the woods ahead and around the blind curve. Reynard brings the horses to a stop. The men draw their weapons and slowly go around the bend. There stands a thick bearded Asbjarnarviki, his stance wide like a bear with a bloodstained axe in hand. In a circle around him are four dirty men, slouching and twisted, and wielding long knives.

"Just hand it over Northling!" One of them cries prodding at the air with their knife.

"You all better fucking run," Winters calm voice booms at them.

The four dirty men all look towards Winters. With no hesitation from the sudden intervention of the group, the Asbjarnarviki sinks his axe into the back of one highwayman's head. With giant strides Dequande hurtles towards the men with shocking speed. One highwayman tries to stab at the Asbjarnarviki but he glances it away with his axe. He quickly spins around and glances away another one of the highwayman's strikes. The first one he had deflected starts thrusting towards him again, but he is oblivious as Dequande's axe meets his guts with incredibly force. The highwayman the Asbjarnarviki is engaged with takes a step back, only to find his head pulled back then his throat slit wide by Aeris' dagger. The last man, so far frozen in shock, turns and runs towards the treeline. One of Milo's arrows enters through his spine and goes through his chest before finally getting stuck into the bark of a nearby pine.

While Winters goes back around the bend to tell Reynard it is now safe, Milo throws the bow back over his shoulder and approaches the men. Aeris sheaths his dagger and the Asbjarnarviki his axe, and the two stare tensely at one another.

"Is that… Aeris Wynterfang?!" The Asbjarnarviki bellows.

Milo touches the hilt of his sword. The man laughs and, for the first time, Aeris gives a small smile. The two share a quick hug.

"It's good to see you Thanic," Aeris tells him.

Milo raises an eyebrow as he asks, "You two know each other?"

"I am Thanic Karthan, the two of us worked for Ferdinand Vehrack back in the day."

Aeris' resets to its regular scowl. "I thought you were living back in Bjartrtun with your wife?"

The happiness in Thanic's eyes fades to sadness. "Amria is no longer with us, old friend."

Winters and the wagon come up on the men. "Is everybody all right?"

"What happened?" Aeris asks Thanic.

Thanic glances at Winters before saying to Aeris, "That is a long story. Say, I am heading south to start my own trading company. Would you come join me like old times?"

"Yes," Aeris answers without hesitation.

"Wait! What about helping Tyros?" Winters says in shock.

"I apologise," Thanic says. "I don't mean to steal him away if he's already sworn to you."

"I'm not," Aeris says.

Winters opens his mouth to object, but Milo intervenes. "Just let him go." Winters sighs and nods his head to Aeris. In silence Aeris and Thanic start back on the path south. Paulin waves to the back of their heads as they vanish around the bend.

"Well shit…" Reynard says after they are out of sight.

Winters merely continues forward on the path, and the others follow. Throughout the day the wind begins to kick up. The tall conifers sway back and forth and strong gusts cause pine needles to rain down. The men turn west at a crooked post that directs them towards something called Grayrest. Puffs of low-lying clouds begin to blow in, and soon the skies become dark with a sheet of clouds. The world darkens under the clouds and dwindling sunlight. The caws and low gurgling croaks and shrill calls of the birds dwindle until the only sound is the wind whistling through the trees.

Under the fading light they peer down the road and see a shadowy conglomerate blocking the road, flickering light coming from within. As they near, the thing blocking the road becomes more clear. Parked in a circle are three strange carts. The varied jumble of brightly coloured woods and canvases hurt the eyes, the sides of the carts curve to grow wider and narrower like the shape of a mushroom, and their front wheels are comically thrice the size of their rear ones. And spiring up between all three is a faded green and yellow tent, smoke from a fire fuming from the many tears in the canvas.

"What the hell is this?" Milo asks as he tries to process the chaotic sight.

"Fucking Elves…" Winters mutters.

The wagon stops as they get right on top of it and the men stare at it in a sort of wonder. An Elf stumbles out from between the carts, scratching his chest hair through the opening in his half untied orange tunic. He pulls his prick through the fly of his brown trousers and starts relieving himself, unaware of the onlooking group. Milo clears his throat.

Continuing to relieve himself, he casually turns his head towards the group. "Oh hello there." The men uncomfortably look away, but the Elf continues shamelessly. "Is there something I can do for you?"

Winters says, looking away from the man as he speaks, "Well we were wondering if you could move your carts so we can be on our way."

The Elf finishes and puts his prick back into his trousers. "The Sun has already begun to set my friend. You would be more than welcome to share our fire and stew for the night."

"He's right. By the time they got everything moved, it'd be too late to travel anyway," Reynard says from atop the wagon.

Winters looks around apprehensive before saying, "Fine, we'll stay here."

"Great! Come on in," he says joyously, waving the men in as he re-enters the strange cart-tent.

"I've never met Elves before!" Paulin exclaims.

Winters gives him a sharp scowl, "You're staying out here."

"But-"

"Don't you argue with me." Paulin gives a sour face before jumping back into the wagon and laying on his stomach. "Somebody else needs to watch our stuff."

Milo is about to volunteer when Reynard speaks up, "I'm wide awake from drowsing off at the reigns all the time."

Winters hesitantly enters the cart-tent, then Milo and Dequande follow. Inside there are three benches forming a triangle around the fire. Sitting at the farthest bench from them is the Elf they just met. Next to him is another Elf with longer and pointier ears than the other, solid dark blue clothing, and his legs spread wide with a brown haired She-Elf's heading bobbing between them. On another side of the triangle are two She-Elves, one with long golden hair and the other with short brown hair. Winters, Milo, and Dequande fill up the remaining side of the triangle.

"You didn't tell me you had invited guests for supper," the darkly dressed Elf says with a laugh.

The first Elf begins, "My friends this is Calanthír. The Elf currently pleasuring him is Miracyn, and those two are Fensys and Asinia."

"You never did say who you were," Milo comments.

"Ah my apologies. I am Adcan. Who might you all be?"

"Well I'm M-"

Winters cuts him off, "Just some road weary travellers."

"As you wish," Adcan says somewhat disappointed.

"I believe the stew is done," Calanthír says in his gravelly voice. The blonde She-Elf, Fensys, gets up from the bench and climbs the steps into one of the carts.

"How d'you get these wagons here?" Dequande asks.

"Well our horses," Adcan tells him.

"I don't see any horses?" Winters comments.

"We have them hidden in the woods," Calanthír rasps. Fensys returns from the cart with a stack of bowls in her hands. She sets them down on the bench beside Asinia, the short brown haired one, and takes a seat. Asinia ladles thick soup into the bowl and passes it to Fensys, whom in turn passes it to Calanthír, until it gets to Milo. They pass another and another until everybody has a bowl. Miracyn pulls up from Calanthír's crotch, gulping loudly as she returns his manhood to his trousers. She grabs the last empty bowl as she passes Fensys and scoops the stew directly from the cauldron. Everybody digs in—except for Winters.

"What is in this?" He asks suspiciously.

"It is simple sheep stew my friend," Adcan tells him.

"And where are these sheep of yours?" Winters says before cautiously trying the stew.

Calanthír loudly slurp up some soup. "With the horses. You are awfully paranoid."

"I don't particularly trust you *Knife-Ears*."

"It was said Ateria was a place of tolerance. In the years since, we Elves have learned that tolerance only applies to you Humans," Calanthír says.

"Long ago we were a great race," Adcan says. "Our kind traversed the stars, travelling between the many worlds. We lived without disease, famine, or even to an extent death. Communication was silent; a language was not needed. Your kind came from the dust before our eyes, and on occasion we saved you from extinction."

Winters leans in closely, "And it was your kind that caused the convergence, right? Without your kind there would be no Goblins, Trolls, Wyverns, or otherwise. Even the Dwarves scorn you for tearing apart their homeworld and throwing them into ours."

"You are not wrong. As we crossed between worlds, the majority of our kind failed to see the tears we were creating. But there were those who predicted such an event and pleaded with the others to cease such travel. It was our ancestors who sacrificed themselves to save your world as the multiverse began to collapse on itself."

"Your kind has only ever infected our world with your perverted ways. Lust and envy is in your blood, and your sheer arrogance that you are better than Humans is revolting. Since before the time of the Three Empires your kind has been more Human than Elf anyway."

Milo's head begins to swim. The world wobbles around him. For a split second he is afraid but then he is overtaken by extreme calmness.

Calanthír speaks up, "And it is you who destroys any kind of society we try to set up for ourselves. Since our kind stranded ourselves to save *your* world, Humans have been tearing Elves down. Forced under the rule of man, into the ghettos of man's cities, and even subjected to slavery. Some may have integrated, but we all know they will never be accepted into Human society... not truly. The rest of us have wandered the world as nomads, constantly fleeing and trying to build a life free from your oppression the best we can."

Somewhere inside Milo he is alarmed by the escalating situation, yet his world feels as calm as a warm spring day in Adros.

"Tonight you will repay us," Calanthír says.

Burried deep inside his instincts tell himself to get up and run, but he feels paralysed in a state of near bliss. The world spins around him. The Elves laugh amongst one another, their faces becoming hellishly exaggerated in his delirious state. He finds himself unwillingly chuckling, then everybody is laughing together. Next thing he knows he is brushing away the advances of Fensys. After a few unsuccessful attempts to get Milo's trousers down, Fensys gets fed up and goes to kiss Miracyn as she sits atop Dequande. Milo his world fades into nothingness and he comes back to Fensys now riding Dequande. Turning his head slowly as being stuck in Molasses, his world fading as he tries to make out the shapes of a women bobbing up and down.

Milo comes to as he is shaken awake. It is daylight now and the men are laying in the open road, everything is gone but their own wagon and horses. Rubbing the back of his head, Reynard is standing above Milo.

"What happened?"

"I don't exactly know. I heard something behind me, but before I could turn to see... Well, from the feel of it they hit me on the back of my head."

Groggily Milo sits up and shakes Winters awake. He rubs his eyes and stumbles to his feet. "Damned Elves," he spits. "Was anything stolen, Reynard?"

"Not that I can see. I can't figure why they attacked us?"

"I'd... Rather not talk about it," Winters says with disgust as he struggles to remember the night before. "It must've been in the food."

Milo shakes Dequande, but he does not wake up. He shakes him harder this time, and he briefly opens his eyes only for them to drift back shut. Milo just sighs. Paulin wanders over from his seat in the cart and Winters turns pale.

"Did those Elves harm you?" He asks Paulin.

"No. After a littleI just went to sleep. When I woke up, they were already gone!"

"Thank the gods, your mother would have killed me."

◈ CHAPTER ELEVEN

"Milo," a man's voice calls out. He opens his eyes to the Sun shining brightly above. The cart he lays in moving and wonders if he is waking up to that first day in Dalarus again. When he sees his breath steaming, he knows that he is still in Tyros. Part of him wishes it was that day again, that everything was a dream. "We're here," Winters says. Milo sits up from the cart and looks at the town of Charlesworth.

Before the town is a large field of green wheat swaying gently in the ocean winds. Charlesworth itself is built up onto a gradually rising peninsula, the keep built at the top of the cliffy protrusion. Wrapped around the town from shore to shore is a palisade made from sharpened tree trunks.

The wagon rolls down the narrow road between the vast green fields scattered with working men with wide brimmed straw hats. They approach the palisade's gatehouse, two square wooden towers with a walkway spanning over the large double gates. A loud scraping sound comes from behind the gate before they are slowly pulled open. "Welcome back, Sir Carwood!" A soldier exclaims as the wagon passes pass through the open gate. Two soldiers push the gate closed after them and work together to lock the gates with a large wooden log.

They travel up the road, taking in Charlesworth. The streets are filled with mud and Human waste thrown from the windows of the surrounding houses. Many of the houses are impoverished wattle and daub buildings, their bottom floors dedicated to livestock. In a small market circle there was a bakery, a seamstress, a tavern, a small run down forge, and a few seemingly abandoned buildings. Milo noticed there was a distinct lack of a church anywhere he could see.

Reynard looks over his shoulder to Milo, "Take the reins would you?"

Milo hops over the backrest of the bench and sits next to Reynard, who then hands him the reins. He jumps from the moving wagon and approaches a small single-storey house. Outside is a woman cradling a babe as she uses one hand to wash the family's clothes. The woman spots Reynard and smiles brightly. He takes the babe from her arms and gives her a kiss. Two little girls playing a few feet away watch the stranger kissing their mother with puzzled looks on their faces.

The men pull up to the castle and stop. Built on the edge of the peninsula, it is a square stone keep with a large round tower coming out of the back-right corner. The pair of wooden doors to the keep swing open. A little girl flies out of the keep and runs to Winters. Grabbing onto his leg tightly she says, "Cawood! I was woowied about you!"

Winters smiles brightly as he tells her, "About me? You really think I'd let anything hurt me, Alexa?"

"Awe you back faw good?" The little girl asks.

"I shan't leave that long ever again," he reassures her.

Two more men emerge from within the castle. One is an older man, his hairs long ago greyed, his face was covered with prickly grey stubble, and a stern scowl worse than that of Aeris'. Beside him is a young man who heavily resembles him, though his hair is brown, his cheeks clean shaven, and while he has a serious expression, it is much more friendly.

Winters looks up to the men. "Lord Xandercus, Lord Bartholomew. I have returned from my long errand. How fares Margaret?"

"You took longer than expected Sir Winters. What exactly did you spent these past months doing?" Xandercus bitterly questions.

"Did you not receive my message? I sent a bird," Winters says, all the happiness he had a moment ago fading away.

"I did not," Xandercus states sourly.

"Apologies my Lord. Things did not go well with the King."

"I would have thought King James would want to help us…"

"Well he did in his own way."

"I don't see any soldiers standing before us? I only see these two… whatever they are."

"Oi!" Milo cries.

"I am Dequande, the-" Dequande starts.

Xandercus cuts him off, "I don't care who you are."

"My Lord, the King didn't give *us* any men. But he has sent his armies to-"

"Then what use are they to us?"

"They must be of more-"

Xandercus quickly grows impatient and interrupts, "Why did you bring these two peasants with you?"

Gesturing at Dequande, Winters tells Xandercus, "This is Dequande, a famous gladiator. He-"

Xandercus cuts him off again. "And the other man?"

"This is Milo Khan, somewhat of a hero to Dalarus."

"I wouldn't call-" Milo tries to say, but Xandercus continues to interrupt everybody.

"I had expected more from you, Winters." Turning around and walking back into the keep he shouts, "This was a waste of time."

"Well isn't he just a bundle of happy welcomings," Milo jests.

Bartholomew Hale sighs, "I apologise for my father's behaviour."

"He is more full of anger than when I left," Winters says looking at the keep in sadness. "I presume Margaret has only worsened?"

"By the day I am afraid…"

"When we left your brother had suggested the Arch-Druid see her?"

"The Druids are a cautious society my friend. They fear doing so would allow their highest ranking member to be captured."

"They know House Hale has always been friends of the druids!"

"You must remember, they have spent the past millennium in persecution."

Milo speaks up, "They won't even let you take her to them?"

Bartholomew shakes his head, "She's too sickly to get out of bed, let alone taken to who knows where."

"May I introduce the two of you to Lord Bartholomew, heir of House Hale," Winters tells them.

"Hail," both Milo and Dequande say simultaneously. They look at each other awkwardly.

"My father seems to think little of you two. You may not be what we were hoping for, but I believe we can use every man we can get. I invite the three of you to dinner, we can talk specifics there."

"Alright," Milo says.

After the man turns and retreats into the castle after his father, the little girl shyly approaches Milo and extends her small hand. He drops to his knee and gently shakes her tiny hand. "My name's Milo. What is yours?"

"Alexa," she tells him, now not so shy.

"Hail there," a soft woman's voice says. Milo looks up to a beautiful young woman standing above him, lush brown hair draping to below her shoulder blades, and deep blue eyes like that of sapphire. Her hands are gently clasped at the front of her cornflower blue and rose red dress. "I am Elara," she says blushing softly. Alexa runs off somewhere.

"I'm Milo," he tells her.

"I am Dequande!" The giant bellows, offering her his hand. She extends her small and shakes the giant's hand nervously.

Milo just notices another woman, younger in the face than Elara yet taller and muscular. She shakes Dequande's hand with a stern grip. "Sarah Hale."

"So Milo…" Elara begins.

"Yes?"

"What is it that you do?" She asks a little shy.

"This and that. Apparently I'm a hero now."

Elara giggles softly at that, her smile briefly showing her white teeth.

"Pardon me, my Ladies, I need to speak with these two gentlemen." Elara shoots Milo a smile before turning around and heading back into the castle with her warrior sister.

"There's a spare room in the castle that you can use. If you follow me, I can show it to you?"

*****

Elara smiles at Milo as she sets a bowl of beef stew down on the table in front of him. "I hope it isn't too bland for you. Sir Carwood told us you are from Dalarus."

"I'm not actually used to crazy spiced foods. I'm sure it's great."

She smiles as she retreats around the table and to her seat. Alexa whispers something into her ear and the two girls giggle. She then flashes him another smile. Sitting next to Milo's left is Winters, who leans in and quietly tells him, "I do believe Lady Elara fancies you." Milo just looks at him with an eyebrow raised. Elara passes a basket of bread to her Alexa on her right, who in turn passes it to Sarah, then to Bartholomew. Bartholomew passes it to his father, who slowly digs through until he finds his preferred slice of bread before passing it to Winters. After it finally gets to Dequande, he takes two pieces of bread and sets it in the centre of the table.

"Shall we begin?" Alexander says.

Dequande is the first one to start spooning the beef stew into his mouth, and everybody else follows suit. Milo sees that Lady Margaret and the Dylan Hale are both not present. *'Great, last time there was somebody missing from the table, they ended up being a Vampire.'*

"Dequande and Milo, you are here to help us cleanse the evil from my family's land, correct?"

"Something like that," Milo says after swallowing the bread he was chewing.

"I assume you expect payment? We do not have much, but we will try our best to duly compensate your work here."

He shrugs. "I'm not in it for the coin."

"So we don't have to pay you? Looks like there is one good thing about you," Lord Xandercus states.

"Father!" Elara exclaims. "We can not make somebody work without fair compensation. It is only right that we pay him what we can!"

"He says he will do without pay. Why would we pay him then?"

"Both of you!" Bartholomew snaps. "The men will be paid. We shall give you lodging and food for as long as you work for us and don't cause any problems."

"There'll be no need to worry about that from me, you're not Lord Nasir. I can't be sure about my companion here..." Milo places his hand beside his mouth between him and Dequande, though speaks loud enough that the gladiator can still hear him, "He's been known to break table."

Bartholomew raises an eyebrow, "What do you mean he breaks tables?"

Before Milo can explain his joke Xandercus Hale stands from his seat. He slams his hands down onto the table and scowls at Winters. "You these men you recruited, Sir Carwood? Some wild-looking fellow and a brute who breaks tables!" He kicks the chair as he storms off, his stew only half eaten.

"Father," Elara cries as she gets up and scurries after him.

Milo gulps before saying, "I didn't mean to start anything."

"It is not your fault. My father has been temperamental since our mother became sickly. I'm sure the two of you will be fine. Even with your friend's history of breaking tables." Bartholomew smirks slightly at his words.

"Maybe I shouldn't ask for another cup of ale?" Dequande tries to whisper, though everybody can hear him.

Bartholomew furrows his brow and looks somewhat wide mouthed at the giant. Winters chuckles to himself then sighs. Shaking his head he says, "Perhaps it is time we retire for the night?"

Bartholomew gets up and leaves the room with a sigh. Alexa starts to collect all the tableware. As Sarah Hale leaves the room, she stops in the doorway and looks back to Dequande. "Tomorrow morning, let's spar?"

"I am looking forward to fighting this warrior women."

She exits the room and Winters follows. Milo turns to Dequande, who is quickly stuffing his face with the last bit of food he can. "Do I really look wild?"

◈ CHAPTER TWELVE

Milo is laying on the straw bed in the room the Lords has provided him. Outside the window is the Sun just starting to disappear beneath the horizon. He holds the tiki mask, running his fingers through the intricate carving. It is the hundredth time he has looked at it, yet something about it is still alluring and makes him want to learn all its secrets. He sets it down on his chest and stares at the ceiling. Over a week has gone by, and no word yet. Winters and Bartholomew have been discussing plans, but each time Xandercus Hale has resisted them.

Despite his efforts to stay out of the grumpy Lord's way, Milo has run into him a couple of times. The last time Lord Xandercus caught him passing in the hall, Milo tried politely to tell him, "Good day, my Lord." The Lord stopped in his tracks and looked at him with enmity. "What do you want, peasant?"

A flustered Milo responded, "I just wanted to tell you good day."

Xandercus stomped away, muttering to himself, "How do you know what kind of day it is?"

Milo wonders if the several month journey will have been for naught. Then the door of his room flies open. Winters barges in excited. "Milo, it's finally time!" Before Milo can even respond, Winters is already out of the room. He sits up in bed slowly then gets up and strolls into the hallway. Walking down the corridor, he stops in the doorway, peering through to get a glance of who is in the Throne room. He feels somebody tap him on the shoulder. Looking back, he finds only a hairy shirtless chest at eye level. He looks up at the one person that this could be.

"Are you going in?" Dequande asks.

"Yeah," he says before moving through the door. First, he is in the main hall of the Keep, then he turns a corner and goes under an open arched doorway into the Throne room. Situated at the base of the tower, it is a circular room with nothing in it but the Throne sitting on a round dais. Behind the Throne is a simply patterned glass window, and above that are much larger holes that let in light along with the fresh sea air. Dequande enters after him.

"Milo, we will speak with you first," Winters says from below the dais.

"Alright. What is my task?"

Bartholomew Hale is standing next to the Throne that his father sits in. "Have you ever heard of the creature known as the Kedragora?"

"Can't say I've fought a monster that sounds like a cat's fur-ball."

Bartholomew nods to Winters, who in turn exits the room. A minute later he comes back escorting a peasant in torn, blood-stained rags. "For long the people of Tyros have feared this beast. Those who see it typically do not live to tell the tale. This man is just the latest victim of the scourge."

"A-aye. Tis true my Lords," the man stammers. "Yesterdays I was tending to mah goats when a shadow came overhead. I-its cry pierced me ears and I ran to the cellar I d-dug last season. When everything grew quiet, I crawled out and I found the whole village…" He pauses and breaths in hard as he tries to contain his tears. "D-d-dead!"

"*Village…*" Lord Xandercus scoffs. "More like three shanty hovels."

"Can thou not be so demeaning, Father?" Bartholomew pleads.

"I only call it as I see it." The young heir buries his face in his hands and groans. Standing up from his Throne Xandercus says, "If you do not like my presence, I shall leave." He stomps towards Milo, nearly clipping him on the shoulder if Milo hadn't moved out of the way.

Turning to the ragged peasant Milo asks, "What can you tell me about this Kedragora?" As he says the name of the creature he thinks, *'Where do people come up with these names?'*

The man looks down at his feet, "I didn't get a good look at it m'Lord."

"Is there anything at all you could tell me about it?"

"Well it sounded like a…" The man's voice trails off as he tries to think.

"A what?" Winters asks.

"I c-can't remember now. All I can thinks about is m-mah wife. So m-much blood…" The man falls to his knees and sobs. He wheezes as he gasps for air between fits of crying. The soldier grabs the peasant by his arm and guides him out of the room.

"I will slay this foul beast!" Dequande proclaims with his great battle axe high in the air.

"Actually you aren't," Winters says.

Dequande's arm drops down by his side and disappointment covers his face, "What do you mean?"

"We have another task for you," Bartholomew says. "For some time now there has been a pesky family of cannibals living to the east. They have been attacking travellers and such for some time now, but my father just gave us permission to rid the world of them. Sir Carwood and four other of my men will accompany you."

"Hold on," Milo interjects. "You aren't sending me to go fight this Kedragora alone are you?"

"Of course not. There will also be my sister, and two of my men whom I don't believe you have met."

"Your sister..?" Milo asks thinking of the dainty Elara. "Oh Sarah!"

Bartholomew gives him a weird look. "Yes. Tomorrow at sunrise you will set out on your assigned tasks. Are there any questions?"

"Actually where is Reynard going to be in all this?"

"Sir Reynard requested that he has some time with his family. After his long expedition around the entire continent, I felt obliged to grant it."

"I completely understand."

"Is there anything else?" The young heir asks. After a period of silence he says, "Then you all are dismissed."

Milo starts walking back to his room, but Winters quickly catches up to him. "You want to go to the tavern with us?"

"You do remember I don't drink, right?"

"Well you could just sit with us. We've got a big day tomorrow. And if either of us fails at our assigned task…"

"I guess I'd just be sitting in my room anyway."

Winters, Milo, and Dequande leave the castle. The cawing of seabirds have disappeared for the night, the Sun retreating beneath the horizon. Half the sky is darkened for night, the moon peering down above them. All is quiet as they walk down the night of the town of Charlesworth towards the market circle. Passing Reynard's house, they hear him and his family laughing and speaking jovially. The men approach the tavern, a decorative wood heater shield engraved with the words, "The Stumble Inn."

Inside the tavern it is cosy. There are two fireplaces on opposite sides of the tavern, though only one is burning at the moment. Humble decorations—of which were probably whatever the tavern-keep could find—are hung on the walls and support beams. A small spiral staircase hides in the back corner leading up to what is probably rooms. A curly haired bartend leans on the counter talking to a couple soldiers. Winters and Dequande sit up at the bar counter, and Milo leans against a nearby beam.

"I've been told you are going up against the Kedragora, Sir Carwood," the bartend says.

Winters points to Milo, "I won't be. He will over there."

The soldier farthest from Winters says tells Milo, "I'm Darren. I'll be going with you tomorrow. Sadly, Simkin here won't be."

"I heard it's covered in great obsidian scales," Simkin says.

"Some of my customers who've seen it say it has three heads!" The bartend exclaims to rile up the men.

"My mum said she saw it once. Had the breath of fire she claimed!" Darren says.

Simkin furrows his brow, "Didn't you say your mum was delusional?"

Darren shrugs, "Never said I believed 'er."

From the back of the tavern a woman storms up. Winters barely turns to her as she backhands him. He leans back and puts his arms up to block as the woman beats on him. "You killed Powel!" She screams as she bombards Winters with her fists. Simkin and Dequande grab the woman's arms and pull her away from Winters. "Get off me!" She hisses.

"Bloody calm down Rosalin!" Simkin shouts. She stops thrashing around and scowls at the men with rage filled eyes. "You better leave, now."

"Fine," she snaps. They let go of her arms and she slams the door on her way out of the tavern.

"What just happened?" Milo asks.

"That's Rosalin. She was Sir Powel's... Lover is probably the word for it," Darren explains.

"Who's Powel?" Milo and Dequande ask at the same time.

Winters sighs, "He's the man who was the assassin killed the night we met..."

"What ever happened to his body?" Milo asks.

Winters face twitches, "House Pyrammus took care of him. Cremated as the White Sun mandates."

"Have you talked to Rosalin at all?" Simkin asks.

"Nay, this was the first I've seen her."

"You should talk to her about it," Milo says.

"I'll go see if I can find where she went." He stands up from the bar stool.

"Now? You sure you don't want to let her calm down?" Milo asks.

"You don't know Rosalin," Darren says. "She's always got a temper on her."

"Now's a good of time as ever with her," Winters assures him.

"Alright but if I find out you're dead tomorrow..."

Winters leaves the Stumble Inn, a cold gust of Tyros air blowing into the stuffy tavern. Milo looks around at the remaining men. They sip on their drinks in silence, looking tired a bored now that the commotion is over.

Milo yawns, "Maybe I should retire for the night."

"You sure you don't want an ale first?" The barkeep says.

"I don't drink," Milo says with a shrug.

"We've got a long day ahead of us, go get your rest," Darren tells him.

Leaving the tavern Milo walks back down the streets of Tyros. Dark clouds roll overhead, and a cold breeze pierces his clothing. With nothing left to do after dark the town of Charlesworth has entered its nightly slumber. It is quite the contract to Dalarus here.

Up the street Reynard and his wife sit outside gazing at the stars. As Milo approaches, Reynard calls out for him, "Hail there!"

Milo had intended to let him sit in peace, but now that he has spoken to him he asks, "How are you doing Reynard?"

"Swell thank you! This is Jenni, my lovely wife."

"Hail there," she says with a smile that reveals her crooked teeth. She's a plainly woman with frizzy brown hair and a flat nose.

"Word is they're sending you guys out finally?" says Reynard.

"Aye. I'm glad they are letting you spend some time with your family."

"It was a long time away from them. The babe's a boy; just like Lord Dylan said!"

"Congratulations Reynard. And Jenni."

"Thank you," she says a wide smile.

"Well I won't hold you up. Best of luck tomorrow!"

"Thank you," Milo says before heading back towards the keep. An owl watches him from a roof above. It hoots before fluttering away into the night. He walks up to the Keep's doors, a single Guardsmen with a nasal helmet and hauberk guarding it.

"Greetings Milo," he says sleepily, pulling his halberd towards himself to unblock the door.

Milo nods to him with a faint smile and enters the castle. The hall of the castle is dark, the only light a candelabrum on a table. He goes up to the table and picks up on of the chambersticks next to the candelabrum and uses one of the candles in it to light his chamberstick. He finds his way to the door that leads from the main hall to a secondary corridor until he gets to his room. Still burning he sets it in the windowsill, nothing should catch on fire in the middle of the two foot thick stone alcove. Before stripping down he reties the tiki mask he had left on his bed onto his belt. Jumping into bed, he quickly drifts away into a dreamless sleep.

He wakes up the next morning to a knocking on his door. His room is still dark as it faces west, but he can tell from the faint light out of his windows that the Sun has begun to rise. Dequande rises from his bed and rubs his head.

"You want to get it?" Milo asks.

Dequande shakes his head. Milo gets up and opens the door. Winters stands on the other side, already clad in his armour.

"Get dressed, we are to leave soon."

Milo and Dequande get dressed, with Dequande actually throwing on a vest due to the Tyrosian cold. The two leave the castle. Everybody else seems to have already gathered around and are eagerly awaiting to go. Four horses are grazing at the little grass patches they can find. Winters grabs the reins of a white Pyrammian mare and guides it to Milo.

"Who's this?" Milo asks.

"Elara called her Snowstorm. She's a good steed but the Lady found her too hot-blooded. She wished that you be given her as part of your payment."

"Wait really?"

Winters grins. "I told you she fancies you."

Milo strokes the beautiful mare's soft white hairs. He puts his foot on the stirrup and throws himself onto the tan trail saddle. He clicks his tongue twice, and the mare takes off in a canter. Milo tugs on the reins gently, the bit becoming tighter in the horse's mouth. The horse slows to a trot, and he swings her in a circle around the group. "Whoa," he tells the mare, and she comes to a stop.

"Do you like Snowstorm?" Elara asks. She is now standing a few feet away from him, her dress a soft yellow.

"Very much so. I'm not sure I can accept your horse though."

"I only ever ride my Faringdon Warmblood. She'll get better attention from you I'm sure," she says with a flirty smile.

"Thank you Lady Elara."

The peasant from the attack limps over to the men, still dressed in the blood-stained rags as the night before. He wipes his nose with his hand.

"I w-wish you the b-best…" The man's voice trails off as he stares at nothing in particular, his eyes slowly drifting apart. Nearby a rooster squawks at another, charging at it to defend his territory. The man flops to the ground, screaming in fear. Everybody stares at the peasant.

"What in the name of the Gods is wrong with you?" Winters questions with a furrowed brow.

"I d-don't know!" The man cries, nearly incomprehensible through his tears. He curls up into a ball and shakes violently.

"Get yourself together!" Winters snaps with disgust.

"Maybe he needs some sleep?" Milo asks from atop his new steed.

"What's the point?" The man sobs.

"A lack of sleep can be detrimental to your health," Milo explains.

"I meant in living!" He sobs even louder. "Just leave me to die!"

Winters throws his arms up and stops away shouting, "Fine!"

Dequande approaches the man, his face covered with pity. He picks up the peasant like a limp rag-doll and throws him over his shoulder. Vanishing inside the castle he softly says, "It will be okay."

"Do you think he will be alright?" Elara asks Milo.

"As tasty as he looks, I doubt the cannibals will be able to take him," Milo jests.

Elara chuckles softly, "I meant the other man."

"I couldn't say about him…"

Sarah Hale trots up on a red-roan Thoroughbred, "Can we get going now? Or are the two of you still chatting?"

Milo clicks his tongue twice and the horse gets going. Sarah Hale quickly follows after him. "Come back safe Milo!" Elara bids Milo as he goes down the road. Another two horse and riders catch up to them.

"Greetins again!" Darren says to Milo.

"Ello. I don't think I've met him," Milo says gesturing to the last rider.

"I'm Riker," he says with a nod.

The group spends a good part of the day riding. They travel north towards the Division. The day begins sunny but slowly the clouds creep in. Crows and other birds coo and caw ever so ominously from the dark treelines. Late in the afternoon they ride into the attacked village.

Laying outside the village are a couple moderately sized pastures. A wood fence surrounds them in disarray, falling apart from age. Inside the pastures is little more than the bones of sheep that have been slaughtered and devoured by some great beast. The village itself is made up of four buildings, the wattle and daub walls covered in scratch marks from a giant beast clawing at them. Thatch has been thrown everywhere from the beast ripping apart the roofes. A goat's carcase lays torn in half in the middle of the road, and a doghouse sits eerily empty. Carpeting clouds turn the world dark and monotone, adding to the eeriness of it all.

They come across a smashed chicken coup, the chickens all free and pecking at the bugs in the dirt. "Looks like the chickens did it to me," Milo jests.

"*Ha ha*, very funny," Riker says thick with sarcasm.

Milo halts Snowstorm and jumps off. The others dismount their horses too as Milo enters one of the small houses, its door bashed inwards despite open out. Guts and appendages are thrown everywhere, ripped apart and feasted upon by the creature. The walls and destroyed furniture are caked in dried blood. Milo quickly turns around and stumbles out of the building. A few feet from the door he falls to his knees and empties the little he had in his stomach. Darren grabs Milo's arm and helps him back to his feet.

"What, did you see an army of Frost Trolls in there?" Riker quips.

"Sod off," Milo spits.

"Hey what's that?" Riker points.

"I'm not in the mood for your crappy jokes," Milo spits.

"No look Milo," Sarah Hale tells him.

In the distance is some black creature with a red head flying towards the mountains. Milo struggles to quite make it out. At first Milo believes it is just a bird, but as it moves he can figure that it is much too massive to be any bird.

"Could that be the Kedragora?" Darren asks.

"There's only one way to go find out."

Milo jumps back onto his steed and starts moving in a trot. The others quickly follow. They travel through the hilly landscape of Tyros. The wind kicks up the farther they get to the Division. Between two mountain slopes they ride through a valley, gradually gaining altitude as they enter the Division. Rolling overhead are darker and darker clouds.

They reach the top of the slope, two ridges still towering above them. A hundred yards from them the land dips steeply. Between a circle of peaks and ridges of the surrounding mountains forms a deep basin, a single plateau rising out of it. Spanning across the basin to the plateau is an old rope bridge. The group ties their horses to some nearby trees so they can investigate the strange area. They start towards the bridge and find there is now an old hunchback crossing the bridge. With a bowl clasped in bony fingers the man nears until he meets the group at the other end. His eyes are devoid of colour just as his skin is. Milo thinks the man is blind first, but that only leaves him wondering how he knew the group was coming.

"Hail there!" Sarah Hale calls out to him.

He does not respond.

The hunchback gets uncomfortable close to Riker and he holds out one of his arms as if asking for a hug. An uncomfortable Riker looks to Sarah Hale for guidance. Quicker than Milo thought possible from the old hunchback, he draws a dagger from his belt. Repeatedly he sinks it into the unsuspecting man's guts. Milo, Sarah Hale, and Darren draw their blade simultaneously.

"What the fuck?!" Darren cries.

Riker looks down in terror as he tries to hold his guts in. The hunchback places the bowl up against his throat and slits it wide. Blood flows out and into the bowl. He places his knife hand behind Riker's back and holds him in place until the bowl is nearly full. Letting go of Riker his body topples down to the earth.

The remaining members of the group carefully step towards the hunchback. He raises his hand and claws his fingers. "Stay back," he growls. His soulless eyes watch the group as he chugs down the bowl of blood. Squatting down, he sets the bowl on the ground.

"Cross," the man commands, his teeth red with blood. He raises his boney hand and points across the rope bridge.

"Aren't you going to ask us three questions?"

"Go now!" The man hisses.

Milo leads the way, slowly crossing the creaky bridge. Darren follows suit, and Sarah Hale crosses last, carefully back-stepping as she watches the eerily still hunchback. Sarah Hale looks behind her shoulder for a brief moment, and when she looks back the Hunchback disappeared.

"We should've killed that bastard," she says.

Milo looks around the plateau. The only thing around are the cliff faces and a crumbling wall from a building that used to stand at the far edge. Inside the basin it is eerily quiet, the wind blocked by the mountains surrounding them. Suddenly Milo feels a draft.

Looking up Milo says, "The chickens did do it!"

Fluttering down from the peaks above is a chicken the size of a small house. Long black feathers cover its body, except for a red head and beak. A horrible shriek comes from its mouth as it drops in front of them. Sarah Hale turns to run, but in a powerful slash of its gigantic foot it cuts through her backplate. She collapses to the ground a couple paces later. Milo nocks an arrow and shoots it into the beast's neck. Somewhere in the swath of feathers it vanishes. Its great wings flap out and knock Milo backwards.

Milo slings his bow over his shoulder as he sprints towards the old building. The Kedragora's eye follows him as he runs and disappears behind the crumbling stone wall. Then it looks towards Darren.

"Oh cock," he says.

The Kedragora pecks at him, but he dashes under its enormous breast. It looks between its legs and tilts its head as it watches the man run towards the stone wall. It raises its head high into the hair and crows monstrously. It dashes after Darren, clucking as it tries to peck at him like an earthworm. Milo watches through a hole that was once an old window and can't help but laugh at the sight.

Darren dives through the old window and mere seconds later the wall shakes as the Kedragora slams into it. Stone bricks crumble and rain upon the men, and large cracks form across the wall. All goes silent. Darren stands on the other side of the window from Milo, his eyes darting between Milo and the wall. Milo raises an eyebrow as he begins to peak his head around the window.

Suddenly the giant chicken head is stuck through the window with barely enough room. It watches the men with its shiny black eyes, licking its beak with its tongue. Milo slowly pulls the warhammer from his back. Just as he gets it in the air and is about to strike, it quickly pulls its head back out from the window. Milo returns the warhammer to his back and the men stand frozen for what feels like an eternity. Milo's heart is beating in his chest harder than he ever felt before. He's gone up against a lot of different things, even stone men, but how does he escape a giant chicken?

Milo builds up his courage and pokes his head to look out the window. He doesn't see anything. Darren pokes his head through too. Then they hear some stones falling from above. Milo and Darren look up to the Kedragora perched on the stone wall. It tilts its head as it looks at them.

In a quick movement its beak dashes down towards them. Milo lunges backwards. To his dismay he watches Darren get picked up by the monster, screaming for his life. Milo bolts back out of the building and begins running across the plateau, the screams of Darren disappearing with hideous crunching noises. Halfway across the plateau Milo looks over his shoulder. The Kedragora is scrapping its foot against the dirt of the plateau, getting ready for a charge.

Milo grabs the bow from his shoulder and nocks an arrow. The Kedragora shrills as it charges Milo at great speeds. Milo draws and shoots another arrow at the monstrous chicken. It is even less effective than the last, merely deflecting off the chicken's beak. The chicken prods towards Milo with its sharp beak. Milo shuts his eyes tight. He grabs for something—anything—to protect himself with. He pulls up the tiki mask and holds it to shield him from the fatal blow. Nothing happens.

Then finally something crashes into his feet and flutters about. He opens his eyes and looks around. The Kedragora is gone. Sitting at his feet now is a black and red chicken. Giving him a dirty look it crows before running off.

"Can my life get any weirder?" He chuckles almost insanely. Remembering Sarah Hale he rushes over to where she lays. The claws cut through the armour and deep into her back. She is alive now but there is nothing Milo can do to save her. A sense of sadness and defeat overcomes him. He sits next to her dying body, feeling overcome with helplessness and grief.

Something taps him on the shoulder. Looking up he says a young man with soft, saddened eyes. Milo opens his mouth to ask who he is but no works come out.

"Let me help," his gentle voice says. He kneels over her near lifeless body and waves his hands over her wounds. The stranger turns around and walks out of Milo's sight. Milo tries to get up but can't. He finds pulls everything inside himself to get onto his knees. Looking over Sarah Hale's body he finds the wounds have been healed.

Milo sighs in relief and chuckles sadly, "Lucky for me, it *can* get weirder."

He stands up and searches the plateau for the man with his eyes, but he is gone. Milo crosses the bridge and gathers some wood and tinder. He builds a fire next to Sarah Hale and waits for her to wake. The world turns truly black under the clouds and night sky. Thin droplets drizzle down on them, waking Sarah Hale.

"What happened?" She asks, reaching over her shoulder to feel the gashes in her backplate.

"The Kedragora basically killed you, and it ate Darren."

"Was... That a giant chicken?" She asks scratching her short brown hair.

"Yep," Milo says, the rain pouring down a little harder.

"You said it killed me..?" She asks, her thin eyebrows furrowed and her small lips open wide.

"There wasn't anything I could do to save you. Then some man came out of nowhere and healed you."

"Where is he now?" She asks, looking around into the blackness.

"I don't know."

"How does such a monster come to exist, Milo?"

Milo shakes his head, knocking loose the beads of water forming in his hair. "It wasn't a monster. Just one big, cursed chicken."

Sarah Hale gazes off into the darkness of the night. Brushing some of the droplets of water off her face, she asks, "Do you think Sir Winters' task went any better?"

◈ CHAPTER THIRTEEN

Earlier that day...

Winters is kneeling down at the top of the hill. Down below is a quaint village. There are at least two dozen people—and that's just what Winters had counted so far. "This is a family?" Winters grumbles to himself.

Dequande bumbles up the hill. "What did ya say?" He asks in his booming voice.

Winters waves his hand towards the ground and whispers, "Get down!"

"Oh," he says as he sits down with his legs crossed.

Winters puts his spyglass back up against his eye and scans the men. They have pitchforks and axes, but he has seen no real weapons yet. He knows with this many it will still be harder than anybody initially thought.

His train of thought is interrupted by an inhuman scream. Throwing down his spyglass he looks over to the source. A disfigured boy is standing with a bucket of water in hand. His head is misshapen and one of his eyes is lower than the other. The disfigured boy drops the bucket and runs off towards the village, screeching perpetually. The villagers look towards the hill. Winters ducks below the hill's crest, but the villagers are already pointing. Dequande's massive silhouette protruding from the hill didn't help much either.

Grabbing the tools around them and shouting for more men, the villagers head towards the hill. Spying what they have, Winters first finds they are armed with pitchforks, axes, and sharpened sticks. They then begin appearing with swords and flails. Some of them are only armed with ropes tied into lassos. More and more men come out of the hovels and a sizeable mob builds up.

Winters waves and a soldier runs up the hill. "Get ready for a fight, Nerro," Winters tells the soldier. He unclips the knife from his belt to hide it in the back of his trousers. Rising to his feet, he blows a small horn. Three more soldiers emerge from the treeline to the east and charge at the mob.

"If we can each kill at least ten, I think we can take them. Can you do that Dequande?"

Dequande takes off his vest, "Easy day." Bellowing a menacing war cry with his axe in hand he barrels down the mountain to the mob.

Winters and Nerro follow his lead, moving nowhere near as quick despite being half his size. Dequande splatters the head of a stunned simpleton as though it were a melon. When Winters catches up to Dequande, one villager swings a hatchet at him. Winters sidesteps and cuts down, chopping into the villager's wrist. Half-swording he guides the sword back up and into the soft spot under the villager's chin.

From the side, another villager thrusts a pitchfork at his head. Winters leans back the weapon a mere hair's breadth from his cheek. The villager pulls back the pitchfork. Winters lunges forward, pushing the pitchfork away with his free hand and sinks his blade into the man's stomach.

"Fuck this!" He hears Nerro shout. He glances over and sees Nerro disengaging from combat before turning around and sprinting off. The men surround Winters with pitchforks and sharpened sticks. Throwing his hands up, he lets his sword drop to the ground. He looks over at Dequande. The warriors axe-hand has been lassoed as he held it high. He yanks against the rope, dragging the unprepared villager several feet forward, but cannot break free. Another lasso flies out from behind to secure his axe-hand. Dequande reaches up with his other hand to grab the axe, but they lasso that one as well.

Winters hears a dull whistling sound then everything goes black.

*****

The villagers dance and laugh to festive folk music. The drinks are flowing freely and everybody is getting drunk. Village people of all ages are quickly hooking up, and openly fornicating throughout the village. A large bonfire roars in the centre, above it a large iron cauldron boiling stew, the odour of which smelled of burnt flesh.

Tied up to wooden poles facing one another, Winters and Dequande are forced to watch this twisted festival. Sheering pain rules Winters head. Since waking up he has managed to free the knife from his trousers, and with great strain he is slowly cutting away at his bonds. When he woke up his men were already dead and being butchered for the stew. At first he thinks Dequande and he are the only two alive at this point, but then he remembers Nerro.

"Fucking Craven," he spits.

One of the cannibals hears him and walks over from the bonfire. Crouching down in front of Winters he asks, "'s all this talk about?"

Winters spits in his face. An urge to slit the man's throat with the knife in his hand fills him, but he is not yet free from his bonds.

The cannibal slowly brushes the spit away. Gently he strokes Winters cheek with his middle finger. "You're next," he says before digging his fingernail into Winters' skin deep enough to draw blood. Slowly he licks the drop of blood from under his yellowed fingernail. He springs up and scurries over to Dequande. He kneels over the tied up bull. "And big guy here will be a feast of his own," the cannibal says licking his lips.

Dequande squints angrily at the cannibal.

The cannibal slowly looks over Dequande with a hungry look. He notices a bulge in his pocket. "Whatsah dis?" He says with a dopey grin on his face. Reaching into Dequande's pocket, the giant man thrashes around like a crocodile. Eventually the man grabs a hold of the contents and yanks it out. In his hand is a small doll that a little girl would carry.

Both Winters and the cannibal are visibly perplexed. Blood vessels popping from his temple, Dequande's eyes fill with a rage that Winters has seen in no man before. "That is my little girl's!" Dequande thunders so loud that the entire village goes silent. The village people all stare, a couple frozen in the middle of porking.

The cannibal's face turns to a spiteful smirk. He calls out to some nearby children, "Hey kids, here's a toy!" Tossing it towards the children the doll lands face down into the mud.

Dequande rises up, the ropes binding him travelling up the wooden pole. The cannibal simply watches with his dopey grin. With a roar mightier than any man or beast Winters has ever heard, Dequande uses every muscle in his body to snap the rope. Within the instant of snapping free, his hands are wrapped around the cannibals head. In the next, the cannibal's head is facing his rear.

The limp body still clenched in his right hand the giant charges towards the cauldron. One cannibal with a pitchfork tries to stop him, but Dequande hurdles the limp body and knocks him over. Another two cannibals jump in front of his path weilding a sword and a mace. Dequande leaps several feet into the air, grabs them by the faces, and brings them to the ground with a handstand. Their heads explode between the ground and his immense weight.

From his handstand he does a backflip, landing and dodging a thrust from a sharpened stick. He grabs the stick with both his hands and rips it from the cannibals grip. He swings the stick like a bat into the man's head, both the skull and the stick cracking loudly. Again he roars, echoing throughout the surrounding silent hills.

A small child wearing a burlap sack stupidly runs right past him. He reaches out with his enormous hand and grabs the child by their calves. The child trips and claws his fingers into the ground as he tries to escape Dequande. In one arching movement he picks the boy up into the air and swings him into the boiling cauldron. This time Dequande's roar is harmonised with the bloodcurdling screams of the child trying to escape the boiling waters.

The inbred mother slams the door shut and bolts it right in the face of an older boy trying to flee the Bull's wrath. Dequande walks up behind the boy with giant strides. Without knowing what hit him, Dequande punches the boy in the back of the head. His face collides violently with the door and his limp body slumps against it. With a single kick Dequande breaks down the locked door. Stepping on the body, he enters the building with another menacing roar.

Winters can only hear the screams as he slaughters the people within. Two more cannibals masked with burlap sacks poke up from behind some barrels. They see Winters and slowly approach him. He strains to cut his bonds faster. Trying to channel his inner Dequande, he pulls on the ropes to no avail. He cuts more desperately as they get closer. Right as they are atop him he snaps free.

Flying forward he catches them off guard, slashing one's carotid artery. The cannibal topples to the ground desperately clasping the blood squirting artery. The other one throws their hands up in surrender. Winters kicks him in the crotch before grabbing him by his shirt collar. He drags him towards the cauldron and bashes his skull into the cast iron side. There was no cracking sound, which Winters feels a depraved disappointment in.

❖ CHAPTER FOURTEEN

Milo and Sarah Hale ride through town on their steeds, each guiding one of the dead men's horses behind them. It is the following night. The storm clouds had broken away late this morning and they set back to Charlesworth. When they reach the keep they dismount their horses and start tying all the horses to the troughs. Parked next to them is a small wagon, a young man in brown and green fleece robes unloading a few boxes of herbs and viles from it. His head is bald and tattooed with druid symbols, and a thick brown beard hangs down to his chest.

"Hello!" he calls as he approaches the two.

"Oh great, I thought I left you people behind in Dalarus?" Milo remarks. Sarah Hale and the stranger laugh together. "Did I miss something?"

"Greetings stranger. I am Dylan Hale," he informs Milo, his hands knitted at his front.

"So you aren't a Vampire!" Milo says out loud.

"Why would he be a Vampire?" Sarah Hale asks.

"It's an inside joke."

Sarah Hale just gives him a weird look.

Dylan Hale asks, "So are you going to introduce yourself stranger?"

"I am Milo Khan. Your family, uh… Recruited me to fight the things in the woods."

"Father considers him Winters' pet," Sarah Hale says with a cheeky smile.

Milo is taken back. "Wait what? Pet?"

Ignoring Milo with a smile Dylan Hale says, "I should get to unpacking my things. It has been too long since I last saw you, sister."

Sarah Hale nods and walks to the keep. Milo watches her disappear into the fort with a look of shock. "Pet..?"

As Milo walks up to the doors of the keep the Guard lowers his halberd to block him. "The Lord wishes to speak with you immediately."

"He's still awake?"

"Aye, and awaiting your presence in the Throne-room." The Guard pulls his halberd back close to him and unblocks the door. Milo walks down the dimly lit hallway and turns into the Throne-room. The chandelier that hangs from the ceiling lights the room alongside the beams of moonlight breaking through the clouds. Halfway across the Throne-room is Sarah Hale, whom Milo stands beside as he enters. Sitting in the chair with his usual scowling face is Lord Xandercus Hale. His coarse stubble cheek is leaned up against his tight fist.

"You summoned me?" Milo asks.

"No Winters did," Xandercus says sarcastically.

"When will he be here?" Milo mocks.

"Enough. You know full well I summoned you. How did your mission fare?"

"We lost Riker and Darren Father," Sarah Hale tells him.

Lord Xandercus glares at Milo, "Good for you my daughter did not come to any harm." Milo and Sarah look at each other nervously. "And what of the Kedragora?"

"Dead my Lord," Milo proclaims.

"Good. Sarah, You may leave us now."

"Yes Father," she says. She turns around and leaves the room. Luckily for Milo Xandercus was too busy scowling at Milo to notice the claw marks in his daughters armour.

"I have another mission for you…" Xandercus pauses before rasping, "*Milo*."

Milo waits for him to continue. When he does not he asks, "Yes m'Lord?"

"Have you heard of the cyclops?"

"I've heard tales of one eyed men in Tyros; don't know if they're true."

"A great many have been hunted down over the centuries. Only a very few survive to this day. One of these few is the one they call Borogom."

"I see where you're going with this. You want me to kill him, right?" Lord Xandercus gives a single nod. "Who else will be coming?"

"Two of my… *Soldiers*," he says with disgust. "Nerro and Ajax."

"What about Dequande or Winters? Shouldn't there be more men to fight such a dangerous foe?"

"You vowed to serve us did you not?"

"Yes my Lord, I just-"

"Then get out of my sight. The three of you will ride at daybreak."

"Aye my Lord," Milo says, turning around and walking out of the Throne room. He's getting real fed up with the Lord's grumpy attitude all the time. He goes to the room he shares with Dequande and sets down his things. With his back against the stone wall he sits on his straw bedding. With the moonlight pouring in from the window he sees Dequande using a wet rag to clean his doll. Despite finding it odd that a grown man has a doll he doesn't ask about it.

"How'd your mission go?" Milo asks the giant man.

"We got captured," he replies, focused on cleaning his doll.

"Well you're here now. Clearly you made it out."

Dequande looks up, a sort of fire in his eyes, "Aye. I did."

"I got a new mission from the Lord."

Dequande continues to clean his doll, "Am I going too?"

"No. Just these two. Nerro and Ajax I think he said."

Dequande looks back up in concern, "Nerro?"

"You know him?"

"He was on our mission. He ran when things got tough."

"Great," Milo moans as he lays down in bed fully dressed. He quickly falls asleep from the past couple days.

The world is submerged in darkness. A swirl of rain and sleet crash into the ground. The trees shake violently, and the animals of Tyros dart around trying to find cover. In the middle of all this chaos is Milo. He is looking for something, but he can't figure out what. An ancient woman emerges from the tree line. Her back is grotesquely hunched and her every bone protrudes from her flaccid skin. She hobbles back into the tree line and Milo runs after her. Every part of his body hurts from the freezing rain and wind as he runs through the twisting and spinning woods.

The treeline suddenly stops, and he finds himself before Charlesworth. He runs through a chaotic battlefield with men killing each other with no clear sides. He runs through the battlefield and into the city of Tyros. There he finds his friends all defending Charlesworth. Dequande, Winters, Westman, Arnold, even Templar Fortis are all there. He stops running and the sounds of battle stop. Looking around, the men are frozen in time and the attackers have turned into shadows and otherworldly monsters.

He turns around and continues towards the keep. A man red haired man jumps out and tries to grab him, but Milo just barely passes him.

Milo enters the keep and heads to the Throne room. There he finds a black dog chained up, barking and growling sporadically, white foam pouring from its mouth. The dog stops and walks up to him with sad eyes. One by one Milo removes the chains until it is free. The dog bites him in the throat. Milo jerks awake.

"I'm not sure which is worse, the real world, or my dreams!"

"What?" The soft voice of a woman asks.

Milo sits up quickly and finds Elara standing next to his bed. The dawn has just barely broken he can tell. "How long have you been there?"

"Only a minute. I was having second thoughts on if I should wake you. Father told us he's sending you to fight Borogom!"

"He is. That's what I signed up for isn't it?"

"He's sending you with Ajax and Nerro!" She cries. She sits on the straw bedding and leans against him.

"What is it Elara?"

"Nerro. He's a scoundrel!" She whimpers.

"So I've heard."

"All he does is cause trouble. My father wants to have him hung or at least exiled. Crone taketh his soul!" She rests her head on his shoulder and moans, "And then there is Ajax…"

"What of him?" Milo says, carefully putting his arm around her shoulders.

"He's the worst boy we've ever trained! He's strong but I doubt he could react to a *snail*." Elara looks up into Milo's eyes. "Promise me you will defeat Borogom."

Milo can't help but notice her pink lips and beautiful blue eyes. "I've been in worse situations, one time I was trapped in this weird magic temple with crappy incorporeal guides."

She laughs and Milo's heart beats faster at the sight of her pearly white smiles. Gazing into her eyes he holds her a little tighter. "Another time I was stuck in a cave with a crazy wizard and his minions. Actually- that happened twice!"

Elara laughs again before her face turns dreadfully serious, "Milo, promise me!"

Snapped out of his lighthearted nature he says, "I promise." The two stare longingly into each other's eyes for a long time. Elara leans in slightly just before someone pounds energetically on the door. "Wake up call, wake up call, wake up call for My-low!" A servant shouts. Elara Hale springs up and out of Milo's embrace.

"My father's doing," she whispers, glaring at the door.

The servant again bangs on the door rapidly. "Are you awake My-low?" He shouts through the door.

"I'm as awake as the first time you attempted to bust down my door!" He shouts in annoyance. Dequande on the other hand is snoring through the ruckus.

"Ah good! We expect to see you on your way in five minutes." Milo can hear him walk away.

Milo sets his hands gently on Elara's shoulder. "I'll see you when I get back." She nods with disappointment plastering her face. Grabbing his things he leaves his room. Elara leans in the doorway and holds her hand up to wave goodbye. When Milo vanishes from the corridor without looking back she sighs.

Pulling open the castle doors Milo looks out and sees two men on top of their motley steeds. He unties Snowstorm from the trough and mounts the trail saddle.

One man is dressed in black dyed clothes, black flowing hair and beard too neatly trimmed. "Finally ready Sir Sleepsalot?" He prods.

Milo waves his hand at the sky, "Its barely sunrise!" The man takes off down the road and Milo follows. "Who are you anyway?"

Washing her clothes covered in sudsy water one woman waves to the man. "I am Nerro. You may have heard of me from the women you unsuccessfully tried to gain fancy from."

Milo looks to the other young man trailing behind them. His skin is saggy and covered in birthmarks, and his lack of a chin makes it hard to figure out where his face ends and his neck begins. His arms though are the size of a blacksmith's. Slouched over the young man reminds Milo of a turtle. "So you must be Ajax," Milo asks.

Ajax's vacant eyes slowly drift towards Milo, "I am."

As they ride past the town brothel, the various whores wave and blow kisses to Nerro.

"I hear Borojom is even larger than that big lad," Ajax says.

"Aye. Cyclopses are big fuckers!" Nerro shouts.

"They say he eats the flesh of men."

"So they do," Nerro affirms. A young woman pops out of the window of a nearby house. She quickly unfastens the front of her blouse and exposes her large breasts. Nerro puts his hand over his chest, closes his eyes, and leans back to act as if he passed out. A hand pulls the young woman back into the building, and a second later an old farmer pops his head out. Shaking his fist, he shouts, "Stay away from my daughter Nerro!" He just ignores the old farmer.

"I hear Borojom has two eyes," Ajax says.

Milo nearly falls off his horse in laughter.

"What?"

"A cyclops has one eye boy. That's why they're called cyclops," Nerro informs him.

"Oh…" Nerro says, his droopy face turning red.

They pass through the gatehouse, the gate opened and closed for them. Halfway through the fields Milo says, "Wait." The men stop their horses.

"Get cold feet?" Nerro asks with a smirk.

Milo shakes his head. "Does anybody know where we're going?"

The three turn back.

*****

Standing guard is Milo. Nerro and Ajax sleep around the glowing coals of a burnt out campfire. A full moon high in the clear night sky illuminates the land. After returning to the keep they went to the region Borogom is most frequently sighted and explored until they found massive footprints that eventually led them to the mouth of a cave. Tired, hungry, and roadweary the men went back to the woods and setup camp.

The horses stomp at the ground and snort. Hearing rustling Milo's head snaps to the nearby treeline. Nerro is in a deep sleep on his bedroll, but the bushes a few feet away from him shake around as something moves behind them. Milo reaches for his bow. A pine cone drops into the bushes and something yelps. Milo looks up into the trees and sees Goblins climbing through the branches. His hand springs for his bow and his other grabs an arrow from his quiver. The Goblins jump out of the bushes and down from the branches.

A cacophony of horrid screeches as they charge wakes Nerro up. Springing up from his bedroll he grabs his sword. Before he has time to use it, the Goblins swarm around him, bashing and prodding him with crude weapons.

Ajax on the other hand slowly gets up from his bedroll. He stands unreactive as the Goblins charge him. Liquid drips slowly from his trousers, clearly having urinated himself. One Goblin bashes him on the top of the head with a large stick, and another dives into him. Within moments they swarm the poor boy and tear him apart.

Shooting one arrow after another Milo tries to pick off as many Goblins as he can. In the massive swarm of the scrawny devils he cannot hope to kill them all. He tries to get atop Snowstorm to ride away but the mare is too busy dancing around and bucking in fear for him to get close. The Goblins, done tearing apart the other two, rush towards Milo and the horses. Dozens of Goblins charge at him, flails and swords and other crude weapons in hand.

Crack. Crack. Creeeeaak.

A lofty pine topples over and crushes the vanguard of the Goblin rush. A giant more than twice the size of Dequande emerges from the treeline. The Goblin war cries turn into cries of terror. He wears armour made of scraps of barrels and wagons, and a helmet somewhat akin to a Morion has a single eyehole cut into its faceplate. The giant swings a massive wooden bat and sends a swath of Goblins flying into the air. He smashes the bat down at the ground a couple times before all the Goblins have run off.

The horses screaming and bucking behind him, Milo raises his bow and nocks his arrow. The giant looks at him then stomps off back into the trees.

"So that's Borogom. Seems like an interesting fellow."

Milo follows Borogom back to his cave, keeping at a good distance. Hiding in the treeline, Milo watches Borogom makes his way through the clearing and to the mouth of the cave. A warm glow comes from deep within. As the giant enters the cave the he looks back. He looks directly towards Milo, but if he saw him there was no indication.

Milo crosses the clearing towards the cave, utterly exposed by the illuminating moonlight, the grass swooshing as its parts around him. He half expects Borogom to come charging back out. This does not happen and he enters after Borogom. A short ways down into the cavern he finds the home of Borogom. A fire booms, swaths of smoke exiting through a skylight above, lighting the oversized furniture constructed from wood scrap.

Milo approaches a cross railed fence that sections off the home, and hides behind it. Borogom gently picks up a sheep that is laying on a bed of straw. Taking it over to the bed he sits down and starts petting it on his lap like it were a dog. Vaulting over the fence, Borogom looks at Milo.

"What do you want?" He asks, petting the sheep.

Milo shrugs. "Maybe to say thank you for saving my ass?"

"You shouldn't have come here. Tyros is an evil place," Borogom's voice booms from within his helmet.

"You aren't the terrible man-eater they say you are, are you?"

Borogom lets go of the sheep, which then jumps gracefully from his lap. He takes off his helmet and sets it to the floor. A spot where his left eye would be if he were Human is scarred over. The eye between his two regularly placed brows is not truly centred and drifting to the right. Long and black curly hair rolls down to his shoulders. "You won't believe me."

"Try me, I've seen a lot of things these past few years not even you'd believe."

The sheep walks up to Milo. It smells him briefly before jumping up and putting its front legs on his chest. Milo shuts his eyes tight as it licks his face.

Borogom grins wide at the sight. "Flossy likes you. What is your name?"

"Milo."

"Milo, I have lived for over two centuries. Long ago I used to help men. I would help them plough their fields and harvest their crops, help built their homes and protect them from the creatures at their gates."

"So how d'you get this reputation of being a man-eater?"

"It wasn't my doing. My comrades allowed our curse to overtake them. With their newfound strength many soon tried to take riches and power. Others were enraged by what had been done to us and let it consume them. And with our great size came hunger; many of us fell to do anything to sate it."

"And thus you became man-eaters."

"You follow. My deeds were soon forgotten. I returned for the harvest one year, and I was greeted with screams and pitchforks. A village I had protected for three generations slowly began to resent me until finally I was told they no longer wanted my protection. By the spring those who had not died abandoned their home. For years after I spent my life in solitude."

"Until?" Milo says, sensing more.

"Winters ago your people fought one another. Soldiers came upon me, and rather than being afraid, they saw me as a potential weapon. Embittered by the way humans had treated me, I agreed to join them. After the first battle I realised I was becoming what the others had. I soon discovered none paid heed to the bodies left behind, so I tended to them all myself."

"You burned every body?" Milo says amazed.

"At first I tried to." Shaking his head Borogom continues, "There were too many bodies and not enough wood. I did my best to adhere to the burial rites of the White Sun."

"That was awfully virtuous."

"Nobody else was doing it. Tell me Milo, what brings you here?"

"This land, Tyros… It's full of foul beasts and worse men. I've met a family of Nobles who want to make it a better place."

"And what brings you *here*?"

Milo sighs. "They sent me to slay you."

"Many have come here to slay me. As you can see none have succeeded. You have been the first to talk to me, however."

"I can't kill you," Milo tells him. "I was sent to kill a monster, and I don't think you're one of them."

"Would you like some food before you go?" Borogom says, pointing towards a skinned Elk spit over his fire.

◈ CHAPTER FIFTEEN

A Seagull squawks loudly before diving from her perch atop the branchless-tree of the floating-man-nest. Halfway down to the waters its pulls up from its descent. Flapping her wide wings excitedly, she flies forwards. Swerving between the masts and rigging of the floating-man-nests, the gull looks out across the horizon. All she can see to the horizon is an endless sea of floating-man-nests, their masts sticking up high into the sky. It was these that brought her ancestors here all several years ago.

She swoops beneath a rolled up sail and another gull joins her. The two girls fly together, swooping around the masts and watching the men working their floating-man-nests. Flapping past another, a male gull spots the two females and takes flight after them. A newcomer, she knows. The two girls continue forward, the male slowly trying after them.

Looking down at the floating-man-nest she sees the one she doesn't like. The mere presence of the man makes her feel scared, and he spends most of the last few days atop deck. When above him, she relaxes her bowls and sends a white stream plummeting down towards him. Her friend quickly follows suit.

Valdus looks to the deck beside him after stream of gull-shit splatters on the deck beside him. Another stream plummets into the nearby waters moments later. He looks up and watches as three seagulls fly away. Standing atop the quarterdeck, he looks back out to the endless ships around him; every one of them is attempting to dock on the sovereign island of Corelyn.

Positioned between Ateria and Accules, the small island was in the perfect position for all trade going between the two continents. It has become the seat for almost every major Human trade guild and company in the world. The island is governed by a council formed of each one of the guild masters, and as such the benefits of basing one's headquarters on the island is fruitful. However so many ships come to dock here that there are thousands at once, most of them left waiting in the sea for as far as the eye can spy.

To his dismay, he was unable to find any ships going straight to Dalarus. But his mission is of the utmost importance, and he decided this ship would be the best choice, despite stopping at Corelyn before going down to Pyrammus. But now he's been stuck here for days, and none of the neighbouring vessels can do him better yet. So now he waits, watching the surrounding sea in boredom.

Rather than moving forward towards the island as most of the ships are, Valdus spots a large frigate manoeuvring between the ships and towards his. Fluttering in the ocean winds are two flags: a golden scale atop a blue field, the sigil of Sovereign Corelyn; and on the mast behind it a black field, with skull with an anchor smashed through and an osprey perched atop it, all in red. On the deck are several ballistas and scorpions, and Valdus can tell they aren't armed with harpoons.

Slowly this other ship zig-zags, Valdus watching it carefully. The sailors of his vessel disappear below the deck, and they return in force with weapons in hand. It closes in, ramming Valdus' ship head to head. Several of the ballistas and scorpions shoot into the crowd of armed sailors. Moments later men from the attacking ship swing onto Valdus' from ropes. The men are armoured in skirted lamellar vests and simple steel helms that remind Valdus of overturned bowls.

A skirmish breaks out. Cutlass meets cutlass. The sound of swords clashing and men screaming scares away the surrounding gulls. More men swing from the other ship onto his, armed with cutlasses and spears. The sailors fight as well as they can, yet they are no match for their opponents. One by one each is cut down, and to no loss of the marines. Valdus watches safely on the quarterdeck, all to his entertainment.

As the men are cut away like a gardener to weeds, another man jumps across decks. He is a tall, large built man similarly dressed, though his helmet has armoured spectacles and a chainmail neck-flap. In his hand he wields a one handed battle axe, though the head is shaped like the letter G. The crew being dispatched by the marines, this man marches his way across the deck and up the quarterdeck. Valdus touches the hilt of his Sabre and raises his chin to the approaching man.

The man stops a good distance across the quarterdeck and speaks, "I am Ramsey Redmont. Admiral of the Sovereign Corelyn Navy. You, Captain Kirill, have been found guilty of fencing pirated goods. How do choose to proceed?"

Valdus clasps his hands behind his back. "I am not Captain Kirill."

"Then who are you?" Admiral Redmont asks.

◈ Chapter Sixteen

Milo rides up to the gate as the Sun sets over Tyros. He waits for a moment for it to open. Looking up when it does not he finds nobody is standing in the towers. Dismounting Snowstorm he pushes on the gate. It opens to his surprise. He guides Snowstorm in and shuts the gates behind him so that no undesirables think they are free to enter.

On foot he guides Snowstorm up the town. Everything is still and empty, everything turned a reddish hue under the setting Sun and low cloud layer. Milo creaks open the tavern to see if everybody is just quietly hiding indoors, but nobody is there either.

Up at the keep, Milo ties Snowstorm to the troughs and she drinks. He is somewhat apprehensive to leave her behind, but through even the larger castle doors she wouldn't fit. He finds it disturbing as he easily turns the handle of the door and freely opens it. Every footstep seems to echo louder than usual as he makes his way to the Throne-room. Empty just as expected. Approaching the door of his room he hears a deep grinding sound within. Quietly he draws the sword from his sheath. Swinging open the door with his heart beating fast, he feels like an idiot realising it is just the snoring Dequande.

He gives the giant a shake to the usual no avail. Shaking him harder, he still does not wake. Milo groans as he releases what he must do. Slapping Dequande hard, the giant wakes up swinging. Having already expected it he jumps back and barely misses the forceful blows.

"Milo?" Dequande says in the middle of a yawn.

"Where is everybody?" Milo asks panicked.

"What do you mean?" He asks confused.

"There is nobody here."

"Yeah this is just our room."

"No, I mean in the town Dequande."

"What are you saying?"

"There isn't anybody here. Not in the town, not in the castle, not even manning the gates! *You're* the only one in the whole town."

"They were all here when I went to sleep?" He questions, looking around the room as if he were to somehow find them.

"So you don't any idea what happened to them?"

"None," he says just as perplexed.

"What kind of help you…" Milo stops himself from finishing. He knows he shouldn't blame Dequande for not knowing.

The giant wanders around the castle looking for anybody. Every room is barren, the only one they don't dare enter being Xandercus Hale's room. Once again no trace. Dequande leaves the keep into the now black night. Milo lights a lantern and follows. As the giant wanders from door to door checking each house, Milo kneels down and looks at the ground. A large number of fresh footprints are all leading to one direction.

"Dequande, come over here!" He shouts. The giant jogs over and looks to Milo afraid. "There's a lot of footprints here."

"Where are they going?"

"Don't know. Come with me will you?"

Dequande shakes his head, clutching tightly onto his axe. The men follow the footsteps to the edge of town. Across the stony shore they follow the tracks to a stone ledge following the cliff face below the castle. The two carefully walk across the wedge, wet with spray from the waves crashing a few feet below them. Near the end of the ledge is a large crack in the rock wide enough for even Dequande to enter.

"You think the entire town is down there?" Dequande asks.

"The opening looks pretty small, but all those footprints lead here."

"What do you think they're doing down there?"

"Dunno, but I know I've had a lot of weird experiences with caves."

Milo enters the crack and has to make a shape left. Dequande squeezes through behind him, almost getting stuck. The tunnel widens somewhat and the two can fairly comfortable walk as it descends twenty feet. Then they emerge at the top of a staircase carved in stone. The entire town fills up a large hall cut into the stoney depths, two large pillars supporting the vaulted ceiling. The entire thing is lit by bright glowing crystals in the walls and ceiling. Carved out of the far end wall is a massive statue of a woman. Standing raised up above the crowd in front of the statue is Lord Dylan Hale, seemingly giving some sort of prayer that Milo cannot hear from across the room.

"You shouldn't be here," Dylan Hale says from behind them. Both Dequande and Milo turn to see him leaning up against the wall next to the door.

"What is this place?" Dequande asks with his normally booming voice.

Lord Dylan stops his prayer and looks up at the men. The entire village then proceeds to turn and looks towards them. The members of House Hale make their way down an aisle formed down the crowd of peasants. Milo, Dequande, and Dylan Hale walk down the stairs and meet them midway.

"Milo! You're back," Elara says, her face bright as the crystals around them.

"How dare you come here!" Xandercus Hale screams as he shoves Milo.

"No need for shoving m'Lord," Milo says, trying to step back from him.

Then Xandercus Hale throws a punch. Milo stumbles backwards and touches his cheek gently. He tries to raise his palms to yield but Xandercus throws another. Instinctively Milo dodges the blow and throws a jab at the old Lord's face.

The Lord topples onto his ass and pinches his nose, blood seeping down his hand and chin. "Fuck you," Xandercus snarls. Dylan Hale tries to help him up, but he yanks his elbow away. He slowly gets up himself and bumps into Milo's shoulder as he storms up the stairs.

Milo looks to Elara. Streams of tears are rolling down her cheeks. She shakes her head angrily at him before running up the stairs. The village folk in an awkward silence begin exiting the cavern in an orderly fashion.

"I'm sorry," Milo whispers as he watches her run away.

"I'd say it is fine, but those aren't quite the right words," Dylan Hale says.

"Father shouldn't have tried hitting you," Bartholomew says. "You have done nought but help our family."

"What is this place, anyway?" Milo asks.

Bartholomew looks around the cavern and takes a moment to soak in its glory. "This is a temple of worship for Nhianneah, our god."

"Did you build it?" Milo asks, surprised that they would have such ability to carve out this much stone.

"Nay. Nobody knows who did. Sir Charles Hale discovered it on one of his expeditions and thus he founded Charlesworth upon it."

Milo walks closer to the great statue of the woman. She is completely nude with perfect beauty, elegant swirls carved across her body. "Beautiful sculpt-" Milo stops dead in his words and gasps as he realises who it is.

"What?" Bartholomew asks, squinting at the statue as he tries to figure out what was wrong with Milo.

"I've seen this woman," Milo says.

"You've seen this statue before?"

"No that's not it. I've *met* this woman," he says wide eyed. "Three years or so ago I was inside this temple we found in the Bleaks... I met a woman- this woman."

"What did she say?"

"Just some things about honour, valour, loyalty, wisdom-"

"-and compassion," Bartholomew Hale finishes.

"Yeah, those were them."

"Those are the Hero's Virtues." He pauses in disbelief. "Milo, you met our god."

"Eh... Why would a god want to meet me? I'm just a wise-ass nobody?"

"Maybe they want you to be more than a wise-ass nobody?"

"My life just gets better and better doesn't it?"

*****

Sitting in his room, he waits patiently for somebody to come tell him he's going to be executed—or exiled at best—by the angry Lord. He had been waiting all day but nothing has happened yet. If he makes it a little longer, Winters' sister invited him to join them for supper. Finally comes the knocking on his door. He gets up from bed and opens answers it. On the other side is Sarah Hale.

"Are you my executioner?" He nervously jests.

She furrows her brow. "What? Lord Xandercus wishes to speak with you."

Milo stammers out a small laugh, "I'm screwed."

Sarah Hale leads him up to the third floor of the keep. "Wait here she says," before knocking on Lord Xandercus' door and entering. "He's here," Milo can hear her say from within. "Let him in," Xandercus says muffled by the door. Sarah Hale returns and tell him, "You may enter now."

Entering the room Milo closes his eyes as he says to himself, "I'm going to die."

"Shut the door," Xandercus commands him.

Milo obliges and says, "My Lord, I am very sorry for hitting-"

"There is no need for an apology. I wish to apologise to you, actually." Blinded by his fear he just now notices the Lord is sitting in a chair next to his wife, who is lying unconscious in her bed. Milo can hear her every wheezing with every breath. Blankets are piled atop her, but even through that Milo can see how thin she is.

'Am I dreaming?' 'Have I gone instead?' 'Is the world ending?'

"You need not apologise to me, my Lord. I am a guest under your roof."

"That does not give me the right to treat you the way I have. I sent you to what I thought would be your death, Sir Milo. Then I unduly hit you for coming to a place of worship." Xandercus Hale pauses and looks down at the floor. "I do not think I was not always this cruel... My dear Margaret has become ever so sick. She does not wake for months; and when she does, it is no longer her I speak to. My mind has become ever so clouded and ill itself." She shakes his head then looks Milo in the eyes. "Everything you've done has been for her."

"I... don't follow m'Lord?" Milo says.

"Cleansing Tyros. Since before we even wed she spoke of how together we would save these lands. Alas we never did."

"My Lord, we've been making great strides so far. And apparently the King's Legions are out there somewhere too. Not I've seen them actually do anything though."

"Margaret once told me a story her parents had. They said there were monstrously sized farm animals that rampaged through Tyros. Then a brave hero united the people of Tyros against them and had the biggest feast the world ever saw. Thereafter the realm was united. Since she was a girl, this story gave her hope to save Tyros. Before falling into her unwaking slumber she spoke to me of this one last time."

Milo tries to cheer up the Lord, "Well we have the giant farm animals."

"I hate who I've become Sir Milo."

"Perhaps you should get some sleep m'Lord. Tis late."

"You are excused," Xandercus says, looking back to his dying wife. A tear forms in his eye and drops into his lap.

Leaving the room Milo, runs into Elara in a white nightgown.

"Milo? Father isn't kicking you out is he?" She asks concerned.

"He actually wished to apologise, strangely enough."

"It is good to see he is coming to his senses about you," she says. She placed her hand on the doorknob and smiles cheekily. "Would you like to come in? Just for a short while?"

"Nay, I think your father would go back to wanting me killed if I did," Milo says only half joking. "Winters' sister also invited me for supper."

She smiles and says, "See you tomorrow then?"

"Of course Elara."

He leaves the castle and heads into town. Following the side streets Milo almost gets lost as he tries to find the house. Finally he stumbles upon a small single-storey house. He knocks on the door and Winters opens it wide.

"We were starting to think you weren't going to make it! Come on in," Winters says.

Milo enters and finds a small table already set with plates of dumplings and bread. A woman sets a pitcher of milk down on the table and the young Paulin is running around. "Sit down Paulin, lest the Crone take you!" She nags him. Looking annoyed he takes his seat at the table.

Winters sits down next to his sister and gestures for Milo to take the last seat, next to him and Paulin. Milo obliges and sits down.

"This is my sister Jaclyn. You've already met her son Paulin."

"I finally get to meet this Milo my brother's been talking about," she says with a smile. "Also felt after what happened last night it would be good to get you out of that keep for a little."

"The Lord actually apologised to me," Milo says, still not quite believing it happened.

"Finally warming up to you, eh? Maybe he'll let you court Lady Elara soon," Winters says with a wink.

"What's this? You and Lady Elara fancy one another?" Jaclyn says excitedly

Milo shrugs it off.

"If you just saw the way the two look at each other," Winters tells her.

"Didn't Winters say you have a husband, Jaclyn?" Milo asks as he eats one of the dumplings.

"Daddy's gone like always," Paulin says, poking at his food with his fork.

Jaclyn scrunches her nose as she watches Paulin play with his food instead of eating it. "Eudas is a miner. He spends most of the time at the mining camp and only comes back home once or twice a month."

"Then there's the eternal bachelor over there," Milo prods, giving Winters a cheeky smile.

"I always try to find my brother a woman, but he won't have any," Jaclyn says rolling her eyes.

"I'm the Lord's most senior Knight, Jaclyn. I'm always getting sent to do this or that; don't have any time for a woman."

Speaking with her mouth full and a fed up smile she says, "Ever think maybe they'd stop sending you on all these missions if you had a woman's needs to tend to?"

Paulin drops his fork, it loudly banging against the plate, then the table, until it hits the floor.

"Paulin!" Jaclyn shouts with a look of disgust.

His eyes roll into the back of his head, only the veiny whites of his eyes showing. "Run, run, run; run she does!" The boy sings, his voice deepened and not like himself.

The candles in the house all blow out at once. *"Ribbit"* From inside one of the dumplings on Jaclyn's plate, a small toad tears its way out and jumps across the table. *"Ribbit."* The door unlatches itself and swings wide open.

Milo springs out of his chair and runs to the doorway. A little girl skips by singing, "Fly, fly, fly; the raven goes!" A plump little boy leaps like a frog into a puddle. Crouching down covered in mud he croaks, "Blood, blood, blood; blood is spilt!"

"Die, die, die," an old woman's voice rasps. Milo looks to his left and sees an old hunchback woman. Her greying hair is thin and stringy, her nose long and bulbous, and her skin droopy. She extends her boney left hand towards Milo. "Death comes for her!" She says, clenching her fist and pulling it in tight.

"Milo?" Winters says from behind him.

Milo glances at Winters then looks back to where the old hag once stood. He runs outside to where she was standing and spins around trying to find her. Winters approaches Milo cautiously.

"Did you see that woman?" Milo asks Winters.

"No. What woman?" Winters goes pale.

"She was old and ugly."

"The Crone," Winters whispers. He bolts past Milo and runs into town.

Milo runs after him and Jaclyn calls to them, "Where are ya going?"

Following Winters they run up the road to the keep. The Halberdier struggles to get out of the way as Winters flies through the doors. On his way through Milo takes the extra second to shut the door behind him. Up the staircase they run, and to the third floor. Winters barges into Lord Xandercus Hale's room and halts to a stop. Milo enters behind him.

"We must get Lord Bartholomew," Winters says, his mouth dropped open.

Hanging from the rafters is the body of Lord Xandercus. In the bed lies Margaret Hale completely still, not even a breath. She's dead, Milo knows.

Knocking on Bartholomew's door, he opens it dressed only in his knickers. "You need something?" Milo doesn't know what to say, and seeing the look on his face Bartholomew asks, "What wrong Milo?"

"Your father and your mother..." Milo can't continue, but there is no need to.

Bartholomew bolts past Milo and into his parent's room. He falls to his knees before his father's hanging body. "Father, why?" He whispers to himself.

"Bartholomew, Milo saw the Crone."

Bartholomew stands up, his face dark with sadness and choler. "You saw the Crone?"

"Who is this Crone?"

"The Crone of Tyros she is often referred to," Bartholomew says.

Winters tells him, "She is an ancient evil that hexes these lands. They say she resides in the deepest forests of Tyros, in lands unseen but by the most evil of beings."

"And you believe in this legend?"

Bartholomew looks around as he sorts his thoughts, "I questioned the truth in it until now. When mother fell ill, my brother said an ancient curse gripped her. And now you say you saw the Crone."

"I saw some creepy old lady, can't say if it was this Crone."

"Milo definitely saw her," Winters says. "Moments before he saw her, my nephew was taken by possession, and a toad birthed from my sister's dumpling!"

"Milo, we have one more task for you," Bartholomew says.

"You want me to hunt down this evil primordial entity, don't you?"

"Yes."

Winters elaborates, "You have met Nhianneah, fought otherworldly creatures, killed the Kedragora, and battled with Borogom."

"Ahem," Milo clears his throat. "I never said I battled Borogom…"

"What?" Bartholomew snaps, his sorrow now stirred with anger.

"He's actually quite a nice guy. He might even help you people if you stop trying to kill him all the time."

Bartholomew scowls at Milo, "Hunt her. I will make sure-"

He is cut off by a scream. Milo turns around and finds Elara standing in the doorway, covering her mouth as she pants. Her eyes begin to tear up. Gently grabbing her arm, Milo tries to lead her back to her room. Instead she throws her arms around him and squeezes him tight.

"I'm going to avenge them, Elara," Milo whispers.

◆ CHAPTER SEVENTEEN

Jumping down from the saddle, he ties Snowstorm to a low-lying branch. Sitting down on the mossy roots below a tree, he takes refuge from the rain. Thick, rainy fog engulfs the dark lands of Tyros. Milo has been wandering around the wilderness for days on end. From his satchel he pulls out the last piece of his bread and some elk jerky he made the day prior.

'How am I supposed to find the crone?' He thinks. *'Just wander around the woods is how they should've described it.'*

The fluttering of a crow breaks the silence of the misty land. Landing in front of him it goes, *"Caw!"* It jumps towards him. *"Caw! Caw!"* Milo throws a crumb of bread at it. Quickly the dark bird pecks it from the ground and gulps it down. Another crow flutters down from the trees.

"No more!" Milo shouts at them.

"Caw!" The first one says stretching its wings.

Then a third one comes. And another. Masses of crows fly in from all directions around Milo. The crows fly into one another, their bodies twisting and bending and breaking. Skin tears and guts pop out of their bodies. Quickly a ball of crow guts and feathers forms and hovers in front of Milo. More crows fly in, seemingly endless. First four sausage shaped appendages stretch from the mass. Then another shorter one protrudes from the top and compresses at the base to form a neck. Compressing and stretching it becomes ever more defined. The innards transform into wrinkly and wart covered skin, and the feathers morph into threads that knot themselves into crude cloth. The amalgamation of crow parts shape and morph until they have completed an old hag.

"I hear you are looking for me," she croaks, wiggling her long beak.

"They say I am. Seems you're the one who found me."

She forcefully smiles to show her rotten and missing fangs. "You cannot kill me. I am as old as the dirt beneath you, bound to it for eternity."

"There has to be some way to get rid of you."

"You killed one of my favourite pets." She claws at her necklace of Human teeth and bird bones.

"Eh... what?"

"The Kedragora was my creation. Alongside the Cyclopes, and others you've not met."

"You made those monsters?"

"You follow," a soft woman's voice says. The world melts away, and he finds himself sitting in a big soft chair. The cabin he is in is warm, a fire burning in the hearth. Something sweet is cooking. In the place of the crone is now a beautiful redhead woman in a silky white dress.

"Oh not this again," Milo moans. "How did we get here now?"

The now beautiful woman ignores him. "That stupid pellar and his pet chicken annoyed me, so I cursed them."

"And the Cyclopses?"

"Soldiers who came here for much the same reason as you. They discovered my wrath just as they did my permanence." The woman puts a finger to her lip. She then sits on his lap and wraps her arms around his neck. "Tell me Milo, what is it that you want?"

"How about you tell me why you killed Lady Hale?"

She moans and rolls her eyes. She gets off him and crosses her arms. "Because he wanted me to."

Milo leans in, "Because who wanted you to?"

She laughs and shakes her head, "He."

"Who is *he*?" Milo asks.

"The Dark One," she whispers with a menacing smile on her face. "You may want to get back to Charlesworth, Milo."

Milo stands from his chair. "Why?"

"News has spread about the Lord's Death," she says. The world melts away back to the foggy woods and once again the woman is a hideous crone. She croaks, "Now that I have you out in the middle of the woods there is nothing you can do. An army gathers as we speak." The woman explodes in a mass of crows, them flying in all directions. Milo ducks down as several nearly fly into him.

Milo runs to Snowstorm and unties her from the tree. He puts a foot in the stirrup and flies into the saddle.

*****

Snowstorm trots down an old dried up riverbank. Large ten foot cuts are on either side, roots from the trees around them tangling throughout. The fog has cleared up, but the monotone grey sky does not bode much better. The slow walk of Snowstorm is killing him, as he wants to make it back to Charlesworth as soon as possible, but he knows if he were to go any faster he would only tire out the mare faster.

A few feet in front of them a large boulder flies down from the cut. Snowstorm rears, but Milo wraps his arms around her neck and saves himself from being bucked off. Goblins jump off of the cut and in front of the boulder, screeching as they hold their weapons high. Milo draws his sword and pulls on the reins to try to keep Snowstorm still. More Goblins emerge from the above treeline on both sides of the cut.

Stomp. Stomp. Stomp.

There are only so many things that can make the earth rumble, such as the marching of thousands of Olfenreich soldiers, or the hooves of a Hoskgradian horde. Yet what lumbers over the bank is a relic of when the forests of the world were dominated by large beasts. It is ten feet tall and as wide as a wagon, covered head to toe in scars that run over its thick green skin, and white hairs adorn its balding scalp. A large axe made from solid crude iron atop a large wooden shaft is reinforced with iron rivets to ensure it is able to withstand a blow from this mighty Troll.

The Goblins chant and snarl at Milo in their crude tongue, covered head to toe in crude iron armour. The ancient Troll lets out a loud snarl as each step brings him closer to the edge of the cut.

A crude tongue cracks from the Troll's mouth like thunder as he speaks, "Dirg find man with sharp club. Solve riddle or Dirg smash and use in stew!"

The Goblins cheer in their screeching voices.

Milo looks around to see his options. Deciding his best option would be to first try and solve the riddle, he shouts up at the familiar giant, "What's the riddle?"

"Dirg gives man riddle. Say right man will pass." Dirg scratches his chin as he thinks up a riddle. "What is big and round and Dirg can throws to blocks man's path?"

Milo raises his sword and points at the boulder blocking his path, "That boulder?"

Milo hears a low mumble of disappointment from Dirg. The creature relaxes a bit, and the Goblins back off a little. The Troll rears his head back and grinds his teeth. "Riddle… Right. Mans goes."

"These are your Goblins?" Milo asks Dirg, holding out from leaving just yet. Snowstorm paws at the ground nervously, but he tugs on the reins to keep her in place.

"Yess. Dirg is bosses," the giant says looking at the Goblins, who are chattering to themselves in their undecipherable tongue. Dirg grits his teeth as he yells to them in the same gibberish.

"How many do you have?"

"Er…" Dirg groans as he scratches his chin, the Troll not actually capable of counting past ten it seems as he tries to count the dozens of Goblins that surround Milo. "Buncha Goblins Dirg say. Why mans ask?"

◈ Chapter Eighteen

Reynard pounds on Winters' door. Horns blow in the distance. He bangs on it again. "Come on... Wake up!" Again he swings his fist to knock on the door, but he catches himself as the door opens.

"What is it?" Winters asks groggily, dressed only in his knickers.

"An army has appeared before Charlesworth," Reynard informs him with a gulp.

Winters immediately sobers up from his sleepy state. "What? Who is it?"

"The savages it looks."

"How many?" Winters asks, his face pale.

"Two maybe three hundred."

"Wake the Lords!" Winters shouts before slamming the door in Reynards face.

He starts running towards the keep. *'Wait, I just did that,'* he remembers. Spinning back around he runs down the street towards the gate. Approaching he finds nearly the entire force of Charlesworth gathered behind the gate, maybe a hundred men if all of them are here. Sarah Hale commanding from the rear.

Reynard pushes his way through the crowd of soldiers. He looks up at the gatehouse, now filled as much it can be with archers. "What can you see up there?" He shouts.

Simkins pokes his head over and shouts down to Reynard, "They are just waiting there it seems. They have yet-"

The sound of breaking glass pierces their ears. Flames explode all over the gatehouse. The men behind the battlements scream as fiery liquid coats everything around. Simkins jumps off the tower and thumps to the ground dead, his clothes still burning.

Reynard steps back away from the gatehouse. Slowly it becomes devoured by the flames. Shuffling nervously the small Hale army murmurs in fear. If they were quiet, they would've heard the marching approach. *Bam.* The flaming gate shakes violent.

"Shield wall!" Sarah Hale screams. Feet away the soldiers line up and kneel, pikes and shields in hand. A second row forms behind them, then a third, these ones standing.

Bam. Bam. Again and again they batter at the gates. Cracks form in the wood as it is burned and battered. *Bam.* The brackets holding the log in place splinter and fall apart, and the gates open to the attackers with one end of the log dragging through the dirt. The horde is funnels in. Masses of men throw themselves at the shield-wall, each one meets a fate at the end of a spear. Reynard watches in horror as the bodies pile up, growing larger and larger.

He makes his way over to Sarah Hale in alarm, "My Lady, the bodies are piling up. This is not good."

Sarah Hale watches in astonishment. "Why are they not retreating?"

"They outnumber us. They can afford to lose some lives."

Soon the bodies pile higher than the shield wall itself. The savages continue to run up, stepping over the wounded as they scream and are slow buried in a pile of gore. One jumps into the air and flies over the curtain of spears. Landing amidst the Hale soldiers he manages to stab two soldiers before getting overtaken. Another follows his lead, then another. Soon many manage to bypass the shield-wall just by leaping above it, turning the town into a bloody melee.

*****

Winters runs up to the main road from his house, now dressed and ready for combat. Bumbling out of the keep is Dequande. Winters runs up to him, wondering what took the man who only dresses in shorts so long.

"What is all the commotion about?" Dequande asks while yawning.

"The city is under siege," Winters tells him. Looking down the road, he can see the gatehouse is in flames, though it has not yet been breached. He looks back to Dequande to see down on the eastern beach there are attackers easily removing the palisade from the sand.

"Dequande this way!" He shouts running down towards the beach.

An attacker comes through the hole they made in the wall. Charging at him Winters swings at his head. The attacker parries and the two men backstep. The man dashes forward and tries to cut Winters across the chest. Parrying the strike, he simultaneously kicks the attacker in the groin. He thrusts his blade into the attacker's heart.

Dequande charges towards the hole. An attacker coming through tries to thrust at him, but he hits it with his axe and sends it flying into the nearby ocean. The foolish man tries to charge Dequande without a weapon. Dequande merely picks him up by the throat, collapses his throat, and tosses him aside to suffocate to death.

Another man comes through and he buries his axe in their chest. He kicks them backwards to free his axe and they fly back to knock over another attacker.

Two more attackers run in side by side. A woman with a dagger charges Winters and a spearman charges Dequande. The spearman thrust towards his gut, Dequande slides out of the way. Grabbing the shaft with his freehand he breaks it with his knee. Turning to run, the man gets an axe to the head.

Winters makes quick work of the woman by chopping her wrist as they tries to stab at him, then thrusting his sword up into her ribcage. Another young man watches these two before him get killed and turns to run. A man in black iron armour walks up behind him and decapitates the retreating boy with a single swing of his Zweihänder. The armoured man stands in the doorway, staring menacingly at Winters and Dequande through his greathelm.

He continues to stand there and begins unscrewing his pommel. Dequande and Winters watch the man as he takes his time, wondering what he is doing. When the armoured man eventually gets the pommel unscrewed, he throws it at Dequande's chest. After hitting his chest it falls to the ground and rolls away.

"The fuck was that?" Winters asks.

The armoured man shrugs. He moves forward towards the two defenders. Dequande charges the armoured man with a swing of his axe. The man uses his large Zweihänder to catch the axe and the two lock up. Winters jumps in to strike, but has a hard time finding a gap in his black armour under the moonlight.

Dequande and the armoured man both take a step back. Suddenly a white horse bursts through the gap. The rider swings his warhammer with one hand, it crashing into the back of the attacker's greathelm. The horse dashes between Dequande and Winters. Falling to the ground the attacker's helmet is burst wide open from the blow. Dequande and Winters turn to the rider.

"Milo!" Dequande cheers.

"No, I'm clearly Lord Nasir," Milo cracks. He jumps off Snowstorm, and guides her to his friends.

"This isn't the time for your jokes Milo!" Winters shouts. "Didn't you see the army at our gates?"

"Don't worry about that," Milo says with a grin on his face.

"I guess I can just go back to sleep then," Winters mocks. "Since you said not to worry about it."

*****

Leading the attacking force of Tyrosian outlaws, bandits, and anarchists is a man named Paha Dohen. Not even knowing how managed it, he banded together many of the various groups in Tyros that had a reason to hate the nobility. Now he has an army thrice the size of House Hale's, all ready to sacrifice to the ends of destroying them.

He is sitting atop a horse at the rear of his army, watching as the men slowly funnel into the gates. One of his men thought of using bottles of alcohol to set the walls alight, but he'll take the credit for it. He honestly hadn't expected it to be as effective as it was.

One of his commanders coming from the front of the attack rides up to him. "Sir, we have taken a great number of casualties."

"But are we winning?"

"Their lines are weakening. Our men seem to have been able to get past the shield wall and has turned into a skirmish."

"Remember to kill anybody who tries to run," Paha demands.

"We may be able to stop a few, but a full rout would be impossible to stop once it has begun."

"I don't know what the fuck that means."

"Sorry Sir- I mean Paha. A rout is when the army breaks and runs away."

"Okay mister soldier, if-"

"Goblings go, stab them till all be dead! Go Goblings!" A deep voice booms. Paha and his commander turn to see the Troll Dirg waving his axe high in the air. A horde of at least a hundred Goblins charge from the woods, shrieking and war crying. The Troll stomps forward, swinging his axe around and accidentally hitting one of his own Goblins.

"Dirg say kill them all, crush their bones, and eat their flesh!"

*****

Lord Bryan Blount waits in the woods. All around him concealed in the darkness is one of the Royal Legions. Two hundred spearmen, one hundred archers, and a hundred mounted Knights are all under his command. They whisper to each other anxiously, their officers constantly having to hush them. Lord Bryan watches as the city walls burn, the massive army outside Charlesworth slowly funneling in.

"Are you sure we should be waiting?" His Lieutenant asks.

"Milo Khan said to wait and attack them all at the same time," Bryan Blount says

"Why are we listening to a peasant?"

Right before he can respond, Bryan Blount hears horrendous shrieking of Goblins. He puts a horn to his lips and release two long blasts. The spearmen charge out of the woods and across the fields. The cavalry goes around the flanks of both sides.

Soon the Knights and spearmen of the Royal Legions are clashing against the savage forces from the east, alongside the attack from the Goblins to the north. Arrows rain down on the attackers as the archers take their positions.

*****

Milo, Winters, and Lord Bartholomew cross the field of the dead. The Sun has begun to rise over the battlefield. Bodies are scattered across it, killed by the variety of arrows, spears, swords, and makeshift weapons used in the battle. Goblins scurry about, looting the bodies for anything valuable or shiny, and taking gruesome trophies.

"Tell me again how you managed to get an army of Goblins?" Winters asks.

"Well, this Troll had me trapped and wanted to do some killing. I passed his riddle and he was upset he didn't get to eat me. I figured he could be useful."

"The Goblins nearly clashed with the Royal Legion at the end there," Winters tells him.

"But they didn't," Milo says.

"The Legions could have defeated them alone," Bartholomew states.

"Yeah but at the time the Goblins were all I had. How could I have known I'd finally stumble across them?"

The three men approach the ageing Troll that is squinting to watch over the Goblins. Deciding to take a seat on the ground, he accidentally crushes the corpse of a soldier. Appearing rather worn, he lets out a loud breath and drops his bloodied axe to the dirt. He snorts at the air smelling the approaching men, and squints to see them.

"Greetings Dirg," Milo says.

"What men want?" The Troll squints at them. His left hand reaches down to take ahold of the crushed soldier's leg. With his mighty Troll strength, Dirg rips it from its socket and crunches down onto the raw flesh.

Bartholomew Hale watches with a look of disgust.

"I believe the Lord would like to thank you for your assistance…" Milo tells the Troll, staring at Bartholomew Hale.

"Uh. Yes I would… *Dirg*… Also if I-"

"Dirg askes why?" He mumbles through a mouth full of flesh, followed by spitting it out at the Lord's feet and discarding the arm to the side.

"Well because…" The Lord struggles to find something positive to say, visibly disgusted by the Troll.

Milo clears his throat and speaks nervously, "We are most grateful that you help saved our city. Without your help, the city might well have fallen."

Dirg's eyes sit heavy as he tries to pay attention as they both speak, only to fall asleep where he is, near instantly snoring.

"Oi Troll!" The Lord pokes the green giant in the arm. "When are you going to leave?"

Milo grabs Bartholomew by the shoulder and pulls him back a little. "You might not wish to disturb him, m'Lord."

Luckily the Troll keeps snoring away. Milo starts walking away, and turns back to wave the men away from the Troll. Crossing the field, the three approach a mighty canvas tent erected on a hill.

"Halt!" A soldier guarding the open tent flap commands. "What might your business here be?"

"That's Lord Hale and his men," a familiar voice shouts from inside.

The Guard steps out of the way, his face turning bright red. Entering the tent, the three are met with the King's uncle, Bryan Blount.

"Greetings my Lord," Bartholomew says with a bow.

"Same to you, my newly ordained Lord of Derwindale. It is a shame to hear about your father's passing."

With a sad smile Bartholomew accepts, "Thank you for your kind words."

"I bring bad news, young Hale…" Bryan Blount says somberly. "You are not to remain the Count of Derwindale for much longer."

Bartholomew's jaw drops.

"What?!" Winters cries.

Milo simply raises an eyebrow.

Bryan Blount's frown trembles a little before breaking into a grin. "I have been authorised by King James to appoint a new Duke of Tyros." All three stand in silence until Bryan Blount has to say, "Are you going to accept it, or should I go offer it to the Troll?"

"Sad to tell you the Troll is deep in sleep... Either that or dead; I thought for sure he would've killed the Lord if he were still alive," Milo cracks.

"Thank you, Lord Blount!" Bartholomew cries.

"I also have been given a royal charter to build a military base up here. With Charlesworth's strategic position at the mouth of the Noble Bay-"

A filthy man scurries from under the side panel and into the command tent. He begins jumping up and down in front of Milo. "The Lady! The Lady! She calls the one called Milo. Calls him to the place where water flows up!"

An officer bursts into the tent from the proper entrance. "Pardon me, my Lord! I was oiling me boots, and he just took off running!"

"What is this about, officer?" Bryan Blount questions.

"This me wife's brother. I've been taking care of 'im since she got the pox a few months back."

"Pox. Pox! Pox!!" The maniacal man shouts.

"What is wrong with him?" Winters asks the officer.

"Back when he went to the Bleaks with some Templars. He came back all screwy in the head."

Milo's eyes widen. "The Bleaks..?"

"The Bleaks, oh Bleaks!" The crazy man shouts. "Milo was there! Have you seen him anywhere?"

◈ CHAPTER NINETEEN

With only the light of a lantern, Milo walks down a dark cave. He follows a stream down into the depths, except the water is magically flowing up and out of the cave. The light from the entrance behind him gets farther and farther until it completely vanishes. Following the water and turning at a fork, he finds himself in a large cavern brightly illuminated by the same crystals as in the temple under Charlesworth. Standing at the other end is a gorgeous nude woman, elegant tattoos swirling around her body, and long wavy hair stretching to the small of her back.

"Nhianneah?" Milo asks the woman.

"So some might call me."

"Are you the crone? I can't tell who's who anymore with all this shape-shifting."

She smiles, "I am not. The crone, as you call it, is an ancient evil bound to the land of Tyros. You have seen me many times elsewhere."

"So you *are* a god?" He says shocked.

"No. I am not quite what your kind defines a god to be."

"So why am I here?"

She moves towards Milo gracefully. "You possess the heroes virtues, dear Milo. Honour, Valour-"

"Yeah, I get it," Milo cuts her off.

"Disaster is coming. Dark forces are at play. You must return to Dalarus and be ready to stop them, Milo."

"You're a god, why can't you just stop it?"

"As I have already told you: I am not quite a god. And there are forces binding me from doing so. We must work from the shadows."

Out of a swirl of unnatural smoke forms a man behind Nhianneah. It is the man he had also met in the temple those years ago. Luckily the man is once again clothed.

"Long ago we met an ancestor of yours. We fixed his family sword. Now it is your's, Milo."

The god-man holds out his hands and a sword appears from the dancing smoke. It is a Claymore with forward-sloping quillons, and a fishtail pommel to be used with either one hand or two. Lacking any rusting or wear, it seems to be fresh from the forge. Engraved on the sides are words written in ancient characters that he cannot read.

"Cædenon is yours," the man says.

Milo reaches out and grabs it. For a second the man is a hunchback and the woman a black knight, but after a blink of the eye they are once again as they were. He draws the Templar sword from the Dwarven scabbard, and places Cædenon in its stead.

"Look at that, it's a perfect fit now." He looks up from the scabbard to the two gods, but they have already vanished. "The whole vanishing act is getting seriously old, guys."

Milo picks up the lantern and heads back up the cave. Waiting for him when he surfaces are Dequande, Bartholomew, Elara, Winters, and Reynard. Dequande is mounted on a grey Clydesdale, part of his payment for helping the Hales. Elara is petting Snowstorm with a somewhat bittersweet look.

"What happened?" Bartholomew Hale asks as Milo appears from the cave.

"I met your Gods apparently. Again."

"So the man wasn't entirely mad," Winters says somewhat with disbelief.

"Yeah. At least this time they didn't send me on an adventure through the Bleaks." Milo looks down at his old sword. He hands it to Winters, "I don't need this anymore. Templar steel, barely used."

"I still prefer an axe," Dequande tells them.

Then to Milos surprise Winters lunges in and gives him a bear hug. "I'm going to miss you friend." He pulls away and looks to Dequande with a sad smile, "And you Dequande. I will cherish these memories for the rest of my days."

"So you're not going to hug the brute?" Milo says chuckling.

Elara Hale then springs onto Milo with a loving hug, saying, "So you aren't going to stay?"

Milo pulls back, but holds her close with his hands on her hips. "This isn't my home, Elara."

She smiles sadly as she says, "You better visit me from time to time." The two gaze into one another's eyes, everybody else eagerly waiting to see if they are finally going to kiss.

III.

THE RETURN . . .

◈ CHAPTER TWENTY

A bottle rolls from one side of the room with the sway of the ship, then to the other. *Clink*, it goes as it hits the cabinets. Then it rolls a few feet away, only to roll back a few moments later to *Clink* again. The noise is irritating Valdus some, but he was too engrossed in his book. Docked in the Federation of Rum, a series of islands ruled by Merchant Lords just south of Ateria, the Captain of the allowed Valdus to go through the small library in his quarters. Some of the books were boring, like the one about an old fisherman and a marlin; this one, however, was an epic story about a group of Halflings trying to get a magic ring to a volcano.

The door bursts open into the Captain's Quarters. A man in a blue nautical uniform and gold piping storms in, a large piece of parchment crumpled in his stern grip. Valdus looks up from his book and at the man with an irritated scowl.

"So this is why you didn't want to come to shore?" Captain Winstanley questions as he slams the parchment down onto the desk.

Clink.

Valdus does not uncrumple the paper from where the Captain was holding it, but he can make out the sketch of his face, below it the word: "Wanted." Years ago, Valdus was involved in an unfortunate transgression, of which led to a bounty of a thousand Aterian Richters being placed on his head. It was unfavourable that he had to come to Rum, but it was the first ship he could find going to Dalarus, and he needed to move quick.

Valdus just stares at the Captain.

Clink.

"The boys were too distracted by their bottles and the 'ores to notice. Lucky you..." Winstanley pauses. "And lucky me."

Valdus looks back down and continues to read his book.

"My boys would've turned ya in. Me, well... I just ask ya for a little more payment. Lest one of my boys slip up..."

Valdus closes his book and stares into Winstanley's eyes.

Clink.

"Fuckin' bottle," Winstanley mutters. He bends over and reaches to grab it, but it rolls away from him. The Captain stumbles after it as it rolls back into the desk. *Clink. Bam.* The Captain headbutts his cabinets. Finally grasping the bottle, he sets it on the desk. "You have until the sun sets to pay me."

Captain Winstanley starts walking towards the door. Standing up, Valdus flicks the bottle off the table. Alarmed by the noise of the shattering bottle, he spins around and gives Valdus a nasty snarl.

Valdus grabs his Sabre.

✳✳✳✳✳

Standing on the quarterdeck is Valdus, the new Captain—a clean shaven man named Larry Schettin— and his quartermaster, a dark skinned man named Hamado. It has been favourable winds since they departed, finally sailing north from the Isles of Rum towards Dalarus. A short time ago they spotted a glowing object coming on a collision course at them.

"What is it?" Valdus asks as Captain Schettin peers through his spy-glass.

Captain Schettin hands him the spy-glass.

Valdus puts it up to his eye and squints at the shiny object. Fighting the brightness, he makes it out; "A ship?"

"Mhm. Painted a bright ass colour too."

The three stay on the deck, silently watching the ship as it closes in on them. None of them say it, but Valdus can tell by the look on the men's faces that they are worried it is pirates. Their fears are confirmed when the ship raises a black flag.

"What should we do?" Hamado asks Captain Schettin.

"Lower the sails," the Captain whispers.

Hamado whistles to get the crew's attention before shouting, "Lower the sails!"

As the men scurry around to lower the sails, Valdus asks, "Why are we stopping?"

"That ship is too fast, matey. No chance at outrunnin'em," Captain Schettin informs him.

"So we fight," Valdus says, drawing his Sabre.

The Captain shakes his head. "My men ain't fighters, matey. And even if they were, I doubt we could take that crew."

"Tis the *Golden Skua*," Hamado tells Valdus.

"I wish Captain Winstanley was here…" Captain Schettin says, defeatedly watching the Golden Skua approach.

"But Captain Winstanley went mad." Hamado untucks his shirt from his leather shorts to reveal a stitched up stab-wound. "Bastard was runnin'round stabbing our men and shoutin' he was the Dread Pirate Ginger, remember?"

"Aye. Though he would've known better than I…"

The pirate ship approaches; a grand Clipper painted gold, its giant cloud of sails spun from cloth-of-gold that glowed hot white in the sunlight. Men climbed through the jungle of rigging, and scurried behind the dozens of scorpions and ballistas lining the decks. Sailing up beside them, the *Golden Skua* fired two of its Scorpions, launching grappling hooks over the gunwales. The pirates pull the ships close together and jump aboard into their bounty.

The last man to come aboard was the Pirate Captain. Wrapped around his head is a red bandana, and two pistol crossbows are holstered in his brown vest. He struts up to the quarter deck, his eyes set on the Captain. Then he sees Valdus.

"Valdus? What are you doing here my friend?" He cheers. The pirate Captain was none other than Henry Thorpe, the most successful pirate of the modern day and alumni of the late Captain Ginger of the *Ginger-Root*. And it happened Valdus knew him.

Valdus shakes the famed pirates hand as he says, "Dalarus. It is paramount I get there as fast as possible."

Henry Thorpe grins, "Lucky for you I have the faster ship there ever was. And I am forever in your debt for saving my life." He then turns to the Captain, "For your courtesy of not making us spill your blood, I shall leave you with your lives and enough food to get you to the nearest port."

"Don't let him do this, Valdus!" Captain Schettin pleads.

Valdus ignores him.

◈ CHAPTER TWENTY-ONE

After months of travelling, Milo and Dequande ride up to the Blue Gate of Dalarus. The outer market is devoid of its hectic soul. Half the stalls are empty of their peddlers, and only a few individuals walk throughout. "Kapooray, fresh Kapooray!" A merchant shouts, but something is missing in his voice.

At the gate a Pyrammian Guardsman shouts, "Halt!"

Stopping their horses, the two riders look to each other. The Blue Gate is always open to everyone.

"What is your business here?" The Guardsman questions.

"Uh I live here?" Milo says.

Milo can see the Guard squinting at him suspiciously from behind the chainmail mask that covers the Guard's face. "And you?" He asks Dequande.

"I am Dequande the Bull. I demand you let us through."

The Guard steps out of the way, eyeing the men as they ride past. Entering the city it is as busy as ever on the main street, but the crowd is speaking lower and lacks its usual cheerful demeanour.

"What is going on here?" Milo asks. "Everybody looks more depressed than Xandercus Hale."

"I've never seen the city like this," Dequande says.

They continue to ride down the main street of the melancholy city. Even the most vibrant of colours somehow seem dull. Riding into the town square, they find *Templars of the White Sun and the White Tree* sitting in the Mosque garden.

"What do you think they're doing here?" Milo asks.

"Let's find out," Dequande asks as he jumps from his saddle. He guides the horse to a small post and ties him to it.

Dismounting Snowstorm Milo asks, "Are you sure it's safe to leave them here?"

Dequande grins as he says, "The punishment for horse theft in Pyrammus is paying its weight in gold. Amongst other things."

Despite still not being entirely sold, he ties up Snowstorm next to the Clydesdale and enters the Mosque garden. As Milo looks around at the Templars, he spots one clad in a suit of armour trimmed with gold and a tabard with the symbol of the church, his head bald though with a thick beard. Milo walks up to the man who is sitting beneath a mango tree using his dagger to cut slices of the fruit for his enjoyment.

The Templar stands up and speaks as he chews on the tropical fruit, "Is that Milo Khan?"

"Templar Fortis, it has been a long time," Milo says.

"About three years it has been, right?"

"You know each other?" Dequande asks.

Templar Fortis tells the giant, "Aye we went into the Bleaks together. Say, what reunites us today?"

"I own some property here now," Milo says. "I was also basically ordered to come back by some supernatural being."

"Supernatural being?" Templar Fortis asks.

"The one I saw back in the Bleaks, actually." Templar Fortis goes pale as Milo says this. "Why are you and your men here?"

Looking somewhat relieved to change the subject Fortis tells him, "There has been some turmoil between the White Sun and the Seven Winds recently. A Monk of the Seven Winds was injured during a riot. We were sent to make sure no more be harmed, even if they may worship another."

"Is that why everyone's so dreary?"

Fortis furrows his brow. "You haven't heard? The Lord is missing."

"You sure Nasir didn't simply run off while drunk?" Milo says with a smile.

Fortis shakes his head, "*Shaqif Amir*, not Lord Nasir."

Milo and Dequande look at each other wide eyed. "We better get going," Milo tells the Templar.

"Until the White Sun reunites us," Templar Fortis says, sitting back down and cutting a new slice from the Mango.

Walking through the array of fruit trees and flowers, Milo notices the normally pristinely trimmed garden is becoming somewhat overgrown. After untying their horses from the post, they mount up and ride through the bustling market square. Despite being as crowded and noisy as ever, Milo still feels something is off.

"You know where any stables are?" Milo asks Dequande.

"This way," the Bull tells him, turning off the market square and onto a side street. They ride a few blocks until they ride into a courtyard. Surrounding them are plenty of stalls, though most of them are already filled with horses. Riding up to a man unloading hay from a cart, Milo can only presume he is the stable master.

"You work here?" Milo asks.

Still unloading bales of hay from the cart the man says, "Ye looking to rent a stall here?"

"My friend and I both are."

The man sets down the bale of hay in his hands and looks at Milo and Dequande for the first time. "What are yer names?"

"I'm Milo and this is Dequande."

The man goes back to chucking bales from the wagon. "I was wondering when you two would show up."

Milo raises an eyebrow, "What do you mean?"

"Your friend rented out stalls for the both of you. Paid for an entire year."

"Who?" Both Milo and Dequande say at the same time.

"Uhh… What was that fella's name?" The man says, scratching his head between bales. "Alexander I think he said."

Milo and Dequande look at each other in shock.

"Alexander?" Dequande says.

"Yeah, supposed to tell you to meet him at the Arid Temptress if you showed up here."

*****

A man dressed in black sits in the Arid Temptress, facing the main entrance. He sips from his flask, enjoying the absolute burning sensation. One of the wenches comes up and stands across the table from him. The dress she's in goes down to her ankles, but it lacks sleeves or shoulder, and an inch of her cleavage is showing. Though he doesn't have any opinion on it himself, he thinks less of the woman because she is disregarding societal standards.

"Are you going to buy a drink?" She asks somewhat annoyed.

Smiling at her he says, "I am waiting for a couple friends, dear." He can see the hairs on her arm and neck rise.

She crosses her arms, "Could you buy a drink while you wait?"

"I'd rather not."

"We have the biggest variety of drinks in all of Dalarus. Wine, whisky, rum, absinthe-"

"I only drink rectified spirits," he says, his thin pencil moustache twitching slightly. He leans over to see the door again. "Now if you could please move, my friends should be here any second now."

The woman rolls her eyes as she walks past him and back out of sight. Right on cue, Milo and Dequande walk through the doors. The man in black waves them over cheerfully. They take a seat in front of him, the looks of their face not very happy.

"So we meet again!" the man in black cheers.

Milo's face does not budge. "How did you know we'd be going to that stable, Alexander?"

"Oh I didn't; I purchased stalls from every stable in the city."

"That must've been expensive," Dequande says.

"Oh it was, but you see I have a great many resources at my disposal. And I don't hold much value in copper and gold." Alexander holds up a gold coin and twiddles it between his fingers. "It's like whoring. And I don't mean just because I don't understand the point of sex. To place a monetary value on anything, let alone rubbing your parts together for a few minutes? It is beyond me..."

"What do you want Alexander?" Milo asks.

"Straight to business it is. I have a secret to tell you…" Leaning over the table with a grin, he whispers, "I abducted the Lord." He leans back and puts a finger over puckered lips. Milo and Dequande hands slowly creep to the weapons at their hips. "He hasn't come to any harm—yet. If you wish for him to be returned safely, there are a couple things I need you to do for me."

"And how can we trust you?" Milo questions.

"There's no way you can for certain. But I always fulfil my promises to the word. Oh and if you don't… Well, then he's certainly dead."

The pesky wench from earlier returns to the table. Alexander's jovial smile quickly turns into a furious frown. "No, and please do not disturb us again."

The wench rolls her eyes and starts walking away.

"Actually I'll have an Ale," Dequande shouts after her.

Milo sighs. "What are these tasks?"

"When I decide it is time I will let you know. I'm sure-" He stops talking as the wench returns with Dequande's ale, angrily staring forward at nothing in particular. She sets the ale in front of Dequande, who in return slips a single 5$\mathcal{R}$ coin between her breasts. Moaning in annoyance, she fishes between her breasts for the coin and walks away.

"I'm sure you remember Gerev Westman? He will be accompanying you."

"Great," Milo says sarcastically.

"Splendid! Meet me back here first thing tomorrow morn," he says as he tucks his flask back into his breast pocket. Without pushing his chair back in he gets up. Milo and Dequande silently watch make his way to the door and exit.

"What now?" Dequande asks Milo.

Milo watches the door for a few more moments to make sure Alexander's gone. "I think we should tell Lord Nasir."

Dequande looks over his shoulder at the door, "Is that a good idea?"

"I think it's an even worse idea to get caught up in this scheme and have the Lords think we were all in on his abduction."

Dequande thinks for a long moment. "If you say so."

The two then leave the Arid Temptress. Looking around outside the building for Alexander, he is gone. They take a long, winding route through the side streets of Dalarus, carefully watching over their shoulders to see if they are being followed. After taking nearly twice the time they reach the Hara'asr. For once the gates are shut and locked, and Milo can feel the many eyes watching from the arrow slits above. A pair of Pyrammanian Guardsmen stand before the gate with spears in hand.

"The Lord is not hearing an audience today," one of them informs Milo.

"My name is Milo Khan. I have information regarding the missing Lord."

The Guard hesitates. "Hand over your weapons and we will take you to speak with Lord Nasir."

Milo is apprehensive to hand over the weapons he has collected on his path. Luckily Dequande speaks up before he has to. "I am Dequande the Bull, gladiator and servant of House Pyrammus. With me is Milo Khan, the man who saved your city when the beasts attacked."

"We cannot let you-"

The other Guardsman cuts him off saying, "Let them in, Aksham."

Sticking his fingers under his chainmail mask he whistles. A complex mechanism audibly cranks from within the gates. The left gate swings halfway open and the two enter. Inside the courtyard a few Pyrammian Guardsmen are trying attacking dummies, and a blacksmith is using his forge's grindstone to sharpen the garrison's swords. They cross the short bridge onto the island and into the garden. The roses and tulips and everything else in the garden is slowly wilting.

Two more Guardsmen open the palace doors. Once Milo and Dequande are inside the doors are closed behind them. Sitting at his desk below the raised Throne is Nasir Pyrammus, piles of paperwork scattered across it. To Milo's surprise there isn't a bottle of alcohol in sight.

"Milo Khan and Dequande, you have returned." He stands up and offers his hand over the desk.

Milo clears his throat as he shakes his hand. He opens his mouth to speak but no words come out. Nasir shakes Dequande's hand and clasps them in front of him.

"We know who abducted your brother."

Nasir holds up his hand and rapidly signs something to his servants. "What do you know?" He asks desperately.

"This man, Alexander. He claims he has taken him and will release him only after the two of us do something for him."

"Where is this Alexander?"

A group of Pyrammian Guardsmen marches down from the nearby stairwell and line up off to the side. The Captain of the formation steps up and half bows to the Lord, "Our men are ready for your command."

"My Lord, I think it would be best if we did as he asks," Milo tells him. "Something's off about him, and I doubt he's working alone."

"What does he want?"

"We don't know that yet. He's going to tell us tomorrow."

"If you believe this to be the best course of action, I will let you do this first. So far you have been a true friend of House Pyrammus. Save my brother."

Hearing this, the Captain takes a step forward, his hands clasped behind his back. "My Lord, I believe we should go on the offensive. The Shaqif's life is depending on us!"

"Let it rest, we will let them do this first," Nasir orders before signing something with his fingers at the man.

The Captain relaxes and looks at the man in the corner of his eye. He then returns to the formation and leads them back up the stairs.

Lord Nasir sits back down. "You may take your leave now."

◈ CHAPTER TWENTY-TWO

Once again, everything feels off on the approach to the Blue Gate. There is hardly anybody walking about, and today it seems to Milo that there are even fewer of the shoddy merchants. Somewhat relieving though, nobody is hollering at him to buy their junk. As he passes by the woman who sells cheap jewellry, a man in a red and cream headdress stops in the middle of his sentence and watches Milo pass by. Milo realises just how much Shaqif Amir means to the city.

Strolling through the city Milo takes in all the sights. He can see the palm leaves that create the streets canopy swaying gently. Smoke fumes from chimneys in the cookhouses. Women sit in window sills above, already fanning themselves in the warm Pyrammian morning. Merchants organise their wares and workspaces, finally having a respite from the typical constant business. The city being in its depressed hibernation allows so much more of the small things to be noticed.

Milo takes a turn onto a smaller side street. The box the preacher used to stand is off to the side, abandoned. Inside the Silken Princess it is as dead as ever. The tables are all empty and the only person in sight is Griselle.

Milo walks up to the counter, "Hail Griselle."

"What would you like to drink?"

"I don't drink, remember. Just wanted to say hello."

The old toothless woman squints at him, "Do I know you?"

"Yeah. I stayed here a long while ago."

Griselle scratches her head with her large wooden spoon. "You were Avannie's beau, yes?"

"Ehm, not quite." Milo looks around the tavern; "Where is she anyway?"

"After you left stupid girl started seeing horney boy. She get pregnant and I tell her I will have no whores in my tavern." The old lady finishes with hitting the spoon on the table.

"I'm sorry to hear that. I have business I must attend to, farewell."

Milo leaves the empty tavern. He makes his way through the side streets, being nowhere near as bad as the main streets even in the city's current state.

Entering the Arid Temptress through the side door, Milo finds Westman in a corner making out with a Harlot. She is still dressed, other than the top of her dress being untied and pulled down to expose her small breasts. Milo clears his throat and Westman stops to look over at him. The girl pulls the top back over her breasts, then getting up from Westman's lap and walks away lacing back up.

Westman checks out the Harlot as she walks away and asks, "Why'd you ruin my fun? Alexander isn't here yet."

Milo takes a seat across from the man. "How'd Alexander get you to work for him? I didn't think you cared about the lives of other."

Westman gives Milo that mischievous smile of his. "I don't. He promised to pay me."

Glancing around the tavern, he sees one wench place a mug down in front of a man with a red and cream headdress. Milo raises an eyebrow as he tries to figure out if it is the same man from earlier.

"Think you can get the whore back here?" Westman asks.

"No," Milo says, still watching the man.

Hearing the doors open, Milo turns and watches as Dequande walks in. The big man wanders around the quartyard, going to each occupied table trying to figure out where he was supposed to go. Dequande looks in their general direction and Milo tries to wave him over to no avail. Finally Dequande bumbles over to them and takes a seat between Milo and Westman.

"When will Alexander be here?" Dequande asks.

"He's right there," Westman says pointing in Milo's direction.

Turning around, Alexander is walking up from behind him. The man in the headdress is downing his mug, watching Milo's table in the corner of his eye. Realising Milo's looking his eyes dart away. Alexander takes the last seat, his back to the wall.

"How are you all doing today?" He asks smiling.

"I'm good," Dequande replies.

Milo does not answer the question. "Are you going to tells us what you want now?"

"Always straight down to business. I like it!" Alexander says. "Your first task will be to retrieve an object for me. You'll find it at the bottom of lake Vivaine."

"And where is this lake Vivaine?"

"You must leave the city and follow the coast westwards. At a point you will come across a heart shaped boulder, turn north at it. From there you should be able to tell once you find the lake."

"And after that you will set Shaqif Amir free?" Dequande asks.

Alexander gently shakes his head. "There will be one more thing you must do, then you have my word I shall return Amir unharmed."

Westman leans in, "And my pay, right?"

"And your pay. Now I must ask that you go on your way."

The three get up from their seats and walk towards the door.

Vallac calls as they leave, "Oh and Milo, on my way here I found an old acquaintance of yours. He should be waiting for you at your stables."

They leave the tavern and go to the nearby stables. Inside a man sits on the edge of an old splintering chair. Milo studies him trying to remember who he is. He has short black hair, a grey jerkin, off-white trousers, and a backsword on his hip. The man stands up and starts walking towards him.

"Arnold?" Milo thinks he remembers.

"Your asshole friend stole my ship," he grumbles.

"What's this about a boat?" Westman asks.

"I was overseeing its unloading when your friend snuck onto it," Arnold tells Milo with a dirty look.

"He's not our friend," Milo corrects him. "But continue."

"I turn my back and next thing I know my ships sailing away, that fuck at the wheel. As I'm going to report him to the Guards, he shows up and tells me I have to do whatever this shit is before he'd return it."

Milo opens Snowstorm's stall and leads her out, "If it makes you feel any better, he abducted Lord Pyrammus."

Following Milo's lead and retrieving his own horse, Arnold says, "So that's why you're doing this?"

Westman bursts out laughing, "So I'm the only one getting paid. What cucks you all are."

Milo jumps into the saddle. Dequande gets his Clydesdale and pulls himself over the horse.

Westman watches as Arnold mounts his horse last. "Hold up, I don't have a horse."

"I guess he'll have to ride with one of us," Arnold says looking to Milo.

"Don't look at me," Milo says.

Seemingly as if knowing what the men are talking about, Dequande's Clydesdale takes a step forward and tries to bite Westman. "Livonius does not like him," Dequande states.

Milo looks to Arnold, "Well you're the one who suggested it."

The men leave the stables and take off to the desert. Westman rides with his arms wrapped around Arnold. Milo can't help but laugh as the two ride miserably as if they were man and wife. They leave the city and follow the shore. Heat nips at them all as the Sun bears down on them, though the ocean breeze keeps them cool enough.

Looking over his shoulder Milo sees a rider on a camel going the same direction as them. For two hours they follow the coastline, the camel rider always on the horizon when Milo looks back. They come upon a valley to the north, an oasis between two hills.

"Turn north, into that valley," Milo instructs the men.

"I don't see a heart shaped boulder?" Westman says.

"The horses need water, there's an oasis over there."

"Good thinking, Milo," Arnold says, turning his Pyrammian Stallion towards the valley.

The men disappear into the valley from the rider's sight. Slowly his camel approaches the mouth of the valley. When he finally reaches it he looks towards the oasis, finding horses drinking from it but their riders nowhere in sight.

"Don't move," Milo orders from the rider's side.

The man in the red and cream headdress looks to Milo, an arrow nocked on his bow and aimed at him. The other men of the group stand beside him.

"Who are you?" Milo interrogates.

"I-I am a merchant good sir. Headed t-to Marakib."

"I saw you in the Arid Temptress," Milo tells him.

"A coincidence it must have been."

Dequande cracks his knuckles, "You want me to break him?"

"Start with his legs," Milo says. "That way if he still doesn't speak he can't follow us."

"Wait! Wait!" The man shrieks in terror. "Lord Pyrammus sent me to follow you."

"You could've gotten Lord Amir killed if Alexander were to catch on," Milo tells him.

The men walk back to their horses, all except Westman. The mercenary takes the waterskin from the spy and empties it in the sand. "Follow us, and next time I'll dump it miles away from fresh water." Westman tosses the waterskin on the ground as he walks away.

Continuing on their way, Milo watches the spy ride in the opposite direction until completely disappearing from sight. They travel for another hour, the sand dunes shimmering as the day gets warmer. Finally they find the heart rock and turn north. Another half hour they ride, until coming over a hill they spot a large oasis.

"Think that's lake Vivaine?" Arnold asks.

Milo looks around from the vantage point. "Only lake I can see."

The men ride down the hill and up to the body of water. It is crystal clear and surrounded with lush grass. Shimmering in the depths of the water they can see a submerged chest. Dismounting them, the horses they drink from the incredibly clean water. Milo kneels down at the water and cups some in his hands. Bringing the water up to his mouth he notices a dark shadow gathering in the water. Milo drops the water and steps back.

"What is it?" Arnold asks.

Three more shadows develop in the waters. Milo points as the shadows emerge from the water, dark spots in the air that take the form of sword wielding men. Milo draws his sword.

"What the fuck is this shit?" Westman shouts as he draws his sword.

The horses stop drinking, screaming and backing away from the water. One of the shadows charges Milo with its sword held high. It tries to swing down on Milo, but he raises his sword and parries it. They slide each other's blades off one another and Milo thrusts it in the abdomen. The shadow dissolves back into air.

Milo watches as Dequande swings his axe towards another shadow's head. The shadow jumps back and dodges the axe. It lunges forward again, swinging its sword from side to side. Dequande catches the blade with the beard of his axe and kicks the shadow in the chest. The shadow stumbles backwards and Dequande runs the axe through the shadows head like the air it is. Once again the shadow dissolves.

Then Milo looks to Arnold. He is moving backwards, holding onto his sword arm with the other, blood seeping through his fingers. The shadow follows him, constantly swinging its sword at him. Arnold manages to swipe away each blow, then Westman steps behind the shadow and thrusts his sword through its chest.

The last shadow vanishing, Westman asks, "What the fuck is going on?"

Milo kneels down back down at the edge of the water, looking at the chest as it is warping through the water. "You'll get used to it."

"This happens a lot?" He asks walking up to the water.

"Not exactly this, but yeah."

Arnold peers into the water, "So you think this is the lake?"

"Between the chest in the water and the disappearing apparitions that came to attack us? I'd say so."

"No need to be an ass," Westman remarks.

"So... Who's going to swim to the bottom of this lake?"

"Nah," Westman says.

"I had to ride with this fucker humping me the whole way there," Arnold spits.

"I would, but I sink in water," Dequande says sadly.

Milo sighs and pulls the satchel over his head, then he unbuckles his belt and drops it to the ground. Setting his bow and battle axe against the satchel, Milo slowly wades into the water. Taking in a deep breath he dives in and grabs the trunk. Filled with water the chest is extremely heavy. He drags it back somewhat, dirt flying up and fogging up the previously clear water. Milo bursts to the surface gasping for air. Once again he dives below and drags the chest. Pulling it far enough back, his head pops from the water and he gasps for air. Dequande runs in and helps Milo pull it to the shore, water pouring out from between each board of wood.

When they finally drag it to shore and all the water has drained out of it, Milo kneels down and flips up the latches. Looking up to the others they give him a nod. He throws it open and peers in. His jaw drops.

"What's in the fuckin' box?" Westman asks, leaning over to look in.

One by one they all peer into the box, only for their faces to contort in confusion and disappointment.

Dequande states what is obvious to them all: "It's empty."

"Maybe whatever it was disintegrated?" Arnold guesses.

"I was half expecting a Human head or something," Milo spouts.

"What now?" Dequande asks.

Milo stands up and looks at Arnold's wound. "Well first we need to get that patched up. Then I guess we take the empty box to Alexander."

Milo takes some needle & thread from his satchel and takes his time to stitch up Arnold. After finishing Milo finishes his medical practitioning, Dequande mounts his clydesdale and the men raise the chest up and give it to the giant to hold. Mounting their own horses they head back to Dalarus.

*****

Alexander looks down at his breast pocket as he pulls his flask from it. Looking back up as he unscrews the lid, the chest is dropped on the table in front of him. He sets his flask on the table and grins.

"So you found it. I hope it wasn't too much trouble," he says to his workers.

"You didn't mention the shadow guardians," Arnold says disgruntled.

"I knew the four of you could handle it."

"There isn't anything in it," Milo informs him.

"Oh I know," Alexander says smiling wide.

"Why go through all the trouble of abducting a Lord and stealing a man's boat for an empty box?"

"*Ship*, Milo. And don't play stupid. You know full well that this is merely a piece of a much bigger puzzle."

Alexander stands up and grabs the chest. He opens it up and reaches in. When his hands reappear from the box, they are clasping a stone tablet.

Dequande scratches his head.

"There was nothing in there?" Arnold exclaims.

At this point in his life, nothing can surprise Milo.

Vallac sits back down and runs his finger over the tablet as he reads it. Unless one of the men he had recruited were secretly an expert in the Eldritch, Alexander is the only one who can read the foreign language written on it. His face gleams by the time he finishes the tablet. "Take the rest of the day to rest up. Our trip will be long."

"*Trip*?" Milo moans.

"Yes, we need to travel to the Duchy of Holwich."

Milo groans. The Duchy of Holwich is a province in the Grand-Dutchy of New Adros. It resides between core New Adros and Pyrammus, and east of the frontier that Milo calls home. "Why is nothing ever simple with people like you?"

◈ CHAPTER TWENTY-THREE

The *Golden Skua* is anchored just outside the harbour of Dalarus. Valdus descends the latter, entering a rowboat with one of Thorpe's pirates.

"I apologise for not being able to take you myself," Henry Thorpe says from the deck above.

"Think naught of it," Valdus shouts back up to him.

"Best of luck, old friend!" Thorpe says.

One of his pirates then rows the dingy towards the bustling docks. The dingy gently sways in the lapping waves, and the water sparkles under the equatorial sun. Slowly they approach the docks, having anchored a good distance away to avoid the Pyrammian officials.

Rowing the pirate says, "The Captain still tells the stories about ya." He waits for a response but does not get one. "Thank ya for saving 'im."

Eventually the dingy get to the docks and they stop at a short wharf. Valdus jumps out of the boat and walks up the creaky stairs to the city. Looking around, he sees the bustling crowd, trading and working. He spots the Arid Temptress and goes to it.

"You there, red one!" A voice calls out. He stops and turns to look at a taxman sitting at a bench in the middle of the bustling streets. "Have any items to declare?"

"No," Valdus says, walking past the taxman and continuing to the tavern.

Entering the Arid Temptress, he makes his way across the courtyard and to the counter. Sitting down, one wench approaches him; an almond skinned girl with brown hair and brown eyes. She wears an off-white sleeveless shirts that cut right above the breasts, a black corset wrapped tightly around her waist, and a brown-orange skirt that reaches down to her ankles. In most other parts of the world, this would be considered indecent, but the Pyrammus heat calls for less material.

"What would you like today, m'Lord?" She asks with a sly smile, likely calling him a Lord because of his elegant red vest and golden harp pendant around his neck. He is not exactly a real Lord, but he is not going to correct her.

"A mug of mead if you have any," Valdus says.

Grabbing an ornate ceramic mug, decorated in pseudo-Asbjarnarviki fashion, she heads over to a barrel and fills the mug. She places it in front of him carelessly and some of it spills out onto the table, "That'll be ten Richters, m'Lord."

"Ten?" Valdus asks in disbelief. Back at his father's tavern, a mug of mead sold for three Richters, and he heard that it had risen to four in recent days. How could he be charged more than double?

"Yes m'Lord."

Valdus stares at her, waiting for her to explain why. When it becomes apparent that she isn't going to tell him, he asks. "Why?"

The woman rolls her eyes, "We 'ave to import it from the north. Costs a fortune."

Valdus grunts and pulls a $10\mathscr{R}$ coin from his pocket. He takes a sip from the mug. It is cheap and incredibly sweet like southern meads are. The woman begins to walk away, but Valdus has an idea. "Wait."

She turns around and pretends to not be annoyed.

"You haven't happened to see a strange man with a thin moustache around here, have you?"

"Sounds like the man Myra was talkin' about. Man gave her the creeps even though he never looked at her. That was probably why actually, there ain't a man right in the head who won't look at a nice pair of teats."

"Who is this Myra?"

"Cute blonde that works here. She'll be back after she finishes with a client upstairs if ya want to talk with 'er."

Valdus gets up, the atrocious mead left undrunk on the table.

"You can't go up there," the wench shouts as he walks away.

Ignoring her, he goes up the staircase. He kicks down the first door and finds the room empty. Kicking down another he finds two passed out sailors naked and cuddling. Kicking down the third door he thinks, *'Skinny blonde riding a cock. Must be her.'*

The woman looks over her shoulder at Valdus in shock. The man sits up and seeing Valdus throws the naked woman off his manhood and onto the bed next to him. He jumps up from the bed and screams, "Who the fuck are you?!"

Valdus ignores the man. He looks over to the woman, who is shaking in fear as she uses his hands to cover her feminine parts. Not caring about her fear or humility, Valdus asks, "Are you Myra?"

"Hey whoreson, the bitch is mine 'till I'm done with 'er. Get the fuk outta 'ere before I bash your head in."

Valdus slowly draws his Sabre and runs a finger across the length of the crucible steel blade. "Leave now, or you'll be the one getting hurt," Valdus warns.

The man scowls at Valdus arrogantly, but slowly moves to leave the room. Halfway across the room he bends over to pick his clothes up from the floor.

"Leave your clothes," Valdus commands.

The man stands back up with rage in his eyes and leaves Valdus with the whore, a skinny girl with light skin. After sheathing his Sabre, Valdus walks up to the bed. She is trembling and tears are rolling out of her soft blue eyes. *This girl mustn't have a hard time selling her body. Somewhat timid though.*

"I was told you know the man with the tiny moustache?" The girl bobs her head up and down a couple times. "Do you know where he is."

"A-ad-Adros," she stammers.

"When?" Valdus asks in concern. They are heading to the caves of Anima, a place of ancient power, he realises.

"This morning," she says, her voice cracking.

It's okay. You're safe.' Valdus thinks, pulling the soft cotton blanket over her exposed body. He leaves her in the room behind, and heads back down the stairs. As he walks across the courtyard to leave, the men in the room get up and gather around him with knives and axes. He looks around, examining the room. The men have encircled him, most of them no older than nineteen. Most of them look confident, but that comes from their arrogance and numbers, not their skill. Wenches are sitting on the counter top, the almond skinned one from earlier drinking the cup of cheap mead. One whispers into a young sailor's ear. "If you fight with valour, I might just let you have my honour," Valdus reads her lips. From across the room he can see the boy's pupils dilating, let alone his other reaction.

The crowd parts and the man whom Valdus chased from the room walks up, still completely naked. Now he has an arming sword in gripped in his hand. Valdus stares unblinking into the man's eyes as he draws his Sabre, the man's eye twitching as he tries to tries to hide his unease beneath his tough composure.

The man steps forward and swipes his sword at Valdus. With little effort Valdus parries the blade. Cracks form across the steel of the man's blade like glass before shattering. The man's face twists with surprise and horror. With a single skillful stroke Valdus opens up the man's throat.

The others scramble away from Valdus in terror. One of the wenches passes out and falls off the counter with a loud thud. Valdus approaches the almond skinned wench at the counter. She sits there frozen in terror. He takes the cup of mead from her hand and dumps it on the floor. Dropping the cup on the floor as he walks away, he leaves the tavern.

Walking through the city he thinks about if he'll be able to catch up to the men. A horse isn't an option, horses tend to spook around Valdus. Lucky for him, Vallac won't be on horse either; they like demons even less.

*****

Milo, Dequande, Westman, Arnold, and Alexander walk down into the depths of caves. For the past several weeks they were travelling to Adros with no idea why. In fact, they still don't know what they are doing here now. Along the way Milo did overhear a villager call the place the Cursed Hills. When he asked the villagers about it they said it's been generations since anybody travelled into the hills and they have since forgotten why they are named that, but he has his suspicions.

Why is it always caves?' Milo thinks.

"So what are we doing here?" Westman questions.

"You will see in just a moment, dear Westman," Vallac says cheerfully.

"Vallac!" An unfamiliar voice echoes through the cavern.

Milo turns around and sees a red haired man with an undercut and pointy ducktail beard, dressed in a red vest with matching trousers. On his belt hands a scabbard, a golden hilt with a black leather grip sticking out of it.

"Valdus! I was wondering if you would ever catch up. It's not like I gave you *months* to get here," Alexander says with a mischievous smile.

As Valdus gets closer Milo can see his two different coloured eyes burning. "Don't do anything he-"

Before the man can finish, Milo finds himself in an enclosed cave lit by five braziers. The only other person in the room is Alexander.

"Who is Vallac?" Milo asks him.

Alexander laughs impishly, "Don't pretend to be a fool Milo. You know full well Alexander is just an alias." Alexander steps closer, "Tell me Milo, what is it that you want most?"

"Hmm," Milo says exaggerated. "How about you free the Lord and leave me alone?"

"You were already promised that once this is over. There must be something you desire."

Milo glares at him, "Your head on a pike is starting to sound good."

*****

"Dequande, tell me what it is you desire most in life?"

Dequande has never liked Vallac. He always felt he is something bad. Dequande ignores him.

"There must be something you want? I shall give you *anything* you desire!"

Dequande's heart beats faster as he hears this. "Anything?"

"Yes!" Vallac assures him with a huge grin on his face.

"Bring my little girl back to me."

Vallac's grin turns into a frown. "You ask me for the one thing out of my power. There must be something else?"

"You can fuck off."

*****

"I would go through the whole spiel of asking what you want most, but you know better than to deal with me."

"I do," Valdus says. "May I ask why you chose these four?"

"The one called Milo will do anything in the name of some silly cause. His enthusiasm is quite remarkable. The big brute would follow Milo into a viper pit, and Gerev Westman would do anything for a shiny piece of metal. I merely found it amusing when I drug Arnold into the mix." Vallac grins and laughs. "My friend, a fish has bit."

Valdus is suddenly standing back in the cave. Milo, Dequande, and Arnold are back as well. Vallac has vanished, and Westman lies on the floor. His body is pale and cold, a single gold coin sitting on his chest.

"How did you let this go on? Do you know what will happen now?" Valdus scolds the group.

"What?" Milo asks bewildered.

Valdus targets Milo, "Vallac Xaphan is a demon of the highest order! Could you not see the evil *radiating* off him?"

"A demon?" Milo asks. Dequande and Arnold quietly step back, not wanting to attract Valdus' scorn.

"Yes, a higher demon! Not your typical demon that plays stupid tricks on you, but a demon whose sole intent is to destroy the world." Milo takes the brunt of the man's wrath. "And you imbeciles helped it become free!"

◈ CHAPTER TWENTY-FOUR

Walking up the staircase of the Lord's Tower is Grand-Duke Hrothgar Silverwood. The Lord's Tower is the highest of all in the castle of Achterdin, the seat of House Silverwood and the citadel for New-Adros. Built at a hundred feet up at the end of the Varlebeck Valley and beside the river that flows down and through the valley, it is regarded as the most impenetrable castle in all of Ateria.

Reaching the top of the staircase he makes his way over to the mirror. Turning his head to the side he looks in the mirror as he undoes his hairband, a tooled leather strip carved with a few flowers. He shakes his silky grey hair out. It covers his ears and reaches down just below his chin.

Swinging open the doors of his wine cabinet he goes through the small collection his servants brought up from the wine cellar. Most are from the Aterian lands of Pyrammus or Holwich, though one is an import from Trevalle and another from the Eidirium. He ends up grabbing the one from Trevalle and pops the cork. He grabs a glass from the cabinet with one hand and the bottle with the other, and gently kicks the cabinet door shut.

Setting the glass and bottle down at a table, he pulls out the chair and takes a seat. Hrothgar pours the wine into the glass wishing it was a finer wine. But those are reserved for sharing with family, and the best of wines for special guests. Then he remembers the exquisite vintage he gave to Nasir with some bitterness, but he has a couple others.

In front of him is a large stained glass depicting an unusual tree of silver colour, like something out of a fairy tale. He holds the stem of the glass and takes a sip, admiring the beautiful window. His grandfather imported it from their homeland of the Olfenreich.

A hand reaches out and grabs the bottle of wine. First Hrothgar believes it to be his wife, but he does not recognise the hand. He looks up and jumps. A thin man in a black suit stands beside him, cradling a wine glass in his palm. The man pours the bottle into his glass.

He takes a sip of the wine. Wiping his pencil moustache with the back of his hand, he looks at the bottle's label, with his reddish eyes glinting in the evening light. "I would have gone with the Eidirium, myself."

Hrothgar jumps out of his seat, knocking over his chair. Drawing his sword from his bedside, he questions the man, "Who are you?"

"My name doesn't translate into your tongue. Vallac will do." Vallac holds the bottle of wine up with a smile, "Would you care for more of my wine?"

Hrothgar stands with his sword arm forward and his left hand placed on his hip. "That is my wine. More importantly, how did you get in here?"

Vallac furrows his brow and scowls at the man. He slams the bottle of wine down on the table. "It is mine now. Just as is this castle."

Having had enough of the man, Hrothgar shoves his sword into Vallac through the stomach. Unphased Vallac, grabs Hrothgar's wrist, and forces the blade deeper. Hrothgar lets go of the blade and stumbles backwards. Vallac takes another sip of wine before removing the sword from his stomach.

"To answer your question, I just kind of appeared here." He throws the sword at Hrothgar's feet. "I can also do this."

Vallac snaps his finger. By his side a creature materialises from the air. It is the size of a large dog, but sharp pinkish scales cover its body. The creature howls loudly with an ear piercing shriek. Hrothgar turns and runs, the monster chasing after him. He flies through the doorway to the stairs and slams the door behind him. The monster claws and bangs on the door a second later.

He sprints down the staircase, descending far into the castle below. At the bottom of the staircase he flies through a corridor and storms into the Throne room. One of his Silverwood Ranger's is walking hurriedly towards him from the other side of the Throne room.

Hrothgar shouts to him, "A madman and some beast are in my room!"

"My Lord, the city is under siege. Strange monsters attack as we speak."

"We must get my family to safety," Grand-Duke Hrothgar commands.

"Of course, my Lord," his Ranger affirms. They run through the first pair of doors that are almost always open and into the lobby. Two of his house Guards swing open the double doors. He puts his hands over his eyes as they adjust to the sun. Looking into the courtyard his Guards and Rangers rush as they try to prepare themselves to fight. A screeching sound comes from the sky. Hrothgar looks up to see strange flying creatures circling the castle.

*****

A man shuffles down the streets of Dalarus. Dirt now coats his once elegant clothing, and there are sweat stains around his armpits and collar. The grime sticking to his face is barely visible on his olive skin. The crowds of Dalarus walk past him, unaware of his existence. Trying to push his way through the crowd he accidentally bumps into a larger man.

"Watch where yer goin' or I'll break yer face," the man says pounding his fist into his palm.

"A-aye," the dirty man says.

The man continues down the streets trying to make his way to the palace as quickly as possible. His stomach rumbles. Hunger is gnawing at the man. Then he hears the sizzling of food being cooked. He pushes his way through the crowd and finds a merchant grilling shashlik outside his store.

"C-can I have one?" The dirty man asks.

"'Ave any coin?" The cook asks with a look of repulsion.

"I am the-"

The cook whacks his spatula against the grill and the dirty man shuts up. "I don't care you who are; no coin, no food."

Defeated and hungry the dirty man steps away from the grill. The cook spits at him as he leaves. He stumbles towards the gates. Two Guardsman stand before the gates of the locked down Hara'asr.

"The Lord ain't taking an audience today," one of the Guardsmen says.

"But I-" The dirty man says.

"Scurry along," he orders.

"Wait Aksham, I think I recognise this man," the other says. The dirty man sighs in relief. "Are you Madri's cousin?"

"Nay Jahar, Madri's cousin has a face like a melon."

The dirty man groans, "I am Shaqif Amir!"

The Guardsmen both laugh. Aksham says, "Oh are you?"

Amir signs a couple of his hand signals.

Jahar, snapping to attention, declares, "Aksham, I think this really is the Shaqif."

◈ CHAPTER TWENTY–FIVE

Snowstorm trots through a deserted village. Not a living thing is in sight. Blood is stained everywhere around, but there are no bodies. Claw marks are scratched into doors and otherworldly paw prints are in the mud. A cart sits on the side of the road, its wheel broken off, and its content of fruits tossed everywhere.

Milo didn't know there was anything out here. He rides through the Duchy of New Olfenia. The province to the west of core New Adros, north of the tropical Royce, and south of the Noble Bay, it is made up mostly of dense forests. While parts of it are heavily populated, he is in a part of it so deep that he can't imagine why Templar Fortis told him to come here.

Suddenly a small child darts out in front of Snowstorm. The horse grinds to a stop as the boy stops in front of him, falling to his hands and knees into the mud. Milo jumps from his saddle and kneels over the boy.

"My parents," the boy sobs. "Please come help them."

Milo looks around the still and quiet village. "Where are they at?"

He grabs Milo's hand with his, "This way."

The boy leads Milo over a fence that has been toppled over and points at a door. Milo struggles to push it open from the damage sustained to the building. Finally it gives and he flies into the room. He pats the dirt from his sleeves.

"So where-" He stops abruptly as he sees the old man standing before him, dressed in a robe sewn from separate red, green, blue, yellow, orange, and purple cloths.

"Greechin's Milo," Albus says.

"You!" Milo hisses.

"Gerev broke the second seal by selling Vallac his soul in the caves of Anima. You must not let him break the-"

Looking down he sees a smashed table, one of the legs broken into a sharp stick. Milo grabs it and plunges it into Albus' heart before he can finish his sentence. "Will this finally kill you?" Milo growls as he shoves it deeper into the man's chest.

Albus stumbles back, the wooden stake pulling from his chest. His eyes water; another blow shaking his tears loose and sending them falling. His flesh shrinks and rots. Another blow into his chest. He falls back, his decaying body collapsing like a burning building. Tearful eyes shut tight as his flesh gives way to bones, then his bones to nothingness.

Hearing a noise in the doorway Milo looks up. The boy is scowling with red, puffy eyes burning with hatred. "You killed my new father, whoreson!"

Milo opens his mouth to say something but the boy runs outside. Slowly he gets up to follow the boy. When he looks outside the boy is running out of the village and disappears into the tree line. Remounting Snowstorm he continues down the road and deeper into the woods.

Half an hour later through the forest untouched by Humanity, a huge stone wall appears down the path. He follows it to the right until he finds a giant wooden gate. Knocking on it a small slit slides open, a pair of suspicious eyes peering through. "A traveller seeks what here?"

"The Sun lit the traveller's path to here," Milo tells him.

The slit slides shut again. A moment later the large wooden gate slowly creeps open. Guiding Snowstorm through, a bald man dressed in a thick leather vest and wielding a Zweihänder steps in front of him.

"Your horse," he says, holding out his hand.

Knowing he isn't asking, Milo hands the man the reins, and he takes Snowstorm off to a place unknown.

Milo looks forward and sees a massive tree in the centre of everything. It is white like ivory, and its lush canopy of leaves is a brighter, healthier green than Milo had ever seen on a tree. Small ponds and streams are throughout the area, ducks swimming in them. Far from the tree and against the walls are several buildings that Milo can only assume act as the barracks for the monks who live here.

Milo walks up to Dequande and Valdus, who are sitting around a pond drinking wine. Valdus looks incredibly bored, but Dequande is happily watching the ducks.

Noticing Milo approaching Dequande shouts, "We were beginning to fear something had happened to you!"

Milo looks at Valdus with a smirk, "You were worried about me?"

Valdus looks at him blankly, "*He* was worried about you."

"What is it like out there?" Dequande asks.

Milo lowers his head, "A lot of suffering and death out there. The King's men are trying to garrison as much as they can, but it's not enough."

Dequande frowns. "What are we going to do?"

"I don't know. I am going to ask Fortis that."

"Thank you, goodbye," Valdus says before taking a drink of wine.

Milo furrows his brow then shakes it off. "It's good to see you guys again. At least you Dequande."

He walks towards the tree, admiring it. Below it sits Fortis in a wooden chair, oiling his blade, a Templar sword not too different from the one Milo had before. Only one thing has changed about the man since the Bleaks, and that is the helmet by his feet is a more modern, rounded topped one.

The man looks up from his blade and smiles. "So you didn't get lost in the woods."

"Lost in the woods is how you found me all those years ago," Milo jests.

"That's not true, you were in a town."

"Yeah and that town was lost in the woods," Milo says with a chuckle.

"We received a bird from your friend Sir Carwood Winters. He said the monsters have him held up in Charlesworth."

"Shame, we could've used his skills. Do you have a plan on how to take on Vallac yet?"

"We are planning a march on Varlebeck. Outside of that, I don't think we have a clue." Seemingly a nervous habit, the Templar goes back to cleaning his sword.

Milo looks up and down the giant tree. "So the White Tree is real..." He says. Milo has an urge to touch it. He extends his hand.

"Aye it is." Fortis looks up from his sword again. He stands from his chair and shouts, "Milo, don't-"

As his fingertips brush the hard white bark, Milo suddenly finds himself transported. The stands in a flat plane. The ground is not nothing, but in his dreamlike state he cannot see it to be anything. Vallac stands feet away from him, his unnerving smile plastered on his face.

"There is nothing you can do to stop me," Vallac says.

The ground trembles beneath them. A terrible faces rises from the ground beneath them. Its grows bigger and bigger until it is larger than any castle. Opening its mouth wide, it swallows Vallac, sending him into an endless void.

"-touch the sacred White Tree!" Templar Fortis finishes.

Milo retracts his hand, his eyes widened in amazement. He blinks at the Templar a couple times then looks back at the tree.

Fortis grinds his teeth. "Only the Vicar of the White Tree himself is allowed to be graced with its touch!"

Milo looks to him, unperturbed by his shouting. "I know how to stop Vallac."

Fortis raises his eyebrows and clears his throat. Calmly he asks, "You do?"

"The White Tree, it gave me a vision. Or would it be the White Sun?" Milo thinks for a moment before snapping himself back into it. "I don't know how to describe it. If you can get me to Vallac I can stop him."

*****

Two hundred Templars, along with a handful of volunteers, are crammed into a single large hall. There are enough tables for everybody to sit at, though not comfortably. They feast upon chicken soup and bread, and the drinks are flowing. By this point almost everybody is drunk, but Milo can hardly blame them; it is quite likely the last feast they will have in this world. Tomorrow at sunrise they begin their march across the Grand-Duchy and to the occupied city.

Sitting next to Milo is Arnold, who says, "So they say they White Sun gave you a vision."

Milo shrugs, "Something like that."

"I heard you got it because you disgraced the White Tree with your touch," he says giving Milo a dirty look.

"Nobody told me I wasn't supposed to until afterwards."

"They should have strung you up for it. Or at least took your hand."

Milo drops his spoon into his half eaten soup and gets up from the table. He squeezes through the claustrophobic gaps between the tables. Going outside he hears a dog barking. He walks over and sees a man with a huge chin standing over a chained up rottweiler. The dark barks and bearing its teeth at the man.

"I don't think he likes you very much."

The man looks over his shoulder at Milo, "Most animals don't. They seem to have this sense that people don't. Animals seem things where people only see what something appears to be."

"People. So like the two of us?"

The man steps away from the dog. "It's good to see you again, Milo."

"Do I know you?"

"I don't think we were ever formally introduced. You can call me Bruce."

"Are you coming to fight with us, Bruce?"

"Aye I am. Perhaps we should get some sleep now, we leave early tomorrow. Us people need sleep, right?"

"Right…" Milo says weirded out by the man.

The man walks away and the dog calm down. Milo kneels down and scratches it behind the ear. The dog moments ago in a rage now licks his face happily.

"He likes you," Fortis says from behind.

Milo stands up and looks at Fortis. "I'm sorry."

Fortis is taken back. "For what?"

Milo sighs, "For touching the Holy Tree, freeing Vallac, for everything."

"Everybody makes mistakes, Milo. I wouldn't trust a man who hasn't." Milo furrows his brow as he tries to decipher what Fortis is saying. "A man who's never made a mistake eventually will—and when he inevitably does, he won't know how to react. A man like you knows to take responsibility for his mistakes, and he knows how to deal with the consequences."

"The people out there are dying, and those who are lucky to survive soon after fall victim to plague. All because I didn't stop Vallac earlier."

Fortis shakes his head. "You can't change what has already been done. All you can do is take the next step forward and hope you've learned from the last."

"I broke the sixth edict, that you should take ill."

Fortis places his hand on Milo's shoulder. "You did not break bread with Vallac. You adhered to the fourth edict: Protect those who are weaker than thee; they are under the White Sun's protection; and for you are His sword." He draws his sword. "And tomorrow we set out to adhere to the seventh."

"No evil is to go unremedied," Milo recites. "Fight against enemies of faith, family, and folk."

◈ CHAPTER TWENTY-SIX

"Where's the scout?" Templar Fortis grumbles, muffled through his helmet. Milo notices the Templar's new helmet has a flaw: an open gap between his chin and breastplate.

The Templar sits upon his white destrier, watching closely at the city in the distance. Around him the world is coated with dark ash. Not a single crop stands unburnt, and naught remains of the surrounding buildings but stone walls. Storm clouds brew above, further plunging the world into darkness. Not even the sound of the adjacent river is comforting, its dark waters running thick with blood and ash.

Milo spots a brown horse emerging from the city. "I think I see them," he tells Fortis from Snowstorm. Otherworldly screams, screeches, and howls were echoing about a few minutes ago. Shortly after the scout entered, everything went quiet.

Dequande squints at the approaching horse from atop his Clydesdale, "Where's the rider?"

Halfway across the valley they can hear the hooves galloping towards them. The wind has died alongside everything else in the valley. Two hundred Templars stand behind their leader in a tight formation, and they wait silently for their next orders. The horse grinds to a stop as it is blocked by the army. It screams and runs around in circles before the men.

"There's your rider," Valdus points at a torn off leg still dangling from the stirrups. A steel greave is still attached to the calf.

Templar Fortis turns his horse around and draws his sword. "Swords of the White Sun! Today we fight a shadow cast upon the land of His light. Fear not for the White Sun has given us a mighty weapon: faith in His power. Do not let yourselves fear, for He has a plan for you all today. Praise the Sun!" He raises his sword high into the sky, catching a speck of light and shining briefly.

The men cheer, throwing clenched gauntlets into the air, "Praise the Sun! Rah!" Their powerful collective voice echoes through the silent Varlebeck Valley.

Templar Fortis turns his steed back towards the city. "Forwaaard... March!"

Milo hesitates before moving his horses forward. The Templars march rhythmically, every one of them synchronised to the beat of Fortis' destrier; the only ones out of step being Dequande and himself.

Suddenly three figures appear on the road before them. Dequande shakes his head violently and Fortis leans off to the side sickly. Milo is unphased by their jolt into existence.

Fortis calls, "Templars..."

Dequande grinds to a halt, anticipating the command. "Halt!"

All on the left foot the Templars synchronously stop, and Milo stops a second later.

"Who are you?" Fortis ferociously asks.

On the left stands a woman in a red corset, her eyes red like blood. "You'd like to get to know me, huh? Never fucked a girl with red eyes before?"

Fortis barks through his helmet, "Every Templar takes a vow of chastity!"

"We know you Templars say them words, but does anybody really believe you to keep them?" The woman taunts.

It is the one in the middles turn to speak next, a man in a black jerkin. "Leave now and Vallac will forgive that you ever marched on him."

"So he can slaughter us another day? No, today we fight," Fortis proclaims. He draws his sword from its sheath.

The last one is a stunted man, his face wrinkled like a prune and his eyes are white with blindness. He does not speak in turn, instead giggling. On his note the three vanish back into thin air. Fortis looks around, clearly confused.

"They are demons of the lesser order," Valdus tells him.

Beneath his helmet, Fortis releases a heavy breath. "I once thought I had fought demons in the Bleaks. Now I believe that was not the case."

"The Bleaks was something else," Milo tells him.

"Forward..." The Templars extend their legs and dig their heels into the cobbled road. Fortis pauses for a long time before finally commanding, "March!"

The army continues its march down the road. Leaving the burnt wheat fields behind they enter the city of Varlebeck. Bodies are piled on the sides of the streets; men, women, and children slaughtered indiscriminately. Entire blocks of the city are naught more than collapsed rubble. The tall tudor houses that still stand have their windows shattered, both inwards and outwards. Junk is thrown carelessly about. A shredded abdomen of indeterminate sex is caught in a clothes line, its intestines and organs dangling. And yet in the chaos of destruction, the world seems to be frozen in time. Not even a rat scurries about.

They march into the town square, a large open area surrounded with shops and filled with stalls. On the north side of the square is a Cathedral of the White Sun, its massive stone architecture unscathed by the fiery destruction that destroyed the town. It doors are swung wide open and blood stains the ground from bodies being dragged out.

Milo looks around the square nervously. "Something's wrong."

"That is the evil forces trying to get at you," Fortis tells him.

"No, I mean something's seriously wrong here."

"Yes, you are feeling the darkness trying to break your faith. Do not be afraid, and the White Sun will protect you."

"Fortis listen! The city is a ghost town. Monsters were residing here a short time ago."

Valdus draws his Sabre, "He is right. We came here expecting a battle, and everything up to now pointed towards getting one."

"Maybe he's chosen to sit in his castle than meet us in the field?"

The world is engulfed in a bloody haze. All around them, creatures materialise from thin air. To their every side, within buildings and on the streets, houndish creatures from another world phase into existence. In the skies hellish things like that of a small child but with the head of a bird and giant wings materialise from thin air.

The Templars break formation and clash with the surrounding army. Many run up between the mounted men in the front, defending the horse with their halberds. Milo grabs his bow and shoots one at the flying creatures, his arrows accompanied by bolts shot by crossbowmen. The creature goes down as Milo's arrow pierces its stomach. He turns and shoots another in the head, followed by two bolts in the chest. Then he aims down and sends another arrow into one of the hound-like creatures. He knocks another arrow, but before he can draw it a figure suddenly appears in front of his horse.

It is the woman in red, one of Vallac's demons from earlier. She swings her blade to open up Snowstorm's throat, but then the man named Bruce steps in from nowhere. His blade parries hers. The two desperately push on each other's blades to gain leverage. The woman steps back out of the lock and Bruce strikes at her. A series of quick strikes and parries ensues, the swords sparking and clanging as they meet.

"To Saint Gerard's Cathedral!" Fortis shouts at Milo and Dequande.

Fortis' destrier churches forward, the monsters before him dazed as the horse suddenly blows by them. Milo throws the bow over his shoulder, and with Dequande he storms through the sea of monsters. With his left hand Milo swings his warhammer like a polo mallet, crushing a monster's head; in his right hand he slashes them away from his stead. The monsters mostly hold back from Dequande, his giant horse seemingly intimidating them. One tries to bite at its rear leg, only to get kicked in the face.

Fortis' destrier goes down front first and tosses him forward. He lands in a half controlled roll and springs back up. A monster leaps into the air at him, but he cuts it away with his sword. He runs towards the Cathedral, slashing away at the monsters in front of him.

Milo and Dequande ride their horses through the massive cathedral doors. Milo sheaths his sword and throws his warhammer back over his back. Quickly he reaches for his bow and begins shooting down the monsters. Dequande vaults off his stead, landing on the carpeted cathedral floor with a slam. Fortis runs in. He and Dequande quickly slam the doors shut, moments later the monsters crashing into the door and clawing away at it.

"Get something to block this door!" Fortis yells at Dequande.

Dequande lets off the doors and the monsters send the doors flying back. Fortis narrowly catches them and uses all his weight to keep the monsters out. Dequande picks up one of the bulky wooden pews and Fortis moves as he slides it in front of the doors. The pew shaking and slowly moving back Dequande places another one behind the first, and then a third one atop them. The two back away from the door.

"The White Sun will not let the darkness in here," Fortis tries to reassure the two.

"Oh. In that case, I suppose I should leave," a man's voice says. Standing before the doors is the dark dressed demon, now with a one handed Flamberge sword.

Fortis charges the demon, swinging his sword with all his might. Easefully the demon raises his sword and parries. Before Fortis even knew it was coming, the demon draws a Misericorde from his belt, and sends it up the narrow gap beneath Fortis' chin.

The demon slowly draws the blade from Fortis' chin and the body drops to the ground. He gazes at the dagger in admiration, blood dripping down the length of the skinny blade. Then Dequande's axe falls upon his wrist, sending his hand and the dagger to the floor. The demon tries to swing on Dequande, but he knocks it away with his axe.

"Run Milo. Go fight Vallac!" Dequande shouts.

Milo tugs on the reigns and faces Snowstorm at one of the Cathedral's large, arching windows. "Ha!" He shouts, applying great pressure with his legs. Snowstorm sprints forwards towards the window. Milo draws the bow and shoots an arrow. The window shatters and crashes down in a great clamour. Snowstorm leaps through the large shattered window. Snowstorm gallops throughout the city, the screams of men and monster alike behind him.

He reaches the end of the city. Towering high above the valley is the castle of Achterdin. Great towers spire high into the air, the Lord's tower above them all. Beside it is a great waterfall, below it the river bends in front of Milo, cutting him off from the castle if it weren't for the stone bridge between the city and the castle.

Riding towards the bridge, the last demon appears on the other side. The stunted imp giggles as it holds a torch. It drops the torch and a line in the earth sparks and flashes. Next thing Milo knows dust is blinding his eyes and his ears are ringing. Snowstorm rears and he topples backwards.

He ears still ringing he slowly gets up off the ground. As the dust settles he looks upon the bridge. It has been demolished, only the two foundations on each side and a single pillar in the centre remain.

"I'll be back for you," he whispers to Snowstorm, petting her snout.

Then he runs towards the bridge. He leaps into the air and lands on the central standing pillar. Stones shake free as he lands at the edge. He backs up and takes another leap. This time he narrowly misses. The crumbling stones break as he slides down the side. He reaches out and grabs at the top of the bridge, his arms hitting the stone hard. Painfully he pulls his body up and onto the other side.

He walks up the earthen ramp leading to Achterdin. At the top of the ramp he finds the drawbridge raised. What his plan was if this was the case, as he suspected it most likely was, he did not know. But he had to at least try.

As he stands in defeat, the draw bridge begins to lower. Vallac is inviting him in. When the drawbridge sets down in front of him he crosses it, the portcullis raising for him. Walking through the gatehouse he looks up and wonders if the murder holes above would be his end. Then the next portcullis raises as well. He walks through the courtyard and enters the main hall. Except it isn't the main hall of Achterdin now.

In its place is the Royal Throne room, a large hall with monstrous pillars lining the walls, a tall dais at the end with a grand Throne atop it. Seated in the Throne is King James, his chest ripped open and his heart in his lap.

"This is what I will do to your King James," Vallac's voice says from nowhere yet everywhere at once.

Milo crosses the long hall until he is at the steps of the dais, staring up at the King's body. Suddenly he finds himself on a beautiful, sunny beach in Pyrammus. A cog is shipwrecked like a beach whale. "This is where Arnold's ship is. I would ask you to fulfil my promise for me and tell him, but I'm afraid you won't be alive to do so."

Then Milo is standing in an empty plain, utterly flat and void except for a single tall mountain spiring into the sky, atop it a small black tower. Everything is covered in a perfect blanket of snow, the cold more bitter than anything Milo had felt before. Approaching the mountain he finds the mouth of a cave. He enters it for shelter from the cold and finds a spiral staircase leading up. Step by step he walks up the staircase, it being seemingly endless. Finally he reaches a door at the top. He pushes it open, the freezing metal knob stinging his hand. Entering he is now at the top of the Lord's Tower.

Standing across the room from Milo is Vallac, a golden chalice cradled in his palm. Milo looks around the room for anybody—or anything—else, but it is just him and Vallac.

"Would you like some wine?" Vallac asks before taking a sip. "I will spare you one last drink."

"I don't drink," Milo spits.

Vallac takes another sip. "A Hero's sacrifice, amidst a field of blood. You played into my hand so perfectly!"

"So all this was the final seal? You knew we would come?"

Vallac laughs. "Now you are figuring it out! Yes, you Humans are so predictable; easy to strategize against."

"What are you going to do now that you are free? Bring about the end times?" Milo asks.

Vallac slowly walks towards Milo. "I am merely the vanguard."

He takes a sip of wine, still creeping closer. "Night is falling, the darkness is nearly upon your world. You are standing in the dusk."

Vallac stops inches away from Milo. "There is nothing you can do to stop it, just as there is nothing you can do to stop me."

Then Milo smiles. Vallac cocks his head and furrows his brow. Milo slowly raises his tiki mask at the man. Vallac's face first looks at the mask puzzled, then it warps into horror.

The bottle of wine on the table begins vibrating. Everything in the tower starts bouncing, even Milo. The massive stained glass window shatters, but the shards stay suspended in the air and spin violently. The walls and roof of the tower tear seemingly as if paper. In a vortex the shards and tears swirl violently around them, the various objects in the room being sucked in and crumpled. Suddenly the unnatural debris is blasted away far and wide, Vallac simultaneously disappearing from existence.

Milo's fair hair gently falls over his forehead. Walking to the edge of the destroyed Lord's Tower, he combs it away from his forehead with his fingers. He sits down and lets his feet dangle off the edge. In the distance he can make out that the Templars are getting the upper hand. He looks down at the tiki mask in his hands, "Thanks disappearing peddler."

It is finally time to go home. But something inside him was forever lost.

◈ Epilogue

"Are you sure you wish to go in alone, my Lord?" Asks a man with a horribly scarred face and soulless grey eyes.

"Yes, Vladimir. There is naught you could do but get yourself killed," Valdus tells him.

"As you say, my Lord."

Valdus descends into the darkness of the cave. He digs around in his pocket and pulls out a small cloth pouch. "*Saat bute drike sveka*," he whispers before tossing into the air. "*Ka!*" The pouch bursts into flames and turns into an orb of light, illuminating the cavern.

He continues further into the depths of the earth, the orb following him closely. Reaching the end of the cavern he reaches a solid wood door set right into the stone. He turns the handle slowly before suddenly throwing the door open. He peers in for a moment, assessing potential traps. He enters the massive hall lit by numerous braziers and chandeliers, the orb cowering behind the door. Walking down the hall slowly he peers at beautiful tapestries that drape the walls. Every one of them depicts events in the world's history. The worlds converging on one another, to the war against the Fomorians, to the discovery of Ateria. The tapestries become more recent as he continues down the hall, events such as the Troll Wars and the Malbose Revolt. He sees himself in the roots of the pale tree, but he pays little mind to it. Then the battle against Vallac. He stops dead in his tracks to take in the final tapestry.

"Fucking hell."

"You like them?" Albus asks, sitting on his dais a few feet away. Valdus turns his head towards the old man and glares at him. "So you finally found me."

"Last time I said if I saw you again I would kill you. Would've saved a lot of trouble if I had hunted you back then like the mad dog you are."

"You do not understand!" Spit flies from his mouth. "I needed a champion to defeat Vallac."

Valdus walks up the steps of the dais until he is looking down upon the old man. "He would not have been a problem if you had not released him."

Albus thrashes around in his seat and throws a cup of wine at the wall. "The sisters demanded it! Weaved it tightly into my fate!" He calms down and begins to comb his beard with his long fingernails. "Weaved Vallac's release into my fate the black haired one did. Yet the fair haired one entangled it with her own thread."

It becomes clear to Valdus why Albus would release a higher demon. "You shouldn't have peered into time. You knew it would drive you mad."

"A lie. Our masters before us merely feared to wield such power."

Valdus scoffs. *'He thinks he's fine.'* He gently touches the hilt of his Sabre. "It's time I put you down, Albus."

Faster than Valdus thought possible for such an old man, Albus jumps from his throne. His arms spread wide he shouts, "I am immortal!" Just as he finishes his throat is cut open with one skillful swipe of Valdus' Sabre. Albus continues to grin wider than the gapping cut across his throat. His hand trembles as he slowly reaches to feel the cut across his throat. Instantaneously his face turns to horror as he desperately tries to make his trembling hand hold his throat closed. His body topples to the ground, and it lays still in mortal slumber.

Valdus starts to walk away. He pulls his handkerchief from his vest pocket and wipes the blood from his blade.

"*Versparde svedalt.*"

For a moment everything goes black as every one of the fires in the room go out at once. Then all the tapestries in the room spontaneously ignite. The walls of the great hall are engulfed in a violent inferno. Finding his Sabre adequately clean of Albus' blood, he sheaths it. Tied to his other hip is his black tiki mask, its sinister face exaggerated by the flickering light of the hall of flames.

And here the jester takes his bows;
He exits the stage, yet the play...
The play is not yet over.
Let us descend into the darkness.